LAURA L. SMITH

IT'S
COMPLICATED

LAURA L. SMITH

Birch House Press
Est. 2015

IT'S COMPLICATED
Copyright © 2013 by Laura L. Smith

Cover Design ©2013 Angela-Designs.com

Cover photography by: Kelci Alane Photography

Scripture quotations in this publication are taken from the following: the *English Standard Version*. Copyright 2001 by Crossway Bibles, a division of Good News Publishers. *New Living Translation*, copyright 1996, 2004. Used by permission of Tyndale House Publishers, Inc. Wheaton, IL. *The Message* by Eugene H. Peterson. Copyright 1993, 1994, 1995, 1996, 2000. Used by permission of NavPress Publishing Group. All rights reserved.

It's Complicated Status Update Series (Book 1) / Laura L. Smith. –2nd ed.

This is a work of fiction. Names, characters, places, and incidents are a product of the author's imagination. Locales and public names are sometimes used for atmospheric purposes. Any resemblance to actual people, living or dead, or to businesses, companies, events, institutions, or locales is completely coincidental.

ISBN-13: 978-0-9961801-9-1 ISBN-10: 0996180192

[1. Dating—Fiction 2. Sexual Assault—Fiction 3. Christian life—Fiction 4. College—Fiction 5. Romance—Fiction 6. Roommates—Fiction]

Birch House Press
Est. 2015

IT'S COMPLICATED

For Ally and M.E.H. – thank you for sharing your personal stories, so that other victims may find hope and healing. You are strong, beautiful and courageous.

"I devoured the whole book in two days, and can't wait to hear more about these girls. It's like a Christian *Sisterhood of the Traveling Pants*." – Jessa Bertone, college junior

"Laura Smith speaks for the broken. With a voice that's warm and true, Laura gives words to those rendered speechless by issues that high school and college girls should never have to deal with—but so many of them do. In writing that's raw, relevant, and real, Smith goes where few authors dare to go: straight into the heart of today's young woman." – Amy Parker, best-selling author

"YA author Laura L. Smith has crafted a story that lets readers learn along with her four female characters—and the lessons aren't hollow. Tough issues that follow girls to college—like beauty, physical relationships, underage drinking, and loneliness—are treated with Smith's usual grace and humor. Fans of Jenny B. Jones and Sarah Dessen will love IT'S COMPLICATED!" – Laura Anderson Kurk, author of GLASS GIRL

"Laura Smith has the rare ability to capture the rawness of her characters' emotions in IT'S COMPLICATED. Through Claire, Kat, Palmer, and Hannah readers learn that loss comes in all different forms, but with the strength of God's love and power of His plan they can get through it." – Ally Hunter, date rape survivor

PROLOGUE

"YOU HAVE A TEN MINUTE BREAK before your parents rejoin us for the dormitory tour." The peppy girl at the front of the room sounds like she's leading a cheer. All she needs are pom-poms. She smiles and closes her notebook with a light thud.

That's my cue to head to the bathroom. Mingling is not my thing. Especially in a group like this, where I don't know anyone, where I'm not sure if I belong. I mean I'm really excited to go to Clarkston University—considered the best state school in Ohio—this fall. I was nervous about getting in. Now that I'm in, I'm nervous about fitting in. Everyone here seems rich and beautiful and smart and totally pulled together.

I'm the smart part, I guess. But pulled together? I work hard at just trying to keep it together. And rich? Not even close. Mom and I struggle to get by. I'm here on partial financial aid, partial academic scholarship, and partial wing and a prayer.

I adjust my floral tank in the mirror and tighten one of

1

my long, sandy blonde braids.

"I love your hair!"

"Thanks." I smile gratefully to the girl with sparkling hazel eyes, wavy auburn hair, freckles, and a wide grin.

"I could never get away with it." She shrugs. "My hair is so crazy and out of control. It would just look poufy. See?" She grabs the ends of her hair and pulls them outward past her ears.

I can't help but laugh. This girl wearing silver bangles, the sundress I swear I saw in the window of J. Crew, and pink nail polish that matches the pattern in the dress perfectly is one of the girls I'd labeled as "totally pulled together."

"I copied it. Have you heard of Holly Starr?"

The girl wrinkles her forehead. "Actress?"

"Musician. Anyway, I love her music, and she always wears braids with big, cool headbands." I straighten my own headband.

"What kind of music does she play?" It's getting crowded by the mirrors, so smiley girl leads the way, and I follow her out of the bathroom to an empty space along the wall.

I'm not used to girls like this starting up conversations with me, let alone continuing them. "Upbeat and slow. A little of everything. She inspires me."

"Cool." The girl nods. "I like a little of everything. I'm Hannah, by the way."

"Claire." I manage.

"There you are, Hannah." A PTA-ish looking woman wearing white capris, a turquoise silk top, and pearls slides her arm around Hannah.

"Hi, Mom. This is Claire."

"Nice to meet you." I give Hannah's mom a quick handshake.

"Hello, Claire. Nice to meet you too. How do you girls know each other?"

My cheeks warm. I was trying to get away from conversation, not dive into it. "We just met. I'm from Cleveland."

"Hi, I'm Lauren Lassiter." My mom appears. I cringe. I never know what Mom will say or do, but it usually makes me uncomfortable.

"Polly Trager." They shake hands, sizing each other up.

"Last names starting with A–K follow me," calls Cheerleader Girl, who ran our last session about dining halls.

"Last names L–Z follow me," announces the boy with Clark Kent glasses and plaid shorts, who helped with the opening session.

"They must be alphabet top heavy," Mom says. She looks like she could be a student with her broomstick skirt and chocolate brown tank. Since Mom's so young, for a mom, and we're both petite, we share clothes. It stretches our budget and wardrobe. Bone structure and clothes are hopefully all people think we have in common.

"Yay, we get to be together!" Hannah cheers, tipping my balance as she hooks her arm in mine. "Plus, we get the cute tour guide. So, this is what I know about the dorms," she starts, while our moms chat two steps ahead of us. "My best friend, Palmer, was here last week for orientation. We couldn't come together, long story. Anyway, they have doubles, which are like military barracks, or they have these sweet four-person suites."

"Sweet suites?" I ask, feeling a little awkward walking arm in arm with this girl I hardly know, but also a little relieved she's leading and talking and apparently in the know.

"Well, for one thing, they have their own bathroom, so you don't have to share the locker room style showers down the hall. Nasty."

"Nice." I nod.

"And, for another, they have two rooms, plus the bath, so it's like a little family room and a little bedroom. So cute. I guess they're both small, but it gives you a place besides your bedroom to hang out."

"Space is good," I say as we cross the street. I picture a room with bright beanbag chairs and posters on the walls, like something out of a Pottery Barn Teen catalog.

"Palmer and I are going to room together," Hannah continues, chomping on her gum. "We were going to go lottery for two other roommates, so we could live in one of those suites, but what would *you* think about being our third?"

My heart jumps inside my chest and I feel my face flushing. I'm sure I can't afford the more expensive room, but am grateful someone as nice as Hannah wants to room with me. I thought it was going to be so hard to meet people. "*Umm.* Wow, that would be cool, only I d-don't," I stammer.

"Here is the standard double room, complete with trundle beds that fold into couches, giving you more living space," our guide says. "Feel free to break up and peek in any of the rooms in this hall."

Hannah drags me into a room on the far right. "See. They are itty-bitty. Living space? Hardly! No place to run, no place to hide, and you'll gag when you see the community bathroom."

"The trundles are cute," I say.

"What do you think?" Mom asks, rubbing my back. I stiffen at her touch interrupting a rare "me making a friend" moment. "They're bigger than your bedroom."

I tense tighter. "They're fine," I answer. Did Mom have to point out how rinky-dink my room is at home?

"Hannah's mom has been telling me about the quads. They're a little cheaper and give you some options for living space." Mom's voice quivers. I can tell she's worried about something. Maybe the higher rent? Wait. Did she say cheaper?

"Cheaper?" I almost spit out the word in surprise.

"Yeah, isn't that hilarious?" Hannah laughs. "It's like a sale at Macy's on designer shoes. The cooler rooms cost less."

"Some weird University accounting." Hannah's mom swings her purse. "Anyway, Hannah and her best friend, Palmer, are getting a quad. College costs a fortune. It doesn't hurt to save a little where you can."

"And Claire." Hannah grins, squeezing my elbow. "She's our third. Right? Promise me you'll be our third!"

"Yeah, sure." I smile, twisting one of my braids. "Is that okay, Mom?"

Mom exhales, and even from behind her giant sunglasses I can tell she's relieved. I exhale too. Cutting costs is a good thing. Mom agreeing to let me room with Hannah is an even better thing.

"Now, we'll take these stairs to the second level, where you can see the other option of four roommates," Glasses Guy says.

"He's so cute in a nerdy, collegiate kind of way. Don't ya think?" Hannah whispers in my ear.

"Not my type." I smile. "But, cute. Definitely cute."

Back on the street, our tour guide gives one last spiel about how to log in online to sign up for dorm and roommate preferences.

"Now, you're all free to roam around our downtown area for lunch. I suggest Mr. Burger—the best hamburgers anywhere!" He smiles. "Next session is in two hours back at the main room of the student center. See you there."

"I'll be there early." Hannah bats her eyelashes in his direction, even though I don't think he hears her.

"Care to join us for lunch?" Mrs. Trager asks.

"That would be great. I'm famished," Mom agrees. "Since the girls are going to be roommates, we should probably get to know each other."

"How about we skip Mr. Burger." I'm a vegetarian. "I bet every last person in orientation will swarm there."

"When I went to school here there was a delicious bagel shop. You could get anything you wanted on them. I hope it's still here. How does that sound?" Mrs. Trager asks.

"But, you went here a jillion years ago, Mom." Hannah wrinkles her nose.

"Sounds de-lish." I smile, thrilled to avoid a crowd and beef at the same time.

"You went here?" Mom asks.

"It's where I met my husband. It's special to have Hannah carry on the tradition." Mrs. Trager gives Hannah a squeeze. Hannah rolls her eyes, so just I can see. "How about you?"

"I got my degree from Ohio State," Mom answers. "I teach high school history."

"Hey, I know that girl." Hannah motions toward the other side of the street. "She was new at my high school this year. I didn't know her very well, but she always seemed sweet and laid back, you know? Her name is...something cool...oh what is it...Karly, no, K-K-Kat."

"Kat Wiley!" Hannah calls.

The girl with dark hair, pulled back in a ponytail, sporting Umbros and a Clarkston Soccer T-shirt stops and looks around.

"Kat, it's me, Hannah from Hoover High." Hannah waves frantically.

"Hey." She crosses the street toward us. "Are y'all comin' to school here, too?" she drawls.

"Go Clarkston!" Hannah cheers, pointing to Kat's shirt. "This is my new roommate, Claire. We're rooming with Palmer Ruscilli too. Do you know her? We're here for orientation and all that. Do you play soccer here?"

Kat nods slowly. "I know Palmer. The gorgeous one, right? We had Calculus together. And, yeah, I can't believe it, but I made the team. We're trainin' all week every week, but I've been headin' home on the weekends to hang out with my folks. Coach can't officially call it practice 'til August." Her voice is slow and sweet and Southern.

"That is so awesome! Making a college team is like ultra hard to do." Hannah grins. "Do you get to hang out with the football players?"

"There are athletes all over the place. And, yeah, I'm amped. Clarkston has some strong players returning this year. We should have a great season."

"You don't by chance, have a roommate yet? Do you? Please tell me you don't have a roommate," Hannah grabs Kat's arm.

"I've been thinkin' about livin' in the athlete dorm." Kat tightens her ponytail. "But I don't know. The girls I play with seem great and all, but I might need a break from the intensity sometimes, ya know?"

"We need a fourth!" Hannah can barely contain herself. She's actually jumping up and down. "You can be our fourth. We'll have one of those adorable quads, and it will be so much fun!"

"For real? Y'all need a fourth?"

I nod.

"For real!" Hannah jumps again.

"I'm in." Kat gives us each high fives.

"I have to text Palmer!" Hannah squeals. "She'll be *so* excited!"

1
CLAIRE

"*BONJOUR, DEUX CAFÉS AU LAIT, s'il vous plait.*" My voice shakes as I try out my French for the first time ever outside of the classroom.

I've never left Ohio before, and here I am on the other side of the world at the Charles de Gaulle airport in Paris. I've been taking French since third grade. Back then it was colors and numbers. Now, as I listen to French words flurry off the tongues of the crowd pressing around me, I realize the language is still colorful and infinite.

"Is that it?" Mom asks eyeing the small, flimsy plastic cup of coffee I hand her. "How much was it?"

"Two euro a pop," I toss my long, curly hair over my shoulder with a lean and a neck flip, careful not to spill our caffeine. "That's about three dollars, or a venti with a shot of flavored syrup at Starbucks." I say.

"This doesn't look like a venti or a grande or even a tall! It looks more like a teeny! I hope Arnot plans on picking up coffee most mornings, because if we're relying on my salary to pay our way, we'll have to do without." Mom's fingers tremble as she wraps them around her cup. I remember the first time I ever saw her fingers tremble like that. It was the first night Dad didn't come home. I was seven. I came out of my room one morning in my Cinderella nightgown thinking it was strange no one woke me up for school. Even weirder was that Mom wasn't dressed, and Dad wasn't reading the paper. Dad wasn't even there. Mom just sat at the kitchen table in Dad's blue terry cloth robe with her coffee mug in her hands, but it was clattering against the table as her fingers shimmied up and down. They've been like that ever since.

I sip my coffee. The foamy milk tickles my lip. It is the smoothest, richest drink I've ever tasted.

"*Mmm*," I sigh. "I see why they charge two euro. It's amazing! *C'est magnifique!*" I take another swallow, savoring the warmness as it eases down my throat.

"I'll text Arnot and tell him we're here. Thank goodness he's picking us up. I don't think we'd ever make our way out of this jumble." Mom pulls out her phone. "I still can't believe he flew us over here, Claire. Can you? He's a keeper!"

I force a smile. Mom's had a long line of "keepers" since Dad left. Let's just say I would have never even slotted any of them in the "want to date" category. Mom is smart, and she's pretty with her pale blue eyes and shoulder-length straight hair, the same sandy color as mine. But the number of guys out there looking for a single, unstable woman in her late thirties who teaches high school and has an eighteen-year-old daughter must be almost nonexistent.

I watch the other travelers scurrying by from every

nation on earth. Would one of them be a good match for Mom? I try to guess their nationalities. I try to memorize how they tie their scarves, how they gesture while they talk and kiss each other on both cheeks to say hello. Everyone here has an air of style.

"Claire." Mom looks at me impatiently. I have officially spaced out.

I open my eyes wider and nod exaggeratedly. "Sorry."

"Arnot says to take the moving sidewalks to Concourse A, go to the escalators, ride them to the main lobby, and follow the signs to baggage. From baggage, go out the doors to the right of the taxi stand." She exhales, blowing the golden wisp of hair that's fallen from her loose ponytail away from her face. "He said it would take us about forty-five minutes—just to walk through the airport! Sounds complicated, but he's such a seasoned traveler. I'm sure he knows what he's talking about."

"No more complicated than an American airport." I put my arm in hers. "We can do this." I say just as much for my benefit as Mom's.

Arnot's directions are perfect. With the help of my basic French and multiple signs printed in English, we maneuver like mice through a maze, find our luggage without many complications, and roll it out the doors.

A chilly gust stings my face. I pull up the collar of my denim jacket and start digging in my suitcase for my pale gray scarf. I didn't expect August to be chilly.

"He said he'd be driving a dark blue Peugeot. What's a Peugeot look like?" Mom bites her lip.

I laugh, watching all the tiny, boxy cars driving through the pick-up lanes. "I'm guessing small and squarish."

Mom laughs too, as I keep digging through socks,

sweatshirts, and, *Aha*! I pull my scarf out of my bag just as an angular, navy blue Peugeot pulls up to the curb.

Mom laughs again, shrill this time. "You guessed right."

As I knot my scarf around my neck, Arnot gets out of the driver's side wearing a black leather jacket and contrasting white wool scarf. His black hair is slicked straight back like a vampire, and he's suspiciously tan. But he's all smiles. He rushes to Mom. It's hard to tell who's moving faster, because they collide somewhere in the middle—Mom all tiny and pale almost tripping on her long, flowy skirt and Arnot, thick and confident. Arnot wraps his arms around her and kisses first one cheek, then the other. "*Bienvenue*, welcome, *ma cherie*!"

He turns to me and does the same. It's all so French, and I'm still in a semi-slumberish state from the two or maybe three hours of sleep I got on the overnight flight. Plus I'm a bit giddy with the reality of being in Paris. I'm so muddled that I actually kiss him back.

When Arnot steps back I see someone else kissing Mom's cheeks. Then, that someone turns to me. He looks like Arnot, but younger and taller, at least six feet, and way hotter! This guy's complexion is dark like Arnot's, but on him it seems European, Greek maybe, not fake-baked. A five o'clock shadow accents his jawbone, even though it's only around 9:00 a.m. His black hair isn't slicked, but gelled upward with bangs that almost—but not quite—cover his dark brown eyes.

He smiles, the same broad, welcoming smile of Arnot, but instead of seeming like a used car salesman, it makes me smile back. "Hi. I'm Phillip, Arnot's nephew. You must be Claire." He puts out his hand.

Thankfully he doesn't go in for the hug and cheek smooches. I'm a bit off balance already. It might have knocked me over. I'm hoping he's just along for the airport ride. I shake his hand tentatively, feeling my face flush. "Yes, I'm Claire. Nice to meet you."

No one said anything about a nephew. Let alone a dangerously cute nephew. I mainly avoid boys. My Dad is such a loser; he kind of spoiled things for me. I've always sworn I'd never end up like Mom. And after one horrible relationship "no boys allowed" has become my strategy.

"*Enchant*é," Phillip says with a practiced French accent and squeezes my hand before letting it go. "I'm studying abroad at Regent's College in London. I have a few days off before I head back for summer term exams. If it's okay, I'll be spending a lot of time with you these next couple of days."

I swallow hard and blush. I should be thrilled, but honestly, I'm nervous.

2
HANNAH

I WONDER IF I'VE GONE down the wrong strip of shops as my flip-flops slap against the boardwalk and my ponytail bounces back and forth as we walk. But, no. Here it is.

"*Ta da.*" I smile swinging open the door of Double Dip. The rush of icy air conditioning hits my face, along with the sweet scent of waffle cones baking, as the bells tied with red string to the door jingle our arrival.

"I love this place," I say. "Don't you guys? You can each get one scoop. What flavor do you want?"

"Superman!" Owen says. He pumps his eight-year-old fist in the air.

"How about you, Sammie?"

"What flavor are *you* getting?" my twelve-year-old sister asks.

I glance along the rows of creamy concoctions in the freezer case: Moose Tracks, Cookie Dough, Vanilla Bean. I hone in on the fruity section. "Black raspberry," I say.

"Me, too." Sammie sidles up beside me and locks her tan arm in my freckled one.

"I'll take three cones, one Superman, and two black raspberries," I tell the clerk, who looks like he's as young as Sammie.

Ice cream in hand, we turn to leave the shop at exactly the same moment the guy in a skin-tight, bright green T-shirt walks in. My heart plays hopscotch as I remember his muscular chest, which I saw while he was riding his skimmer board at the beach earlier today. Ohmygosh ohmygosh ohmygosh! Should I say hi? I have to say hi!

"Hi." I smile and feel myself bounce.

"Purple stripes, right?" he asks, running his hand, laden with string and rope bracelets, through his sun-streaked curls.

My ears get warm. He recognizes me and remembers my swimsuit! Okay, this is too good to be true. If only I could stash my little brother and sister somewhere, like in the freezer case, just for a minute, just long enough to find out his name. Maybe I can pretend they're not here.

"Hannah!" Owen calls from behind me.

"Just one sec, O." I brush him off.

"Kids." I laugh, putting down my sibs on the spot. "Yeah, purple stripes. That's me." I smile harder than I should at cute skimmer boy. "We're here on vacation."

His green eyes crinkle in the corners. "Me, too. Actually everyone on the beach is. I think all the locals head north during the summer. At least that's what my uncle says. We're staying with him."

"Hannah!" Owen's voice sounds thin and whiny.

"Don't interrupt." I grit my teeth. "So, you're staying with your uncle. How cool is that? Is he your dad's brother or your mom's brother? You were awesome on that skimmer! I wish I knew how to skim. Where'd you learn how?"

"We come every year. My uncle's single and lives in one of the high-rise apartments across the street from the beach. He taught me as soon as I could stand."

Thud.

An icy, soggy blob lands on my foot. I look down at the lump of red, yellow and blue, slipping from my flip-flop to the floor, leaving rainbow tracks on the top of my foot.

"Owen! Look at all of this!" I yelp.

"My ice cream," Owen whimpers. "I tried to tell you it was falling."

Grabbing a handful of napkins from the counter, I know he's right. I feel a sharp pain of guilt in my chest. Owen called my name. I ignored him. I was more interested in flirting. Speaking of flirting, I'm sure this is making a horrific impression. My conscience is pulled between comforting my little brother and impressing the beautiful beach boy. I love my siblings. I really do, but they always seem to have "an incident" at the most inopportune times. I lift my head to laugh things off with Skimmer Boy, but Owen interrupts.

"I'm sorry, Hannah, I really am." Owen's lower lip trembles and from beneath his thick brown bangs, I see his hazel eyes are wide open, like a scared, lost puppy. It's impossible to be mad at him.

"I know you are, O. We'll get you a new cone." I mop up as much of the sticky mess as I can with napkins the consistency of Kleenex, kiss Owen's tuft of dark hair, and toss the papery slop in the trashcan.

The boy has moved on to the line, clearly not

impressed. I swear my heart fell with that scoop of ice cream. Sammie licks her cone like nothing happened—how could she not notice? Owen shakes, trying not to cry. *Please don't cry, please don't cry*, I will him. I approach the counter and the boy, heart galloping, to reorder. Skimmer boy walks past, holding a carton of ice cream in a white plastic bag.

"Sorry about that." I tilt my head toward the scene of the spill.

"Have fun babysitting." He glances at Owen and Sammie.

"Thanks." I groan. "Maybe I'll see you on the beach?" But he doesn't answer. He's out the door.

"Babysitting," I murmur to myself. "This is my life."

"Can I help you?" tween worker in goofy, paper hat asks. *Does he not recognize me from four minutes ago?*

"My brother lost the top off his cone." I huff, holding up the cone with Superman drips around the top. "We need a new Superman."

"One new Superman coming up!" He hands me the new cone.

Wouldn't that be cool? If I could order a new Superman, or an old one, or even just a plain man? He wouldn't even have to be *super*. I'd walk up to the counter and announce, "I need a cute boyfriend, preferably one who can skim."

"One cute boyfriend coming up," the worker would reply, handing me a six-foot, suntanned hottie over the counter.

Unless someone invents that type of shop, I may never get a boyfriend. Being the eternal babysitter to Thing 1 and Thing 2 is a major disadvantage. But college is just around the corner. Just two weeks until I'm at Clarkston and a whole new world of boys will be opened to me. No more younger sister and brother to watch, just three awesome roommates. I can barely wait!

I sigh as I watch my wannabe crush walking down the boardwalk, carrying his bag out of sight.

"He was really cute." Sammie pokes my hip. "Is he gonna text you?"

He was really really cute, like out of my league cute.

"Doubtful," I mumble, popping my gum out of my mouth and into a trashcan. I take a lick of my ice cream, catching a violet streak with my tongue before it slides all the way down the side of my dark cone. The cool sweetness lightens my spirits slightly.

"Why not?" Sammie asks, licking her cone on the side, exactly how I did.

"He didn't get my number." I take another bite.

"Oh well, you'll probably see him tomorrow. This sure is yummy. Don't you think black raspberry is the best flavor in the whole shop?" Sammie continues.

"No, Superman is!" Owen jumps up in the air, his new mound of ice cream wobbling.

"Slow down, O." I tug his arm. "I'm not getting you another cone."

"Black raspberry." Sammie peeks behind my back, taunting Owen.

I take another lick, laden with fresh berries, dancing in cream so sweet and thick it tastes like whipped cream. I might see him at the beach again tomorrow, and with that happy thought, I decide this might be the best ice cream ever. I hate to admit it, but Sammie may actually be right.

3
PALMER

I SET DOWN MY EMPTY ice cream bowl, allowing a million warm needles to tickle the skin on my back as I untie the string to my bikini so I don't get a tan line. *Mmm*. I feel like my cat, Thunder, when she stretches in a patch of sunshine, soaking up its heat.

My body melts into the deck chair. Every muscle in my arms and legs are past complete exertion from lobs, volleys, and serves. Done. Over.

My BFF, Hannah, is scampering around the Florida beaches with her adorable family. Our new, mysterious college roommate, Claire, is off gallivanting on some millionaire's dime in Paris. Our other roomie, Kat, has to train every day with the women's soccer team, but at least she gets to be on campus already. And me? I'm sitting around at home playing tennis with my little sister. Part of me loves it. Out on the courts I feel strong and capable and in control, like smacking that yellow ball puts all of my worries in their proper places. And I will miss Tia when I go away to school, even though sometimes she drives me crazy. But, I'm still jealous of my roommates. I am so ready to be out of here and at school.

I close my eyes and relish the rays soaking into my skin.

"*Woohoo.*"

A catcall softly whistles from behind. I jump out of my groggy doze realizing jerking upward from my belly down pose was a dangerous mistake. Luckily there's only a centimeter or two between my dangling coral bikini top, my chair and me. I drop back flat against my towel.

"I would have come over earlier if I'd known what I was missing." Keegan announces his arrival.

"Hi, babe." I fumble with my tie, trying to knot it quickly and tightly, so I can sit up safely.

"Hello yourself. I'd be jealous if there was anyone around. As it is, I'm just all hot and bothered."

"Stop it." I slide up to sitting and swat his invisible words with my hand. He looks so irresistible in his white baseball pants and royal blue jersey. Even if he is a little sweaty from his game, it just makes Keegan look rugged and playful. He raises his dark eyebrows high above his slate gray eyes.

"Did you win?" I ask, sliding over to make room for him.

"Yup. Seven to four. Two runs scored by yours truly."

"You're such a stud." I bat my eyelashes. My whole body feels as fluttery as my lashes.

He sits next to me, so close, his thigh touches mine and a different kind of heat prickles my skin.

"Are you trying to drive me crazy, Palm?" His eyes,

which normally droop around the edges in a kind of perpetual sleepy look, turn upwards when he smiles. My heart always jumps when they do that.

"What do you mean?" I try to ask innocently.

"I mean, you lay here almost topless, sweat trickling down your back." He pauses and slides his finger down my spine, wet with perspiration.

"I didn't expect…" I try to defend myself, but my words are completely defeated by his soft, full lips brushing against mine. He tastes like tangy Gatorade and salty sunflower seeds—baseball player snacks. I can't help myself. His lips are incredibly soft, and it must be ninety degrees out here! I slide my arms around his neck and tilt my head upward to reach him better. I'm five-eight, but he's a good three inches taller.

His tongue darts between my lips, and his hand slides up my mostly bare back. I feel a twinge throughout my entire body. Where is my cover up when I need it? I'm used to his hands on my back, but with a shirt as a barrier, not with his hands touching my actual skin. Where my muscles were limp from exhaustion before, they're now taut, on the ready.

Ready for what?

To swat him away, like his playful words? Or to lean into him? I feel like a cartoon character with an animated devil on one shoulder and an angel on the other. The devil wants Keegan to kiss me and touch me forever. His fingers slide from my back, to my sides, where my skin is especially sensitive, almost ticklish to his touch. What if they slid all the way around front? What then? The angel slaps my shoulder and wants me to slap Keegan across the face, stand up, and pour my glass of ice water over his head, or maybe over mine. Oh, *stop, stop, stop,* something whispers inside me.

A Bruno Mars melody rings from my phone.

I pull away, panting. Saved by the bell.

"Let it ring," Keegan murmurs kissing me again.

"I've gotta check." I gasp for air. My display reads "Mom."

"Hi, Mom."

"Hi, honey, how was tennis?"

"Good."

"Good," Mom continues, but her voice sounds like it's coming from another planet. I can barely register her. Keegan traces the outline of my thigh with his index finger, staring intently at me with eyes like wet slate. The rosy spots on his cheeks from being in the sun all day give him just enough of a boyish innocence to not come off as devilish. I pull my eyes away.

"Yeah, it was great. Tia totally tromped me, though. Drives me crazy. She went to the pool to hang out after. I needed to chill, so I came home."

"I'm swinging by the grocery on the way home to grab some sushi for dinner. Is there anything else you can think of that we need?"

"*Umm.*" Keegan slides his finger over my hipbone and across to my belly button. "*Umm.*"

"Palmer, you there?"

"Sure. Sorry, Mom. Someone was trying to text me." In one motion, I brush his hand away, stand up, and walk toward the grill. Keegan gives me his best sad face. I stick out my tongue at him.

"Could you get some blueberries? And more ice cream? I just finished it off. It's so yummy and cool and summery."

"Okay, I'll grab blueberries, but let's skip the ice cream. You don't want to gain the freshman fifteen before school even starts. Could you run a load of darks in the laundry for me?"

"Sure." I suck in my stomach and pace around the deck.

"All right, see you in a bit."

"K. See you soon."

I put down my phone and glare at my empty ice cream bowl and then glare at Keegan. "You make it very hard for a girl to have a normal conversation with her mother," I scold.

"I didn't want you talking to *her*." He smiles. "I wanted you kissing *me*." He stands and comes toward me, slipping his hand into the small of my back and scootching me against him. "Like this."

So warm and sweet, but Mom's ice cream comment rubbed me the wrong way, and I feel prickly, like I don't want him too close to my stomach, because maybe he'll notice it's not as flat as it could be. I stiffen, but Keegan doesn't seem to notice. He kisses my neck.

"And like this." He purrs.

I laugh and stretch to reach the top of his head, where I rub his dark buzz cut like it's a good luck charm. "You are so bad."

"And what's wrong with that?" Keegan's smile slides from the corner of his lips all the way across his mouth. "And you are so good." He kisses my neck again.

"I have to do laundry." I step back. "And my mom will be home in fifteen minutes, and she would die if she caught you here."

"I was just driving by. It wasn't planned or anything, Mrs. Ruscilli." Keegan pretends to defend himself to Mom.

"I'm glad you drove by." I squeeze his hand, strolling

off the porch. I head toward the walk that leads around front to the driveway. "But now…"

"But now, you're kicking me out?"

"Something like that." I grin, knowing he gets it. His parents would kill him if they caught us alone too. We walk hand in hand until we get to his Accord parked in the middle of my driveway.

"I'm not leaving without one more kiss. I don't get you alone like this very often." He poses in front of the driver's door, with legs spread apart in a serious stance, like he's ready to catch a ball. All he needs is his glove.

"There's a reason for that." I roll my eyes. "One more." I surrender and stand on my tippy toes, kissing him lightly. But he gathers me up in both of his strong arms and pulls me tight, and the kiss lasts longer than a second, longer than a minute. I'm lost in his lips and the sun, and I gather every ounce of willpower in my body to pull myself away again.

"I have to do that laundry and hop in the shower." I take two steps backward like I'm playing Mother May I? in reverse.

"Sounds fun. I'll help with the laundry if I can stay for the shower."

"Ha! You wish!" I take three more steps back. "Maybe you need a *cold* shower." I laugh.

"Love you," he says.

"Love you too." I step away quickly before I get tangled up in his arms again.

"See you tomorrow?"

"I'll be waiting." I blow him a last kiss as I turn my back.

4
KAT

I TURN. *TAP-TAP*, SPIN. Dang it! The ball got away from me.

I realign myself with the soccer ball. *Tap- tap*, spin, *tap*. Double dang it! That time I nearly had it!

Tap tap, spin, *tap tap*.

"Yeah!" I boot my ball into the practice net set up in my back yard and watch it swoosh into the top right-hand corner.

"Nice shot."

I turn from the goal and see my older brother, Alex, and his best friend, Nicholas, standing by the back door.

"Thanks." I nod toward Nicholas, knowing it wasn't Alex who gave the compliment. "But I was more excited I got this control trick down that my trainer showed me. Wanna see?"

I run to the goal, grab my ball, and place it between my feet. *Tap tap*, spin, miss. "Man! Well, I had it a minute ago."

"No one said we wanted to see." Alex laughs, shaking his head.

"What exactly are you trying to do?" Nicholas steps closer to me and further from Alex.

"At least his friend cares, even if my own darlin' brother does not." I fake pout to Alex. "See, Nicholas, you put the ball between your feet, like this." I reset the ball for the ten millionth time. "Then, you tap with your right, then with your left, so the other team thinks you're dribbling, or getting ready to pass."

I tap the ball with each foot, do a three sixty with my body, regain perfect control of the ball, tap it with each foot again, then shoot it toward the goal. "Nailed it," I pant. "When you turn around like that," I pause to catch some air, "it totally tricks the other team, and when they're faked out and least expecting it, you pass or shoot. Sweet, right?"

"Very." Nicholas agrees. "Can I try?"

"Sure."

He picks up the ball with his freckled hands and sets it up. *Tap, tap*, spin, but he keeps spinning and does a turn and a half, so he's facing the wrong way and is several feet away from the ball.

"Sweet!" Alex claps and whistles. "That, my friend, is why we are swimmers."

"You try," Nicholas taunts, holding the ball out to Alex.

"I said 'we.' That is why *we* are swimmers." Alex's green eyes sparkle like sunlight on a stream as he steps forward.

Alex grabs the ball, sets it between his feet, and taps it twice, then instead of doing the required spin, sneaks off running toward the goal. I instinctively chase after him, cut him off, and bop the ball out from between his feet and to the left. By then, Nicholas is at my side. He gets control of the stray ball and kicks it toward the goal, where it bounces off the post and into Mama's bed of peonies. A tall green stalk folds, making one of the fuchsia flowers bow and rest atop the ball.

"Now that's a cool move!" Nicholas gives me a high five.

I slap him back and pounce on Alex. "You are so cheap." I take him to the ground. "You didn't even try to spin." He rolls over, so I'm pinned to the grass and he's on top of me.

"How's that for a spin, darlin'?" he mocks.

"Stop." I try to kick him with my legs, but he has them trapped. His arms cross over my eyes so I can't see. The smell of freshly mowed grass and damp earth fills my nose. I don't mind being on the ground, but I can't stand it when he wins. "Never call me darlin' on the soccer field! How about 'fast' or 'powerful'? 'Beast' would do." I snap back at him, flailing. Daddy got transferred to Ohio a year ago, but we still sound like we're from Tennessee, and when we go at it with each other, we sound like we're from some log cabin by a creek in Tennessee.

"I'll rescue you, fair lady!" Nicholas pulls Alex off from behind, and they start wrestling and rolling in a ball of masculinity. I am free.

I wipe my grassy hands on my T-shirt. "Thank you, Sir Swimsalot."

Somehow, they untangle. "Sir Swimsalot?" Alex asks, cocking his chlorine-bleached head. "P-lease!"

Later, Alex and I sit on the couch zoning out with *American Idol* on the flat screen. He's a year ahead of me and will be a sophomore at Ohio State this year.

"Whatcha doin' tomorrow?" he asks, sticking his hand in the bag of popcorn we're sharing.

"After church, just chillin'. I think I'll call Palmer, the girl who stopped by last weekend who's gonna be my roommate, and grab a coffee with her. I'm drivin' back to Clarkston later tomorrow afternoon. I have training all week."

"Really, darlin'? 'Cause I thought you might be busy flirting with Nicholas."

Nicholas's face flashes in my mind: wavy red hair, freckles dotted all over his smiley face, bright green eyes— not eerie green like Alex's, but true green, like a green Crayon.

"Hush." I elbow Alex.

"Oh, look at my cool soccer moves. Oh rescue me, Sir Swimsalot." Alex raises his voice about three octaves.

"Stop it now." I crunch on a handful of salty, buttery popcorn. "Like I would ever flirt with Nicholas."

"What do you think you were doing in the backyard today?"

"I was practicin' soccer, and y'all showed up. He wanted to see my trick, and I showed him. End of story. Period," I rant.

"Well, if you're *not* trying to flirt with him, you'll have to try harder." Alex takes a swig of water, his ice cubes clanking in his glass.

"What are you implyin'?"

"I mean all Nicholas talked about once we were inside was you."

I pull my eyes away from Ryan Seacrest and look Alex straight in the eyes.

"Kat's such a great soccer player. You and Kat seem so close. That must be really cool to have a sister you're so close with. All of mine drive me nuts. Where did Kat get those crazy eyes and dark hair? She doesn't look anything like you. It's cool we'll both be at Clarkston in the fall." Alex does a pretty good impersonation of Nicholas's flat, midwestern voice.

I swear there's a piece of popcorn lodged in my throat and another five hundred kernels popping in my stomach.

"I don't like Nicholas. Not like that. I swear, Alex. He's just some guy from school. He's your friend."

Nicholas just graduated like me. He and Alex train at the same pool, so he's around a lot. Whenever Nicholas comes over, he's super easy to hang out with—almost as easy as when it's just Alex and me. But when I picture Nicholas I feel nothing. Honestly, no flutters, no heat, nothing to be embarrassed about, just a smile. Nothing more. Empty radar.

Alex's lips curl downward.

"It's not any different..." I start, but catch myself. I was going to say it's not any different than him acting all friendly when Palmer dropped by to say she was glad we were going to be roomies. Of course, everyone drools over Palmer, because she could be mistaken for Megan Fox, only prettier. But I realize if I say that, it's like admitting I think Nicholas is cute. Which I don't. "It's not any different than me goofing around with you. Nicholas is great. I mean super sweet, but he's your friend. That's all. Well, I guess I consider him my friend, too, but *not* like a guy I'd flirt with. Not like a boyfriend."

5
CLAIRE

AS THE TIRES THUD ALONG the French highway, Arnot, Phillip, and Mom chat back and forth about cathedrals, museums, and restaurants. My ears perk up when I hear the bit about the Parisian ballet, but their words morph into short buzzing sounds as my eyelids tug harder and harder.

"Claire, we're here." Mom ruffles my hair.

"Oh!" I exclaim, brushing her hand away and forcing my eyes open. Pale stucco buildings with black wrought iron terraces and flower boxes line narrow streets. It's like every picture of Paris I've ever seen—like Owen Wilson should be coming around the corner for a scene from *Midnight in Paris*. "We're here," I whisper.

"No cars allowed on our street. I'll drop you here." Arnot parks the car in the middle of a small intersection. "Phillip can you walk them to the hotel? I'll drive around and pick you up in about fifteen minutes. Lauren, you ladies will need some time to freshen up, and maybe a nap to get your body clocks back in sync. We'll meet you and Claire in the lobby at 2:00 p.m.?"

"Sure." Mom nods.

I'm still disoriented as Phillip takes Mom's and my roller bags by their handles and leads us down the cobblestone street scattered with cafes with red awnings. The tables are dotted with people sipping coffee. I try to absorb the clanking of plates, the shouting of waiters and friends greeting one another while keeping up with Phillip as he zigs and zags between tables and tourists. Our suitcase wheels bump over the cobblestones.

"*Voila!*" Phillip turns into a charming pink building. "*Grandes Ecoles*. Arnot and I got settled in last night. Let's check you in."

"Arnot is keeping us in style! This place is sweet!" I whisper to Mom while Phillip approaches the woman with a sharp brown bob, standing behind the desk. He hands our passports to her, gets our key and leads us to the elevator.

"There isn't room for all of us and your bags in the lift," Phillip explains as he pushes the button. "Head on up to the third floor. I'll be right behind you with your luggage."

The door opens, and Mom and I walk into an elevator the size of a shower. I push the number three and twirl a stray blonde curl that's landed on my shoulder. "I told you he's a keeper!" Mom giggles like a thirteen-year old. "And the apple doesn't fall far from the tree. Phillip really seems to know what he's doing."

"Uh, yeah." I have to agree I'm impressed. "Like he completely knows his way around these streets and how to check into a hotel. I don't know any of those things."

"We're really in Paris, Claire." Mom's eyes light up

like I haven't seen them in years. She's always exhausted and nervous. Being a single mom can't be stress-free, but I try to make it easier on her. I studied hard enough to earn a partial scholarship to Clarkston in the fall. I try to tidy up the house and the dishes, although that's not my strong suit. I help teach a dance class for little girls to earn free dance classes and a little savings money at my studio. But Mom rarely seems happy. I hug her tight, because right now, at this moment, Mom seems really happy.

Our little box comes to a halt and the door slides open. We step into the hallway and wait for Phillip.

"We wouldn't be here if it weren't for Arnot. It's a dream come true." Mom shakes her head. "I'm so glad he brought his nephew. It will be fun for you to have someone to hang out with. Plus, Phillip's so cute and a real charmer."

I giggle, caught up in Mom's excitement. Plus, who says "charmer"?

"Here we are." Phillip appears like magic from around the corner.

"*Ahh*!" I jump, wondering how much he heard.

"Speak of the devil." Mom takes her bag from Phillip as he pulls out the key card.

"I've been called worse." He winks at Mom.

Once Phillip leaves, Mom and I feel the effects of little sleep. Everything sounds fuzzy. Our conversation is disjointed. We slide on our sleeping masks from the airplane and crash hard.

I thought Arnot was rude to say he wouldn't meet us for four hours, but as the alarm on my phone plays "Undertow" by Holly Starr, I wish he would have said five or six. I click off my alarm and take in the room. It's small, but clean and pretty, with flowery wallpaper, light mauve carpet and dainty white coverlets on the bed and end table. I stretch and walk barefoot to the window, pulling back the curtains quietly, allowing Mom another minute to snooze. The windows are solid, weighing twice as much as the windows in our apartment back home, and they swing outward like doors. The clouds have cleared and sunshine tickles the pale carpet and my toes.

I breathe in the French air, sticking my head out as far as I dare. I contemplate the adventures waiting for me out there. I text my new roommates. I know I won't be able to text them much from here. Roaming charges are insane, but I promised to send them a message when I got to Paris.

MADE IT! COFFEE'S DE-LISH! PARIS IS GORGEOUS (SO IS MOM'S BOYFRIEND'S NEPHEW) - WISH YOU WERE HERE!

As soon as I send it, I remember it's six hours earlier back home, making it a little before 8:00 a.m. Oops!

I can't believe I've been included in their trio. They all know each other. They all seem like the type of girls everyone knows. I've always been the girl who no one really noticed. I did my thing, danced and studied, and was kind of left alone. I mean, I have friends, but they're friends from ballet and people I talk with on the bus. I've never been the BFF type. I don't have a clique I spend every Saturday with at the mall or every Friday night at the football game. It was all kind of wild how I met Hannah. Fate maybe? I hope they don't regret their decision to include me in their room.

"Mom." I nudge her. "Time to wake up. We're in Paris. Time to meet Arnot."

I slide on a fresh pair of jeans, a pink paisley tank and my gray scarf. A dab of mascara and lip gloss and a spray of

Beautiful, my favorite perfume, finish me off.

Arnot and Phillip stand in the lobby. I can't help but feeling like it's a double date.

"You look beautiful," Arnot says to Mom, kissing her first on her right, then her left cheek.

"I told you, Mom." I smile, but Phillip is kissing my right cheek and my words get warbled. He kisses my left. He smells woodsy and musky and takes me totally off guard.

"If you told her, then I'll tell you. You look great."

I blush deeper than the pink swirls of paisley in my shirt. Where did this boy come from?

"Shall we explore?" Arnot asks, saving me from a reply.

"I'm so excited," Mom starts chatting away. I worry she'll come off too eager and turn off Arnot. But I relax, watching the way he laughs at her jokes and listens to her stories.

"What do you want to see first?" Arnot asks.

"Can we grab something to eat?" I ask. "Even if it's just something I can carry around while we walk."

"You need a *crêpe*!" Phillip explains, as we pass a corner *crêperie*.

Arnot steps up to the little stand with a chalkboard sign. "What would you like to try?"

Mom looks over the handwritten list of choices. "Cheese."

Arnot orders cheese *crêpes*. I watch the worker spread a thin layer of batter on his hot iron and swirl it around until it is fully covered. He tosses a handful of shredded Swiss cheese in the center. When it's done, the crepe man expertly folds the circle into a neat triangle with his spatula, wraps it in wax paper and presents it to Mom.

The melted cheese smells so tangy; I'm almost dizzy with hunger.

"Chocolate for the lady and myself," Phillip instructs the cook in French.

I was thinking cheese, but after one bite of the sweet, rich, gooey treasure in my hand I'm thankful Phillip ordered chocolate. The chocolate is warm and dripping out of the sweet pancake-like wrap. "*C'est delicieuse*," I say, licking my lips and trying to sound like I'm a native Parisian. "*Merci*."

"*De rien*," Phillip says. "There is nothing like a chocolate *crêpe* to add some sweetness to a Saturday afternoon."

I take another bite instead of trying to make a clever comeback. Phillip sounds like a movie script when he talks, not a person. We walk as a foursome, people watching and chatting about the pleasant change in weather.

I gaze in the windows of the shopping district, memorizing the French styles, so I can emulate them back home. Boots with short, flirty dresses, and scarves—more flowing, less structured. I love it!

"See something you like?" Phillip interrupts my fashion fantasy.

"Everything," I sigh, staring in a window strewn with pastel scarves, carved music boxes, silver picture frames, and flirty, flouncy dresses, "but that little dress is so cute!" I squeal, forgetting Phillip could probably care less about dresses.

"Then get it," he nudges. "We're going to duck in here for a minute," Phillip tells his uncle. "There's a dress we have to get Claire."

Arnot and Mom are a few steps ahead of us. "Great."

He smiles and hands me a 100 Euro note.

"Oh, no." I step back shaking my head. "I can't let you buy it. I don't need it. I just said it was pretty." I wish I could say I'd pay for it myself, but I have no idea how much it costs, and I'm pretty sure it's more than I have in my wallet. I take another step back trying to get away from the awkward situation and trip on a pop can, almost tumbling to the ground.

Phillip extends his hand and steadies me. "Uncle Arnie loves spoiling his guests. Don't insult him." His smile is warm.

Arnot winks. "Phillip, make sure she gets what she likes. We'll head toward the garden and wait near the entrance."

My heart pounds uncomfortably as we enter the store, but I relax almost immediately as I inhale the scents of vanilla and lavender candles. A young clerk says something in French too rapid for me to understand.

Phillip answers her in perfect French, and she walks back to the rack where the dress I admired is displayed.

"*Quel taille?*" she asks

"What size are you?" Phillip asks.

I untuck my curls from behind my ears letting them fall over my face and cover my eyes. "I'm really short, so I don't think they'll have my size," I murmur. Maybe my petite frame will be my out of this increasingly uncomfortable situation.

"*Très bien, n'est-ce pas?*" the girl says, holding up a dress that looks exactly my size.

Phillip thanks her and motions me to follow the girl to the fitting room. I close the curtains and peak at the tag. 84 Euro! That's more than $100. Even if I spent everything I brought with me to France I couldn't afford it. As I slide the filmy fabric up around my waist, I realize it's short—really short. So much for worrying about finding one small enough, but it is beautiful.

"Let me see," Phillip calls from behind the curtain. Embarrassed by how much of my legs are showing, I try to think of a reason why I can't slide the curtain back, but come up blank.

I pull the heavy white fabric back and start explaining. "It's really expensive, plus way too short!" I point to the hemline. "Can you imagine if I wore this out in public? I'd be so self-conscious!"

"You look amazing. And it's not considered short in Europe. No one will look twice; it's just the style." He nods to the clerk and says something that includes the word, "*oui*," which even in my nervousness I know means yes.

"I can't get it."

"It's already yours." Phillip laughs. "Now change back into your jeans."

The curtain floats back like a scene in a dream. Did Phillip say I looked amazing?

6
HANNAH

"HANNAH, I'M GOING RUNNING. STILL want to come?" Dad nudges my arm. My eyes adjust to the dark room, with chinks of pale light sneaking in between the slats of the blinds. A cool breeze from the ceiling fan grazes my face. I've burrowed into a cozy spot in our beach condo and am tempted to tell him no thanks. But I know I'd regret it.

"Sure," I whisper, wiggling away from Sammie's body, which is smashed right up against mine in the bed we're sharing. I hear a rustle from below as Owen tosses in his sleeping bag.

"I'll meet you by the door," Dad mouths and points.

I tiptoe to my drawer, rummaging in the dark for running clothes.

Squeak.

I close my eyes, hoping neither Sammie nor Owen heard the drawer close. They'd just want to go with us or want me to stay, and it would ruin everything. I slip on my clothes in the dark bathroom and pull my tangle of wavy hair into a ponytail. I don't even bother brushing my teeth, let alone putting on make-up.

"Ready?" Dad smiles, room key in hand.

I nod, carefully turning the handle to the front door and escaping into the breezeway.

"We should get a great sunrise this morning." Dad's voice sounds like a radio announcer, even though his career is selling some kind of containers to the grocery industry.

"Look. It's starting." I point to the horizon where the washed out light is warming into pastel pinks and yellows.

We stretch in silence, absorbing the fresh, salty air and the whooshing crash of the waves rhythmically hitting the sand, over and over, like they're strumming the beat of their own song. The light gets rosier and brighter by the second as the sun peeks just above the horizon, throwing its blaze across the surface of the water.

"Are your eyes open enough to see that sun?" Dad taps me on the shoulder, signaling it's time to move.

"Almost."

We start running side by side, allowing our bodies to wake up as our hearts start pumping.

"You having fun here?" Dad asks.

"I love it here."

"Anything you want to do on our last couple of days?"

"*Hmmm*. I don't know."

A seagull squawks overhead. I look up. As I avert my eyes back to the beach, I spy Skimmer Boy, wearing nothing but sweat shorts and gym shoes, with a guy who's probably his uncle running toward us.

I feel a zing through my chest at the sight of his tan skin, but oh no oh no! I have on zero make-up! My hair is a frizz ball. I'm running with my Dad! Maybe he won't notice me, or maybe he won't recognize me, or maybe a giant whale jumping out of the ocean will distract him. Please let there be a giant whale!

"Hey Stripes!" he calls, waving.

No such luck. But he did wave.

"Hi." I wave back.

"See you at the beach." His voice trails as he keeps moving.

"Sounds good!" I yell, hoping he'll hear.

"Who's that?" Dad asks, running his hand through his short, steel gray hair. "And why did he call you 'stripes'?"

"Some guy I've seen around," I try to say nonchalantly, between breaths. "My swimsuit has stripes. I don't know. That's just what he calls me." I turn my head to the ocean to hide my bright red cheeks.

"Does he have a name?"

"I'm sure he has a name." I laugh. "I just don't know what it is. I saw him at the beach yesterday. Then when I took the kids for ice cream he was there too. We said 'hi'. That's it."

"*Uh huh.*"

"And I can't believe he just saw me like this. I look disgusting!" I pat my frizzy ponytail.

"You never look disgusting. You're so pretty, Hannah Banana."

"Thank goodness he didn't hear you call me that!" I punch Dad lightly on the arm, secretly liking that he still calls me by my pet name.

"I could make a point of calling you that really loudly when you see him at the beach later."

Is that my heart thudding or our feet pounding the sand?

"No thanks!"

I slip into a daydream of lying on my towel and having Skimmer Boy walk over and ask if he could rub some sunscreen on me. But even in my dream, as I smell the coconut lotion, Dad shouts, "Hannah Banana!" and Owen and Sammie start tickling my crush. I feel my freckles turn pink just thinking about it. All I want is a few minutes alone with that boy. Just to talk without ice cream falling on my foot. Just to find out his name. Just for him to ask for my number, so we can text.

"So there is one thing I'd like to do before we leave," I say.

"What's that?"

"Well, you and Mom are great and all." I'm not sure how to say the rest without hurting Dad's feelings, but Dad always tells us to speak our minds.

Dad keeps running left, right, left, right, left; his Nikes sinking softly into the sand. I keep his pace. Left, right, left, right, left.

"But, *umm*, *uh*, I was wondering if today, if today, I could hang out by myself a little. You know, just have a little time when I don't have to build sandcastles with O and Sam."

"I thought you liked building sand castles." Dad's eyes flash. "Remember the one we built a few years ago that looked like a sea serpent? We spent all day out here toting buckets of sand and water back and forth."

"I was so bummed the next morning when it was mostly washed away." I picture the S-shaped beast in my mind, at least six feet long. We'd drawn scales into its side with a stick and found bright white shells for its teeth and eyes. The next morning it was just a big lump.

44

"Sandcastles aren't forever." Dad laughs. "The fun part is building them."

"Yeah," I admit. "They're fun to build. I didn't mean that. I just want some time to lie out and listen to music and read my magazine. You know? Just some veg out alone time."

"Sure."

"Really?" *Was it that easy all along? All I had to do was ask?*

"When we go out to the beach today, you can wander off a little. Not too far. You still need to be able to see our condo. And then every hour or so touch base with us. Let us know you're all right. Okay?"

"Sure, Dad. Thanks."

"You deserve some time to yourself. Everyone does. I didn't know you needed it."

"Yeah, I guess I didn't know I did either. It's just the kids always want to do little kid stuff, which is fun and all, but sometimes I like to do other stuff."

"Like talk to that boy we just saw." Dad playfully punches my arm. "It's not always easy being the oldest, but you'll be off to college before I blink. And sometimes being oldest has its benefits."

***

BENEFITS LIKE NOW.

As promised, here I lay by myself on the beach. I have everything I need for a perfect day: suntan lotion, earbuds, brand new pack of Extra Polar Ice, nail polish, magazine, bottled water, towel, money and phone. Plus the bonus that I don't have Owen's water gun or Sammie's goggles, just my stuff, no one else's. So far, I've flipped through half of my new *Glamour*, eaten a bagel and painted my toenails turquoise.

I must have dozed off in the warm sun. I check my phone. No texts. Not time to check in with Mom and Dad yet. I have another fifteen minutes or so. I know Claire's in another time zone, and Kat's probably practicing, but where's Palmer? Hello, I have beach news. I want to chat. I click on my Facebook App and scroll down through people's updates, liking and commenting as I go. I post on my status, "If you're looking for me, I'll be at the beach…indefinitely." I stand, brush the sand from my legs and stroll to where my family has set up camp for the day to get my "checking in" over with. Their towels and cooler are abandoned. I scan the ocean and find Mom and Dad floating with Sammie and Owen on rafts.

"Hey!" I yell as I get closer. They can't hear me with the waves. I step in. *Mmm.* The cool water feels amazing against my hot skin. I wade in up to my waist. "Hey!" I call again.

"Look, it's Hannah!" Owen squeals.

"Hey guys. I'm just checking in."

"Get on my raft with me." Sammie scoots to the side of her raft to make room. "It's so fun out here."

I take a step toward her, ready to plop on the raft, then remember this is my Hannah day. I pulled my hair in a cute bun and headband, so it wouldn't look so frizzy in the humidity. I have on mascara, waterproof of course, and lip gloss. If I raft, I'll end up looking like a drowned rat.

"Thanks, Sammie. Maybe tomorrow. I'm going back to my towel for a while."

"*Awww.*"

"Hannah needs some time to herself today," Mom instructs. "You can grab a drink from the cooler, Hannah."

"Thanks, Mom. See you in a while."

I walk slowly, pushing my way through the tide back to the beach. I grab a Diet Coke from the cooler, pop the top and take a sip. It's sweet and tickly on my tongue. Back at my towel I pull out my phone, plug in my earbuds and put on my favorite mix. Owen's favorite Building 429 song comes on. Usually I let him listen in on one ear bud. Oh well, I'll play it for him tonight. I scan the beach for Skimmer Boy. He did say he'd see me at the beach today. It was almost like an invitation. Right?

Kids splash in the waves and dig in the sand. Couples walk by hand in hand. How romantic to take a stroll along the beach! At a Tiki Hut somewhere down the strip, I hear an acoustic guitar playing "Brown Eyed Girl." A group of older college kids play volleyball in a sand pit. Looks kind of fun, but they're kind of drunk and I kind of wouldn't fit in. No signs of the boy. I flip through my magazine, checking out cute shoes and sniffing the potent perfume samples. A sundress in an H&M ad is too cute! Sammie would totally appreciate it, but she's not here. It would look darling on Claire, all sheer and flowing. I grab my phone and text her:

DARLING DRESS @ H&M MAKES ME THINK OF YOU!
YOU'RE 2 SWEET – JUST GOT NEW DRESS – CAN'T WAIT FOR U TO SEE IT – HAVE FUN @BEACH

I tap my phone. How lucky am I? Meeting her at orientation? Claire's going to be a perfect roommate. I take another sip of Diet Coke. Not so tasty when it's warm. It feels thick on my tongue.

I scan the beach again. More couples. *Grrr*—hate them! Oh, but there's Skimmer Boy, in all his sun bronzed glory, riding a wave as it dissolves into the sand. He picks up his board, and I call out, "Hi!" I ditch my towel and trot toward him.

"Stripes. What's up?"

"Nothing, really. Just hanging out at the beach, you know, catching some rays, listening to some tunes." Somebody stop me, I sound like a bad Disney sitcom.

"You ever skim before?"

"Nope."

"Want to learn?"

"Sure." I hope this involves him taking my hand, steadying my waist, adjusting my legs. It can't be that hard, right?

"All right. So watch me one time to get the hang of it."

"K." I'm smiling so big my teeth might pop out of my mouth.

He drops the red board with the yellow starburst pattern flat in two or three inches of water. At that precise moment, a wave comes in and he hops on the board. He rides several feet down the beach until the tide pulls back in, and he's left standing on his board on the sand looking like a stud from *90210*.

"Harder than it looks, I'm guessing."

"It's not that hard. It's all about timing. I'll help." He hands me his board. His fingers graze mine for one slight second, sending a staticy buzz up my arms, which makes it impossible to concentrate.

"So toss it flat in front of you."

Plop. "Okay. It's flat." I didn't fail that part, even though my insides are all warbly.

"Good. Now when the wave comes, jump on it like a skateboard."

"Okay."

"I'll tell you when."

My heart thumps faster than two jump ropes going double Dutch.

"Now!"

I jump on, land on my feet, ride for about two seconds, and tumble, landing like a sea turtle on all fours, covered in sand. I topple onto my rear end. A throb shoots from my behind where it hit the sand. My instinct is to scream "Ouch!" at the top of my lungs. But I've already made enough of a fool of myself in front of this guy. I bite my lip, try to swallow my pain and brush off my hands, like it's no big deal. I swallow hard and force a light laugh. "Much harder than it looks."

"Not bad for a first time, Stripes." He reaches his hand out. It's warm and rough and sends a shockwave down my arm as he pulls me up to standing.

"Thanks." I laugh a real laugh now, completely 100% embarrassed. Between the ice cream and the sand, I'm on a roll. "I'm not so sure about that. And it's Hannah. My name is Hannah."

"Okay, Hannah. Can I still call you Stripes? I'm Reed."

"Stripes works. Can I try again?" I must be a glutton for punishment. I look down at the board, so he won't see me blushing.

"Sure."

"Reed!" a girl's voice calls from a swarm of sunbathers. "Reed!"

I turn to see the tanned beauty with wavy, sun-streaked hair down to her hips.

"Just a sec," he says and waves nonchalantly, like gorgeous model types are always calling his name, which they probably are.

Reed grabs his board and puts his hand on my shoulder. "We'll have to finish our lesson another time."

"Sure. No problem." My heart flops to my toes like a gooey jellyfish.

"See ya around, Stripes." He turns and walks toward the girl, the muscles in his back rippling as he walks. Is it possible she's his sister?

"Yeah. See ya." Whoever she is, she's way more important than me.

7
PALMER

I CHEW ON THE CAP of my pen as I look out my bedroom window at the dark clouds billowing across the sky. The stormy weather matches my mood. I sit listening to the rain thumping against my windows, and try to capture in my journal why I feel so anxious. I flip back through the pages trumpeting my excitement when I got the acceptance letter from Clarkston, detailing the drive to Hannah's to make sure she got hers too. There's even a smudge on the page—hot fudge—from the sundaes we ate to celebrate.

Thunder curls against my legs, her long, silky gray fur brushing and tickling my bare feet. The nervous gnawing that's been biting my stomach all day, chews harder. "I wish I could take you to school with me." I whisper, stroking my kitty's back.

I turn my mind and pen back to my journal and write in thick, black, all caps:

WHY DO I FEEL ALL KNOTTED INSIDE?

I'm going to miss Thunder and Tia, in that order, and my parents and my room and everything I've ever known. I don't know much about my new roommates, except for Hannah, who I love, but the others—unknown. UNKNOWN I doodle in large letters, emphasizing what might be the root of me feeling like there's a lit firecracker bouncing around my stomach. *Keegan and I have vowed to see each other most weekends, but will it be the same? He is my best friend. We do everything together. Day after day without him at my side will be weird. I'm not sure what I'll do. I don't know what to expect.*

Okay, enough of the "bad."

Freedom and new friends, I scrawl. *Freedom means not having Mom tell me I should wear a different pair of shoes when the ones I have on are absolutely darling, or Dad telling me I talk on the phone too much, or Tia stealing my favorite pair of jeans, or having to pretend to eat meatloaf, even though it's completely gross. Freedom means not having to pick Tia up from practice or have her try to hang out whenever my friends come over. Freedom means an extra cup of coffee if I want it in the morning, without anyone making comments, letting my hair grow out a couple of inches, even though Mom prefers it trimmed. But it's more than that isn't it?*

Freedom means diving into my writing and taking journalism classes and getting on staff for a school magazine. Freedom means long, late night chats with roomies and going for a run or to a football game or playing cards together on a Saturday afternoon. And friends? I totally depend on Hannah, but some of our high school friends are stale. I'm so sick of Kaitlyn's constant sarcasm, tearing everyone down, and all Olivia ever talks about is how much she had to drink last weekend—b-o-r-i-n-g. Claire and Kat will be a relief.

CHANGE. NEW. FRESH!!!

I glimpse at the clock and pop the lid back on my pen. It's time to get moving for dinner at Keegan's.

"Change. New. Fresh." I say the words I ended my journal entry with aloud, easing on my favorite pair of dark jeans and my bright yellow tank with the ruffle, hoping to keep a sunny outlook. A coat of shiny coral lip gloss and a squirt of Michael Kors perfume are the final touches.

"Perfect." I wink at myself in front of the bathroom mirror. "Pretty and sleek for Keegan. Conservative for his parents." As I take in my reflection, I notice the empty space around my neck—my cross. I dig in my heart-shaped, porcelain jewelry box and pull out my smooth, silver cross. I love the weight of it in my hand, and hold it for a minute, clinging to its solidness. I slide the chain under my hair and close the clasp. "There. Perfect."

"Mom! Dad! I'm going to Keegan's for dinner!" I call, walking down the steps.

"Where?" Dad's voice grumbles like the thunder outside. Even though Keegan and I have been dating for almost two years, Dad can't let the mention of Keegan's name go without a comment.

"I told you last night." I exhale as loudly as humanly possible.

"Watch it, Palm," Mom says, gently placing her hand on my arm. "She did tell us, honey."

"Why do you always go over there?" Dad growls.

"We could have Keegan over to our house for dinner this weekend?" Mom says.

"Great idea." The sarcasm is thick on Dad's tongue.

"Just what I was looking for."

"Thanks, Mom. Can I help with the menu?"

"Of course. Sound good, Steven?" Mom turns to Dad and smiles a perfectly straight, bright white smile, framed by mauve lips. Mom works on looking flawless, well, for a mom.

"Fine. I like it better when I can keep an eye on him."

"What would we do without you to keep us safe?" Mom leans in and kisses Dad on the cheek.

Seeing my escape, I grab my purse from the hook in the laundry room and head to the garage. "I'm off."

"Home by ten!" Dad bellows.

"Okay!" I yell back.

I hop in my red Mini Cooper and turn the ignition. I can't wait to get away from Dad's watchdog mood. Freedom! I take a deep breath. Keegan's parents are nice enough, but they're real brainy and talk about politics and problems in countries I can't find on a map. I always feel like a moron or that if I give an opinion, it will be the wrong one.

At Keegan's I ring the bell, shifting my weight from my left foot to my right to my left again. *Please let Keegan open the door. Please let Keegan open the door. Please...*

"Hi Palmer. Come on in." Mrs. Holloway steps back from the door, her gray hair pulled back in a sloppy, low bun. Hasn't she ever heard of L'Oreal?

"Hi, Mrs. Holloway. Thanks so much for having me over for dinner tonight." I paste on a smile, my eyes searching the background for Keegan.

She shuffles in her slippers down the hallway toward the kitchen.

The house smells like mothballs and strange spices.

54

Gag. So glad the next time we dine together will be at my house.

I follow, hating the silence, willing her to talk. "Crummy weather today, huh? Especially after all that sunshine yesterday." My words seem to thump off the walls and land on the floor, lifeless.

"Pretty wet," Mrs. Holloway mutters.

Thanks for zero help in the conversation department.

"Palm." Keegan is beside me. His hand slips into mine—big, warm, soft, and safe. My shoulders relax.

"Hey." I smile. All of my attention, my entire world, is focused on him. His T-shirt fits perfectly across his strong chest. It hangs out over his plaid shorts. How can this outfit make my heart flutter? But it does. I squeeze his hand, even though all I want to do is kiss him again and feel those soft lips. But kissing in front of his parents is not a possibility. His droopy eyes lift.

"What'd you do today?" he asks.

"Not alota. Just trying to get stuff ready for school. You know I leave in a week?" I wave my hands around for emphasis.

"I don't like to think about it. What kind of stuff?"

"I found these great comforters my roomies and I could all get. I sent the website link to everyone, but I don't know if Claire can check her email in France. All I ever remember Kat wearing to school were jeans and Converse. I don't have a clue what she likes in the way of pillowcases! We have to decorate our room, and time's running out."

Keegan kisses the top of my head, which is his way of saying he loves me even if he couldn't care less about dorm décor.

We help his mom set the table and pour drinks.

Mr. Holloway appears in a bushy brown cardigan carrying a platter of something steaming and spicy.

"Smells yummy." I nod as the scents of curry, cumin and cardamom waft across the table.

Mr. Holloway passes around dishes, and Mrs. Holloway talks about something she heard on NPR this morning. Meanwhile Keegan's hand slides onto my thigh under the table. It's comforting, feeling him there.

Before I've even served myself, Keegan's dad swirls Saag and rice, heaving a heaping forkful into his mouth. I should be used to it by now. I mean, not everyone prays before dinner, but Keegan goes to youth group with me. I always assume his parents will pray before dinner, but they never do.

Dear God, thank you for this meal and for the chance to get to be with Keegan. Help me not be so nervous in front of his parents. Amen. I run through my silent prayer hastily, so no one notices me just kind of staring at my food.

I tentatively dip a piece of Naan bread in the Korma. It's kind of tangy like a tomatoey bowl of chili, only earthier. Then, smack! The after kick of the spices sets my tongue on fire. I grab my glass of milk and gulp half of it down.

"Is it too spicy?" Keegan's mom asks, in a voice that makes me feel if I admit it's too spicy, I'm clearly not cultured.

"No. It's delicious." I force the words off my flaming lips. "It's just so yummy, and has a little zing."

I stir a healthy spoonful of yogurt into everything on my plate. Keegan's hand runs up and down my leg now. It was soothing at first, but now it's a little tickly. I elbow him gently.

"Did you grow any of the herbs you used in dinner

tonight?" I ask Mrs. Holloway, knowing her garden is her pride and joy.

"No." She smiles at me, as if I'm in first grade. "I get all of my Indian spices from the farmer's market in the summer. There's this wonderful woman with a stall of bulk spices." She heaps more Saag on her plate. "I stock up, so I have enough to last all winter."

Keegan's hand creeps between my legs. I have on jeans, but he's pushing the boundaries. I can't yell at him or slap him. His parents are inches away. I squeeze my legs together, trapping his hand.

"Don't you grow some things, Palm?" he asks.

"Sure. My mom and I plant sugar snap peas and tomatoes every summer in the back corner of our yard. We grow fresh basil, too. *Mmm*." I lick my lips. "I love veggies fresh from the garden."

You would think this small thread of commonality would spark a little conversation, but Mrs. Holloway just nods and says, "Basil? *Hmm*."

I somehow make it through the meal without igniting my face with fiery spices, spilling any green or red sauce down the front of my top or saying anything too stupid. After we clear the dishes, I excuse myself to use the restroom.

While washing my hands, I recompose myself. I tuck my hair behind my ears, check my teeth for any food fragments, reapply lip gloss and smooth out my shirt. Feeling fresher and more in control, I walk into the dark hallway.

Strong arms pull me tight and pin me against the wall. Keegan presses his lips against mine softly, sweetly. All of the tension of dinner melts. I adjust my arms around him and lean in. He kisses me with a little more pressure, and then his lips overtake me, until I can't feel the floor underneath my feet.

Blood pulses hot in my veins while goose bumps crawl up my flesh.

I hear the familiar shuffling of his mom's slippers and push away, breathing heavily.

"*Mmm*. I just love fresh Palmers from the garden," he whispers in his deep voice.

"Stop it." I whisper, shaking my head.

"I don't want to." He leans back toward me, pressing my back into the wall, not hard, but just enough so I'm comfortably trapped. His lips are on mine again, and his hand cups my neck, pulling me closer. Colors flash behind my closed eyes.

"Keegan, would you or Palmer like some tea?" Mrs. Holloway calls from the kitchen.

Keegan releases me, and it takes me a minute to get my bearings.

"Tea?" he mouths.

I nod, not trusting my voice.

"Sounds good, Mom. I'll make it."

"Right after I kiss my gorgeous girlfriend again," he whispers.

"You can't do this!" I mouth.

"Yes, I can," he whispers back. "I can and I will, while I can. You were the one talking about moving away in a week. I need to take every chance I can to have physical contact with you and maximize it." He gets closer with each syllable. He kisses me again, but this time it's gentle and slow and lasts only a second. I need him to stop, but I don't want him to stop. When he pulls away I feel like part of me pulled away with him.

8
KAT

WHOOSH! THE BALL SOARS OFF my head, along with a thousand raindrops, and rolls back to Julia, an incoming junior at Hoover High.

Smack! She sends it back to me with her foot.

With a week break from training at Clarkston before the soccer season officially starts, I promised Hoover High's coach I'd help him run their training camp.

Thump! I take a step to the right and lean, almost slipping, to get that one back to her.

Thud! The ball lands in the wet grass, splashing mud up Julia's white sock.

I lean back and wipe rain out of my eyes, while Julia grabs the ball. "Ready?" she yells, so I can hear her over the now pelting rain. I'm winded and soaked, but want to get this right. I want to get every soccer move I ever make right. "Ready."

Kaboom! Just as she positions the ball, thunder rattles the soccer fields.

Coach Ruiz's whistle screeches. "That's all, girls!" he screams over the storm. "Camp called for lightening. Do 25 push-ups, a plank for two full minutes, and 100 sit-ups to make up for a short session. I'll see you tomorrow morning."

I trot alongside Julia to the bench, grab my water bottle and ball, and head toward the high school locker rooms. My cleats clatter along the black top of the parking lot. My heart pumps inside my chest as I run, hoping I get inside before the lightning strikes again.

A blazing streak lights up the creepy, dark sky, followed by a bellowing *BOOM!*

I cringe. I hate storms. I don't know most of these younger girls, and everyone seems to have scattered.

"Kat!"

I blink through the downpour, relieved to hear a friendly voice. Someone with an umbrella waves at me to join them. The deluge blurs my vision, so I jog toward the umbrella.

"Nicholas!" I shout. "What-cha doin' here?"

"C'mon!" He wraps his right arm around my waist and guides me toward his car just a few feet away. He opens the passenger door, slides me inside and shuts the door.

Once he's in the driver's side, he folds his umbrella and tosses it in back, scattering raindrops on me and the seats. "Whew! This storm is serious!"

"Yeah. Coach'll practice in most anything, but this is downright crazy."

"I had to get some final transcripts from the office and was headed back to my car when I saw you slopping through the storm."

"You didn't have all your transcripts?"

"Long story. Major administration mishap." Nicholas runs his hands through his red curls, then wipes his wet hands on the front of his shorts and puts his key in the ignition.

"When do you head to school for good?"

"Monday. We're officially allowed to start practice come August 1. I'll live in the athletic dorm until my roommates move in." I have to almost shout to be heard over the pelting rain. I raise my voice, "What about you? Do you have roommates or any idea which dorm you're in yet?"

I wipe my face with my T-shirt, inhaling the sweet metallic smell of rain and look up to see Nicholas looking at me funny, just looking, while we idle at a stop sign.

"What?" I ask.

"Nothing." He shakes his head, and there is an awkward pause for what seems like four hours. Finally he says, "So, college soccer. That's a big deal."

"You know I want to play pro, right?"

"Yeah, it's kind of all you talk about."

I grin, proud. "So, this is the next step for me. I'll play my heart out for Clarkston. Scouts show up from the pros to watch the college teams. If they're gonna sit around and score me, I'm gonna show 'em what I've got." I take a swig of water from my bottle.

"We had swim meets where college scouts would show up. That always made me nervous. I don't want to swim in college, though."

"They don't make me nervous, just more determined. And, honest? You're through? I thought you won the butterfly in States every single year." I shake my head unable to imagine quitting my sport.

Nicholas's face turns as red as my T-shirt.

"Butterfly is my best stroke, but I've been swimming since I was five. Since then I've spent every weekend of my life waking up at the crack of dawn, smooshing with a jillion people into stuffy indoor pool complexes reeking of chlorine and waiting around for hours until my events. I'm burned out. I just want a life, you know?"

"Wow." I think of Alex's life. It's pretty much how

Nicholas described, except now that he's swimming in college it's even more intense. Alex has to eat certain amounts of protein and is required to do all this year-round practice. "I never thought of it like that. I guess Alex didn't start swimming 'til he was ten or eleven, though. I remember people telling him he was too old to start." I thump my silver thumb ring woven like a braid against my water bottle. "But he showed everyone." I thump my ring a few more times, enjoying the echo against my aluminum bottle. "If he has five or six more years 'til burn out, he can make it through college and then some. Plus, he doesn't really have a life." I snort. Nicholas knows I'm joking, but he doesn't laugh.

"Well, I want one. I want a life. I want to be an accountant and get my CPA. I was thinking about rushing a fraternity, and I want a girlfriend." Nicholas peeks at me from the driver's seat, then shifts his eyes immediately back to the road.

"Wow. That's a lot of stuff." I look out at the rain. Maybe what Alex said isn't too far off. It's uncomfortable to hear Nicholas talking about a girlfriend. As long as he doesn't talk about *me* being that girlfriend, we'll be all right. I'm way better off talking sports.

"I don't have any idea what I want to major in, or any of that other stuff. I have three awesome roommates and a room to share. Besides that, all I know is I want to play soccer. With all my heart I want to play soccer."

Nicholas doesn't say anything back. The splash of rain ricocheting against the windshield seems to be whispering secrets from his mind I can't interpret. I'm thankful when he pulls in front of my house.

"Thanks for the ride," I bend over to grab my string bag from the floor. "You fixin' to come in?"

"Do you want me to?" Nicholas stares at me again.

"It's up to you." I shrug, trying to act like nothing weird is going on, hoping he doesn't want to come in, but afraid if I disinvite him it would make things even weirder. *Act normal*, I tell myself. "I don't know if Alex is home or not, but you could hang out on the couch. I'd grab you a towel. It's pretty nasty to be drivin' around."

Nicholas glances at our garage door then back at me and finally at his steering wheel. He's kind of freaking me out.

"I better go. My parents will worry." He motions with his hands to the downpour.

"Sure, all right. See ya later. And thanks, Nicholas. You saved me."

"Anytime you feel like being saved, Kat. Anytime."

I see him shake his head as I shut the door and gratefully dash away from our strange conversation toward my house.

9
CLAIRE

WE MEET UP WITH MOM and Arnot just inside the gates of the Jardin de Luxembourg by a giant statue of the Greek god, Pan. I feel giddy, like I could start dancing right here in the marigolds to Pan's wild pipe music. The gardens stretch on and on as we pass by the palace that now houses the French senate. Groups of old men, sitting in green folding chairs, play chess in the shade and children frolic along the edges of the pond launching miniature sail boats.

Arnot makes a great tour guide, explaining the history of the palace and the layout of the entire city. We sit in the garden sipping Perrier in green aluminum cans from a vendor. I'm usually tied to the clock on my phone, constantly checking it to make sure I get from school to the dance studio on time. Checking the minutes while I crank out homework in the basement of the studio between the classes I teach and the classes I take, so I'm not late for any of them. Looking at the numbers as I race the clock to get dinner on the table before Mom gets home on Mondays and Wednesdays, when she takes yoga at the Y. But in Paris, there is nowhere to be but here, now.

"There's so much to see in Paris, and you're only here for a few days. What else should we see today?" Arnot asks.

"Whatever you say." Mom wraps her arm in Arnot's. "Although, I'm dying to see the Eiffel Tower!"

"The Eiffel Tower at night is spectacular!" Arnot agrees.

"What's the thing you most want to see?" Phillip asks, taking my arm in his, just like Arnot leads Mom. It seems natural, comfortable, so I let him.

"The Eiffel Tower is obvious." I sigh. "But I want to live it, you know, like a real French person. I thought, before we came, that what I wanted to do most was see La Tour Eiffel and Notre Dame and the Louvre, but now that I'm here, it's different. Today in the park—this is perfect. I could do this the rest of the trip, just people watch." I lower my head, embarrassed. I shared my thoughts so openly. He must think I'm such a baby. "Sounds silly, right?"

"No, you're exactly right." Phillip's face becomes animated. "You must see the sights, because you are in Paris, but the best part of Paris is Paris itself—its spirit, its culture, its language, its food, the people. It's so different from London."

"How?" I ask.

"*Hmmm.* Even though they're both huge international cities, London is more black and white. Paris is more Technicolor. London seems busier and more formal and more consumed with proving how great it is, parading Princess Kate around in starched dresses, right? But in Paris there aren't any rules, except to love the city. It's less structured, less predictable, more vibrant, more romantic." He winks.

I know I'm staring at him, but I can't help it. Phillip's dark eyes are mesmerizing, like he stepped off a cover of *GQ*. He seems decades older than the guys at my high school, who throw spit wads during lunch, who all got Mohawks before the football championship game and who spend 90% of their conversations talking about ESPN. And he's a gentleman, holding my arm, ordering my *crêpe*, carrying our bags. He understood what I said. He didn't laugh or ignore me. He agreed. I feel like I could tell him almost anything.

"Claire wants to see Notre Dame," Phillip announces. "And I want to show her *Les Nympheas*."

"It's like you read my mind," Arnot answers, then suddenly reaches for his pocket and pulls out his phone. "Excuse me." He steps away and answers, "*Bonjour.*"

Phillip steps away too, pulling his phone out of his pocket to check messages.

I shrug at Mom and take it as my cue to text my roomies. They keep messaging me like crazy about all of our plans for the year, and I haven't been stellar about responding. It's cheaper if I send them a group text.

SIPPING PERRIER OUTSIDE OLD PALACE WITH CUTE BOY, HEADED TO NOTRE DAME. WE'LL GET CAUGHT UP WHEN I GET BACK XOXO

Just as I push send, Mom appears by my side. "I'm having so much fun. Thanks for being a sport and hanging out with Phillip and letting Arnot and I have some private chats too. Not that Phillip isn't a hunk."

"No one says 'hunk', Mom."

"Whether they say it or not, he is one, and you know it. But seriously, thanks for dropping in that boutique and walking with Phillip. I feel so close to Arnot—way closer in one day than I did all those dates back home. He's always stressed and married to his job in Cleveland. But here, he seems totally focused on *moi*." Mom points to herself. Arnot seems smart and sweet, but I'm still trying to figure out why he flew us all to Paris.

"Mom, I'm having a blast. Really! It's unbelievable. Like it was a *favor* for me to let him buy me a dress?"

"But it was. That's the thing." Mom blinks.

"We're just a few minutes away by foot." Arnot is back by Mom's side, sliding his phone in his pocket. "And there are few things more spectacular than Notre Dame."

The streets are packed with people of all ages and sizes, moms pushing strollers, old men walking dogs, and couples holding hands. The city is just as Phillip described, vibrant and alive. I strain to hear fragments of French conversations and translate them the best I can in my head.

We wind our way to Notre Dame where hundreds of others form two seemingly endless lines to enter the cathedral. I pull out my phone and snap a picture of the famous façade flanked by pillars and gargoyles guarding the ledges. The line moves faster than I expected. Once inside, I hold my breath.

Ethereal mist fills the air. Surely it's just dust, illuminated by the sunlight playing through the stained glass windows, but it seems like magic sprinkled in the air. The thick, spicy incense fills my nose, like the cloves and cinnamon of the potpourri I keep in my underwear drawer, rich and intoxicating.

A service is going on, and the deep, rhythmic voice of the priest chants prayers in French. I can only pick a few words out—"Father" and "Holy" and "forever" jump out, but the rest blend together in a sacred tongue.

"I'm not Catholic," I whisper to Phillip, as we find seats half way up next to an enormous pillar.

"Neither am I," he whispers, so closely his lips tickle my ear. "It doesn't matter. Just take it in."

My eyes can't drink in the splendor. The vibrant purples and blues of the stained glass window at my church at home have captivated me since I was little, but the stained glass here goes on forever. There are scenes of the disciples and exquisite rose windows decorated with swirling patterns. Phillip taps me on the arm lightly, pointing at a bird flying over head—a real live bird flitting through the rafters of the church. It alights on the pillar next to us. I smile at Phillip, gazing at our feathered friend.

I stop trying to understand what the priest is saying, but when others fold out little kneelers in front of them, I do the same. I close my eyes and breathe God in and out. This country is foreign to me. This language is foreign to me. Even this denomination of the Christian faith is foreign to me, but God's presence is overwhelmingly powerful in this magnificent place of worship.

I feel Him like a fog rolling over me, surrounding me and filling me with peace and happiness. A rustle of jackets and pants and squeaks of kneelers folding wakes me from my trance. The service is over, but I will myself to remember this feeling, to capture it and save it in my soul.

Outside, my eyes take a moment to adjust to the bright sunlight after the dim interior of the cathedral. The church bells ring, so loudly, I can feel their vibrations in my chest.

Bong
Bong
Bong.

All of France must be able to hear these bells pealing through the hubbub in the square outside the cathedral.

We stroll along the Seine, the river that winds its way through the middle of Paris, and chat and people watch. We buy fresh baguettes from the bakery and cheese from a *fromagerie* the size of a closet. We smear the pungent, delicious cheese on chunks of bread we tear off the loaves and wash it all down with slugs of Perrier.

We ride the subway called the Metro, to the other giant park, the Jardin de Tuillieres, home of the small Impressionist museum, L'Orangerie. Inside I marvel at the beautiful work of the Impressionists, the things I've studied in art history and seen on posters and coasters. But nothing prepares me for the room housing Monet's water lilies.

"Cover your eyes and let me lead you," Phillip suggests.

I shake my head. I don't want to trip or bump into something. I'm also afraid of the dark. Always have been, ever since my Dad left in the dead of night. I've never liked pin the tail on the donkey or covering my eyes to be "it" in hide and go seek.

"Trust me." He smiles.

I look over at Mom and Arnot whispering in front of a Picasso. I am struggling not to look like an idiot in front of Phillip. "All right." I put one hand over my eyes and look downward. Phillip takes my other hand and leads me a few steps through a short hallway.

"Okay." His voice is gentle. "You can open them."

"*Ahh,*" I gasp. I feel like I've been plunged into Monet's garden, surrounded by four enormous paintings, over six feet high. One curves the expanse of each of the four curved walls of the oval shaped room where we stand. Blues, purples, pinks and greens weave together in gorgeous portrayals of flowers floating along the stream outside Monet's home.

"It's amazing," I blurt when I can breathe. "Amazing."

"Just like you."

I feel the blood rush to my cheeks, hot with embarrassment.

"Which one's your favorite?" I ask, trying to change the subject.

"Which one's yours?" He pushes back.

My heart flips like butterfly wings inside my chest. My one high school relationship with Ethan started like this, sweet flirtations back and forth. But that was before everything went sour. I know Phillip must flirt with lots of girls, but he's so charming, and Mom's right, he is a hunk. Plus, he's leaving. What can it hurt?

 After the museum we stroll looking for a place for dinner.

"How about here?" Arnot asks.

A menu describing the specials is posted on a board by the door of a café with a handful of tables pressed against the glass front of the restaurant. With its woven cane chairs, brass doorway, and dark red awning, it looks like several of the other places we've passed. Savory aromas float from the kitchen.

"It looks great." Mom smiles starry eyed. "Have you eaten here before?"

"Yes, a few years back. I remember them having mouth-watering *coq au vin*," Arnot replies.

"What do you think?" Phillip whispers.

"They all look the same to me," I say. "But they all smell delicious!"

"They are all the same," he says. "And they are all delicious."

A waiter brings small glasses of water and hands us menus. Arnot orders wine for the table and pours everyone a glass, even me.

"I'm not 21." I giggle, and push the glass back toward him.

"There are no drinking laws in France." He smiles. "One glass is a compliment to your food. It brings out the taste. Save it to go with your dinner. You'll see. It is part of the culture here. Even children drink wine at dinner in their homes."

I nod, nervous about the prospect of drinking wine. I never have. I'm afraid how it will make me feel. I look to Mom for guidance, but she's intertwining her fingers with Arnot's, oblivious to the world around her. I look back at Arnot, not sure what to say.

He sees the hesitation in my face and gives me a way out, sort of. "If it makes you more comfortable, Claire, adults will often mix water into their children's wine to dilute it."

I twist a section of my hair. I think Arnot was trying to be nice, but he basically called me a child, the thing I'm trying not to come off as. I hesitate and pour some water into my glass, swirling it in with my wine, avoiding Phillip's eyes.

I'm relieved when the waiter returns to take our order. I pride myself in ordering my meal in French.

The thick, cheesy pasta is delicious and exactly what I need after a day of traveling and walking. I didn't realize how tired and hungry I was, but I devour my entire dish as well as several slices of baguette, while listening to Arnot's stories about Paris. I drink my water and ignore my wine, thinking it's safer that way.

I get away with it too, until Phillip raises his glass. "To a perfect day in Paris. *Salut*." Phillip tilts his glass toward mine. I lift my wine glass. As our glasses clink, a shiver of excitement runs down my spine. I take a sip of the sweet, strong liquid. It is warm going down my throat, but comforting, not intrusive.

"*Salut*," I copy, as we all clink each other's glasses, and I take one more celebration sip.

10
HANNAH

"WHAT ARE ALL THESE LITTLE purple things? Are they some kind of toilet paper holders?" Owen comes out of the bathroom holding a handful of my unwrapped tampons.

"OH MY GOSH, OWEN!" I scream, snatching the tampons from him and heading to the bathroom, where I'd stashed a box. "Why were you snooping around under the sink? Why did you unwrap all these? Mom!"

"I dunno. I just wondered what they are? What are they?"

"What's wrong?" Mom sounds exhausted. I wish she'd take a little action here.

"Hannah's all mad, because I opened the toilet paper roll holders. I don't know why we have so many of them anyway. They're kind of weird, with these little strings." He swats a string hanging from a tampon he apparently hung onto.

"*Ahh!*" I scream, stuffing the opened tampons back into their box.

"Owen," Mom starts to snap at him, and then breaks into a full-blown laugh.

Sitting crisscrossed on the floor of the bathroom, I roll my eyes and although I try not to, I laugh too.

"What's so funny?" Owen asks.

"They're not toilet paper holders. They're something Hannah uses to get ready," Sammie says in her authoritative voice.

I peek out of the bathroom, catch Mom's eye, and we both start busting up more.

"How the heck does she use those to get ready?" Owen asks.

"It's a long story." Sammie shakes her head, as if she doesn't have time for these laborious explanations.

"Thanks, Sammie." I tap her shoulder, giving her the gift of thinking she's saved the day.

"Mom," I whisper, "I have got to get out of here before I explode."

"Sure." Mom still giggles a little. "I know we're in kind of tight quarters here. All of you kids sharing a bedroom. All of us sharing one bathroom." She raises her eyebrows. "You want to run out and grab some groceries for me."

"Yes!" Who knew I'd be so excited to run errands?

Mom scribbles a list, hands me two twenties and pulls me into the kitchen of our condo. "Hey, I know it's hard. You've been a good sport. But we're all in this together. Owen and Sammie are sharing space with you too. And this may be our last family vacation." Pools of tears form in the corners of Mom's eyes.

"Mom!" I laugh. "I'll still go on vacations with you when I'm in college."

"I can't believe you're going away, almost the second we get back." She dabs her eyes. "Enjoy your freedom." Mom tips her head to the door. "Take as long as you want, and if you want some time to yourself at the beach again today, you can have it."

My own towel. My own space. Maybe a chance to talk

to Reed again, as long as the model chick doesn't appear. I blow a bubble with my gum and feel a little better. "Thanks, Mom."

I ride the elevator down to the ground and push the glass door of our condo building open. The rush of heat rolls over me like a massage. I inhale a deep breath of salty ocean air and literally feel myself springing down the sidewalk. I feel like a caged bird, released to fly. As I cross the street, I don't have to grab Owen's hand or check to make sure Sammie's with me. I stop and look in the window of a little dress shop and eye a flirty lavender sundress.

Wow! I have to remind myself I can go in and browse. I don't have to ask Mom and Dad if I can stop or tell them where I'm going. Freedom is exhilarating. I pretend I'm already in college and on my own. I might as well get used to it now. I try on the dress and three others. The lavender is by far my favorite. I imagine myself wearing it, walking down the sidewalks of campus with my new roommates arm in arm, or better yet, walking arm in arm with a cute college boy who looks suspiciously like Reed. I run my fingers through silky scarves and hold earrings up to my ears. Adding up prices in my head, I decide I'm going to beg Mom for the dress, and if she lets me get it, I'll buy a pair of dangly earrings with purple beads and a patterned scarf with my own money.

"Could you hold these for me, please?" I ask the clerk.

"We can hold them until 5:00 p.m. After that, we put them back on the rack."

"Great. Thanks so much." I beam. "I was just grabbing a couple of groceries and didn't bring my credit card. I'll be back later." I like the way my words sound, like I'm buying groceries for myself, running errands, like a grown up, like

I'm a grown up.

"What's your name?" The clerk peers at me through her glasses and pulls a pen from behind her ear.

"Hannah."

She prints my name on a manila tag and hooks it over the dress hanger, drapes the scarf around the neck of the hanger and clips the earrings onto the front of the dress.

"Thanks." I bop out of the store and into the sunshine.

Back home, I put away the groceries, slip on my bikini and pack my beach bag as discreetly as possible, before Sammie or Owen start tugging at me, before they can shatter my sheen of independence. I find Mom reading *The Alchemist* for her book club.

"Groceries are in the fridge. Here's your change," I whisper, handing her a handful of ones and coins. "I'm headed out." I point to my bag.

"Thanks, sweetie. Have fun. Just remember to stay where you can see our place and check in every once in a while. That wasn't too bad was it yesterday?"

"*Umm*, how about every other hour today?" I smile.

"*Umm*, how about every hour again?" Mom glares.

"All right." I roll my eyes. "Nothing's going to happen to me."

"Especially if we know where you are." Mom nods, closing the subject.

I anchor two of the opposite corners of my towel with my flip-flops and beach bag near where I found Reed yesterday. I rub on a thick layer of SPF 40 over my freckly, pale skin, not allowing myself to look for him, until I'm all set.

I scan the sand and catch my breath. There he is. Well, there he is with that annoying model-looking girl. No biggie.

I should just act normal, right? She saw him with me yesterday.

I walk right up to the towels they're sitting on. "Hi, Reed."

He looks up and just nods. That's it. Not even "hi," let alone "hi, Stripes." I feel a little woozy, like I've been out in the sun for too long, only I just got out here. The girl glares at me, like I'm one of those annoying vendors trying to sell her a henna tattoo or get her to pay me to cornrow her hair.

"Were we going to have another skimming lesson today?" My voice comes out mumbly and muted, like it got washed away with a wave.

"Not now. I'm busy." Reed shakes his head and turns back to the conversation with the suntanned beauty as if yesterday didn't happen, as if he's Ryan Gosling and I'm a groupie asking for his autograph.

I'm just standing next to them, wishing the sand would turn to quicksand and I could sink into it. Or what if I could slide into the deep blue ocean and float away unnoticed? I have to escape, if only I could move.

"See ya." I gather a scrap of energy to blurt the words and wave foolishly, like he's been talking to me like a normal person, like there is any chance of us seeing each other again.

Walking the twenty steps back to my towel seems like a mile. My face is hotter than the afternoon sun and redder than a sunburn. What a jerk! What a jerky jerk jerk! He's the one who said he'd give me a lesson another time. He's the one who suggested I learn how to skim in the first place. He's the one who gave me a nickname!

I plop down on my towel and stuff my earbuds in my ears, wanting to drown out Reed's nonchalant voice. I wish

LAURA L. SMITH

the music could drown out visuals too. I can't seem to stop looking at Reed and his supermodel, practically nose-to-nose. I roll over onto my stomach, so I can't see them. It would look too pathetic if I packed up all my things and moved now. I'm going to have to tough it out. I don't want to give him the satisfaction of knowing he flustered me like this.

I grab a piece of gum in hopes of chewing away the bitter taste in my mouth.

I hate boys! All boys! I am such a loser. I squeeze my eyes shut to stop the tears from falling out. Why did I think for one second he liked me?

11
CLAIRE

I SLIP INTO THE DRESS. An extra-long string of beads, which I untangle from a jumble in the bottom of my bag, is just the right touch for the flirty short ruffles. With an extra stroke of eyeliner, I add drama to my eyes. I spritz perfume not just on my wrists, but also behind my ears and down the neckline of my dress. My favorite strawberry flavored lip gloss in Mauvelous shines up my lips. I slide the tube in the pocket of my denim jacket to keep them shining all night. This is my first time to the Eiffel Tower and my last night with Phillip. I feel like I'm waltzing across a stage in a new tutu and pointe shoes.

At dinner Arnot orders for all of us in rapid French. Since he's insisted on selecting our dinner, I use the time he speaks to the waiter to talk to Phillip about his classes and my ballet. The way he tilts his head in toward me, the way he nods while I talk and asks questions about my studio and my roommates makes me think he might be as interested in me as I am in him.

The waiter brings wine for the table and pours it in our glasses. Arnot raises his glass. "To the magic of Paris and to lovely ladies." Mom blushes. I learned last night one glass of watered-down wine won't hurt me. I raise my glass and swallow the sweet warmth. I'll dilute it after the toast.

"The Eiffel Tower sounds so romantic." Mom sips her wine. "Do they really set off fireworks every night?"

"They're more like a giant sparkler, all sizzling and white," Phillip answers. "They're spectacular. That's why we must go after dark."

"How will you get back in time for classes, if you're leaving in the morning?" I ask Phillip.

"Easy. Have you heard of the Chunnel?"

It sounds familiar in my head, but I don't really know what it is. "Kind of?"

"It's like an underwater bullet train that goes from Paris to London in practically no time, by zipping under the English Channel. I can take the 6:43 a.m. train and arrive at 7:59 a.m. at the London train station, with the hour time change on my side, and still grab a coffee and make it to my 9:00 a.m. class." Phillip extends his arm around my back and drapes it over my shoulder while he talks.

"That's wild. But isn't it a little freaky being in an underwater train?" I shiver.

"I don't get scared very easily."

"I kind of gathered." I take another sip of wine to avoid the intensity of Phillip's gaze.

The waiter returns carrying something that smells buttery and garlicky and scrumptious. He places a plate between Mom and Arnot, and another between Phillip and me. "*L'escargot*," he announces then disappears.

"*L'escargot?*" I blink hesitantly. Snails!

"Have you ever had them?" asks Phillip, stabbing his fork into what looks like a cheese crusted crouton.

"No, I've never had the chance." Of course, I've never wanted the chance to eat snails, but that's irrelevant.

The flavor that hits my tongue is exactly as it smells, decadent and savory, but when I chew, the thick, muscle-like texture squishes through my teeth. It takes all of my self-control not to spit out the little slug!

I grab my wine, remembering it's still full force, but desperate to wash down the snail.

"So, what do you think?" Phillip asks.

"*Mmm,*" I choke it down my narrow throat. "What do they simmer them in? Garlic and butter?" I feel like I'm six; playing dress up in a Cinderella gown using words that don't fit me.

"Exactly!" Phillip nods.

I smile, swirl some water into my half empty wine glass, and take another sip, better.

"Care for another?" Phillip asks.

I glance at the saucer, thankful there were only four snails on our plate. "No. You go ahead. I'm saving room for dinner." I daintily lay down my fork while Phillip takes the last two *escargots*. I look to Mom, but she's laughing at something Arnot's sharing with her in hushed tones at the other end of the table.

"You could pass for a French girl in that dress." Phillip says.

"Really?"

"Really." He leans in and kisses my cheek.

"*Merci.*" I feel light headed, overwhelmed with the warmth of his lips and of the wine running through my veins.

Luckily, the waiter reappears with water and our entrees, which look like chicken in a dark gravy and smell of fresh herbs and roasting dishes.

"Rabbit, sir," he says to Phillip.

I inhale deeply, swallow and tuck my hair behind my ears. Luckily, everyone else seems busy shuffling plates and glasses to make room for their entrees and don't notice how repulsed I am by eating a sweet, fluffy bunny! While our waiter refills our glasses with golden wine, I reach for another piece of bread and nibble on the crunchy crust.

Soon dinner is over. I've mopped up most of my sauce with slices of baguette. And I've done a decent job cutting up my entrée, pushing it around my plate, and tucking it under a wedge of bread while intermittingly sipping wine to occupy my hands. I feel light and buzzy and breezy, as if this whole trip has been a movie I've been watching instead of my actual life.

Phillip takes my hand as we stroll from the café toward the metro station. His hand feels solid and steady and strong. The ride is crowded and noisy and longer than usual. I laugh as the train stops suddenly, making me wobble. Phillip grabs my waist to steady me, and for a moment we lock eyes.

Arnot leads us up the metro steps, onto the street and past a long row of vendors' carts jammed with every souvenir imaginable. Crowds of tourists meander the same direction as us to the icon of Paris, the Eiffel Tower.

Clang. Clang. Clang.

A guy, who looks like he belongs on the streets of New York City selling handbags and fake Rolex's, bangs a giant ring holding hundreds of miniature Eiffel Tower key chains. "Two euro!" he shouts, in an accent that sounds more

Western European than French. "Two euro!"

"Cool!" I squeal. Letting my fingers ripple through the hot pink, gold and silver miniatures of the famed tower. "I could get one for me and for all my roomies." They seem the perfect memento, small, cheap; my new BFF's could hang them from their backpacks.

"How many do you need?" Phillip asks.

"Four."

"Eight euro." The man puts out his hand.

"One euro each?" Phillip asks.

"No, no, what kind of a joke?" the man asks, in thick broken English.

"It's okay," I whisper, standing on my tippy toes to reach Phillip's ear.

"*Non, merci.*" Phillip turns his back to the vendor and gently turns me away too.

"I want to get those for my roommates."

"You will, but not from him." Phillip squeezes my hand and pulls me along quickly to catch up to Mom and Arnot.

"But," I argue, feeling a little angry. I really wanted those. Phillip pulls me along like a pouting child who can't get her way. Then I see another and another and another guy approaching groups of tourists, clanging their wares, and selling the identical key chains.

"Four for three euro?" Phillip asks a guy who has just been shooed away from a group lounging on a large blanket.

"Four for three? Okay. I give you deal, because she is so pretty." The vendor spreads the key chains out in front of us so we can choose.

"She's so pretty, you should be paying her to take them from you." Phillip laughs. And just like that I'm not even a tiny bit mad. Not only has Phillip saved me five euro, but he said I'm pretty.

I pull my hair over my right shoulder, unable to respond. "Mom, look at these key chains," I call. "Want one?"

"Oh cute," Mom agrees. "How much?"

"Four for three euro," Phillip says.

"I'll get four for my friends at work."

I've seen hundreds of pictures of the Eiffel Tower in books and movies starting back when I was little and watched *Ratatouille*. I knew it was really big, but as I stand underneath the gigantic structure, I realize our entire ballet studio times ten could fit underneath it. There are four lines of people, one for each pillar of the tower, all converging at the top.

"Ooh, let's go to the top." I clap my hands.

"The top looks awfully high, Claire. Couldn't we just go to the second level?" Mom's eyelashes flicker.

"I'll take Claire to the top," Phillip says. "You two go to the second level. It looks like the East pillar is just doing tickets for the lower levels. You can stand in the shorter line and be up sooner. I'll take Claire to the top. The South line doesn't look too bad. Don't worry about us. Take your time. I'll get her back to the hotel."

Mom takes my hand. "Excuse us for a quick mother/daughter conference." She turns us around, so our backs are to the guys and lowers her voice. "Would that be okay, honey? I know we always talked about doing this together, but I think I'd throw up at the top, especially after that rich dinner and all that wine. I know you want to see the top. Are you okay with Phillip?" Mom's voice comes fast and choppy. "Plus," she squeezes my hand so tightly it actually burns, "I think Arnot has something important to tell me. He might just ask me to marry him tonight."

"You think? Really, Mom?" I squeeze her hand, then release it and hug her. "Of course it's fine. It's totally fine."

It usually drives me crazy when Mom acts like the teenager, and I have to act like the Mom, but tonight's different. I have someone to hang out with, someone incredibly handsome and charming to hang out with. What if Arnot did propose to her? Mom would have someone besides me to lean on. Our money issues would be over, and I'd get to see more of Phillip.

"Oh, good. Thanks, honey. I'll see you back in our room." Mom beams. She turns back to Arnot. "We're all set. Don't wait up for us kids."

We wave goodbye, and as Phillip leads me to the ticket booth, lights stream like sparks out of a giant magic wand from the top of the tower.

"Fireworks," I whisper.

The crowd ooohs and ahhhs as the light show pops and fizzes and explodes brightly into the dark Parisian sky.

Phillip and I take a series of elevators, squeezed way too tightly into spaces with people speaking countless languages, but at last we make it to the top.

From here we can see the entire city of Paris, lit up like a map made out of Lite Brites. Phillip points out Notre Dame and the Luxembourg and Tuillieres gardens. He retraces our footsteps over the last two days along the Seine, through the Latin Quarter, everywhere we've been and wraps his arms around my waist.

"This is the most beautiful thing I've ever seen," I sigh, not sure if I've spoken out loud, dizzy from the lights and the height.

"You're the most beautiful thing I've ever seen."

Phillip's lips touch mine lightly for one second before he gets bumped from behind by a group of about twenty Asian tourists armed with cameras.

We both laugh at the interruption. I catch my breath and stare out at the city.

After several still, timeless moments, Phillip asks, "Ready to go?"

"I'll never be ready to go." I lean into him. "I guess I can come back, though. I'll come back later this week."

"Too bad I can't come back with you." He takes my arm and leads me back inside. "How about this? Promise me when you come back, you'll think about me and about tonight?"

"Promise."

The metro ride back to our hotel seems faster than the one to the tower.

"I'm glad you're with me," I confide. "I don't' think I could have found my way back if it weren't for you."

"Sure you could have." Phillip points to the maps of the metro routes adhered near the ceiling of the train. "Everything is color coded. You just need to know where you are and where you want to end up. Then follow the colors and count the stops to get you from A to B." He talks me through our rides today, and it all makes sense when he explains it.

"I've been so excited about Paris and everyone else seemed to know where we were going, I hadn't been paying attention," I admit.

"I've mostly been paying attention to you," Phillip says, brushing his lips against mine just long enough for me to catch a hint of their warmth and a taste of his breath. "What's your story, ballerina girl? Do you have a boyfriend back home?"

"Hardly." I shake my head.

"Hard to believe."

"I had one, Ethan. But we got too into each other, you know, spending every second of the day with each other. If I wasn't dancing, I was with him. "

"Sounds intimate."

"Well, sort of. I mean, I thought so, but it got too intense." I hesitate. I don't usually share much of myself with anyone. "Well, after my dad, I wasn't used to being dependent on anyone, and I kind of freaked. He didn't understand why I needed to step back and slow down."

I never tell my Cleveland friends much. Maybe that's why I don't have any close friends. Not that I've ever minded, but I'll be starting over soon. And home seems so far away. So does reality.

"That wasn't enough for him," I continue, too deep into the story to stop. I scrunch my nose for the count of ten to hold back the tears that come with the memory of emptiness and betrayal. "So, he found someone else to be his one and only."

Did I just bare my soul to Phillip? Maybe it's the lingering effects of the wine. Phillip squeezes my hand as we get out of the subway and begin climbing the stairs to street level. He doesn't say anything. I can't tell what he's thinking, about me, about my ex.

"I've pretty much sworn off boys altogether," I laugh, trying to lighten things up. "How about you? A saucy British girl waiting for you back at school?" I say in my best British accent.

Phillip laughs. "A few. Nothing serious. Euro girls are so much more relaxed than American girls. There's no one special."

He opens the door to our lobby and nods to the clerk behind the desk. "*Bonne nuit.*"

"*Bonne nuit, monsieur, mademoiselle.*"

"*Bonne nuit,*" I say.

"But you're special, Claire."

"*Hmm,*" I sigh, almost laughing at the irony. "But the fairy tale ends here. I tell you goodnight, and you head back to England tomorrow, and that is that."

"It doesn't have to end quite yet." Phillip squeezes my hand and pulls me past my room and down the hall. "Stay with me a little longer. Your mom and Arnot won't be back yet anyway. Keep me company while I pack."

"Okay," I agree. He leads me to his room and slides his key card. The green light flashes, and he pushes open the door.

12
PALMER

THE AROMA OF FRESH BAKED bread layered with brewing coffee makes me sigh. What to choose—coffee cake swirled with cinnamon, muffins oozing with dark blue, almost purple berries, apple strudels drizzled with streaks of white icing? I default to my all time fav—a flaky chocolate croissant with dark chocolate dripping from both ends and an iced coffee. Somehow the sugar-free vanilla syrup in my coffee makes me feel less guilty.

No Kat yet. This could be a bad sign, a very bad sign. What if she's one of those "always late" kind of girls, or worse, one of those "not that dependable of a friend" kind of girls? I don't know much about her from one boring hour of Calculus each day senior year. For all I know she could be a party animal. Wouldn't that be a nightmare! I never paid much attention to her social habits. I slide into an upholstered booth near the door where I can see her when, that is *if,* she arrives. I shiver from the air conditioning blasting from a vent above my head. Great. Now she's making me freeze.

I check my phone to see if one of the texts I got while driving over here was from her.

Nope.

Figures.

Three from Keegan:

1. XOXOXOXO
2. MISSING YOUR KISSING
3. I NEED YOU

And one from Hannah: I HATE BOYS!

I text back Keegan: SMOOCH!

I text back Hannah: ANY PARTICULAR REASON?

TOTALLY HUMILIATED BY GUY I'VE BEEN FLIRTING W/. GOT MESSAGE LOUD & CLEAR – HE'S NOT INTERESTED!

SORRY, SWEETIE!

"Hey, sorry I'm late." Kat slides into the seat across from me with her tray. How did she sneak in without me seeing? I've only been texting for about thirty seconds and she already has her order?

I look up from my phone. Her dark hair lays thick on her shoulders. I don't think I've ever seen it out of a ponytail. She's wearing a pale blue cotton sundress and has a streak of shimmery teal eyeliner against her dark lashes.

"Wow! You look like one of Jack Sparrow's mermaids." I stand and hug her, impressed and the slightest bit jealous. I thought she was supposed to be the sporty one. I was supposed to be the pretty one.

"Thanks." She looks down at herself. "I don't usually make much of a fuss when getting ready for school. I'm usually rushin' from a workout." She shrugs. "But Mama always makes us get fancy for church. Says it's respectful to God. I came straight from there."

Her words chase away the clutter in my brain. The clatter of the café seems to fade far away. All the people and conversations and rustles of newspapers dissolve and there is only Kat and I, at our little table.

"You came from church?"

"Yeah. We've been goin' to Mount Pleasant Church since we've moved here. It's near our house."

"That's cool." I nod. Lower chance of her being a party animal if she just came from church. Some of my roommate anxiety slides away. Maybe some of my moving and change anxiety lessens too. Why do I get my panties in a wad about things that I don't even know if they're problems or not? *Thank you God,* I whisper in my head. *A Christian roommate is exactly what I need. It makes everything less overwhelming.*

Be not afraid. I go before you always.
Mmm.

"Cool?" Kat picks up her bagel smeared with cream cheese.

"Yeah, you know, we had Calc together all year, but, I know this sounds stupid," my words come slowly, "I really don't know much about you, except you always wear awesome nail polish. I remember the first day you showed up in our class with outrageous neon orange nails." I offer a genuine compliment to atone for my negative thoughts.

Kat smiles and holds up her nails, displaying mint green polish. A warm melty feeling, like the chocolate in my croissant, replaces my cold tension.

"And, somehow, you going to church, I'm a Christian too…" I slide my silver cross back and forth on my chain, "makes me feel like us being roommates is going to be a really good thing. Like a God thing, you know?"

"It is wild how it all worked out. I was just walking down the sidewalk on campus and Hannah was wavin' at me like crazy, standin' there with Claire. Five seconds later we were all roommates. But, ya know, if you and me hadn't sat near each other in Calc, if I hadn't already known you, I would've been less sure when Hannah asked me to room with her. I mean, I knew who she was from Hoover High, class president and all, but I don't think we'd ever talked."

My coffee is strong and sweet and cold on my tongue. "Right," I nod, feeling my slick pony bounce against my neck, "like God knew we had to have math together, so we'd feel comfortable enough to accept Hannah's matchmaking, so everything could fall into place."

"Right. God's amazin' like that."

"I know, right? Really amazing like that." Goose bumps run up my arms.

Kat takes a sip from her cup.

"What are you drinking?" I peek.

"Chai Latte. It's my favorite."

"I've never tried one." I raise my eyebrows.

"Get out." Kat laughs. "Here." She pushes her mug my way.

"You sure?"

"We're roommates, practically sisters, right?" Kat leans back completely surrendering her cup to me like Tia would.

It's sweet and frothy and spicy. "*Mmm,* super *mmm.*"

"You like, really?"

"Love it!" I lick the foam off my lips. "So, Mount Pleasant? I know a lot of people who go there. Do you like it?"

Kat nods and breaks off a bite of her bagel. "Daddy's been transferred three times in the last six years, so we've switched churches a lot. I haven't gotten really rooted in one church or one group of friends." Kat swirls her cup. "I'm glad we're gonna live together, Palmer."

I lick the stray fudge from my lips. "What's it like—moving? I'm super close to my family, and I'm totally in love with my boyfriend, and I have no idea how I'm going to handle being away from all of them." The words fly out of my mouth faster than I'd intended. I check her expression, but she's just nodding, like she gets it. Kat feels more like an old friend than a new one.

"Everyone at Hoover High knows about you and Keegan. Y'all are so hot, you're sizzling. He's not goin' to Clarkston?"

"No." I shake my head and try to remember to breathe. "He got a scholarship to play baseball at Polaris State. He's going to start as a freshman. He had to take the opportunity."

"I get that. I'm playin' soccer for Clarkston. I only looked at schools with top-notch soccer programs and where I thought I could get a scholarship." Kat's fingers are adorned with all these incredibly cool silver rings. She slides a chunky one on her pinky back and forth across the surface of her cup. "So, Keegan's okay with you not followin' him? Where does that leave you two?"

"I'm not sure where that leaves us. That's the whole problem." I slap my hands on the table and blink the unexpected tears back as quickly as I can, struggling for composure. "I'm a journalism major, and want to be on the school paper, or maybe write for one of those cool, glossy student magazines." I square my shoulders. "I didn't want to go to Polaris. It's so small and kind of dumpy, and they don't even have a journalism major, just English. Plus," I lean back, "Hannah and I have planned to go to Clarkston together since we were like ten. Keegan and I are going to see each other almost every weekend." I nod, trying to convince Kat and myself that I have it all figured out, that I've made the right decision, even though I have no idea if I have. "You know, I'll go there one weekend. He'll come to Clarkston. We'll both meet at home some weekends. And we'll Skype every night. I'm just a little nervous, but I'm sure it will be fine, right?"

"I think if y'all are as crazy about each other as you say, y'all will find a way to make it work."

"That's exactly what Hannah says, when she's not suggesting I drop Keegan altogether to go on a manhunt with her around campus. I'm sure it will be fine." Eager to stash my pitiful emotional rant far away in the recesses of my mind, I turn the subject and my mood. "Kat, college is going to be so much fun!"

"A blast."

13
CLAIRE

THE HOTEL DOOR CLICKS BEHIND me.

"I need to use the restroom."

"Right there." Phillip points.

I was fine while we were walking around, but once in the dimly lit room, exhaustion hits me—maybe from not eating enough, maybe from the wine, maybe just from a long, exhilarating day in an enormous foreign city. I splash cold water on my face, apply a fresh coat of lip gloss, and step back into the room.

It is dark. Too dark.

And quiet. Too quiet.

"Phillip?"

"Claire." His voice comes from directly in front of me. My eyes adjust, and I find him only two or three feet away standing in his boxer shorts. I look away, embarrassed. I thought he was packing. Maybe he was changing. But he's not scrambling to pull on his jeans or pajama pants. He's just standing.

Something is very wrong.

"What are you doing?"

"Waiting for you," he purrs, stepping forward. His arm is around me, and he steers me around so we've traded spots. His lips mash mine, and they are warm and wet. It doesn't feel anything like our kiss on the Tower. It is the opposite of that. I try to step back, but he holds me close to him. Too close.

"Hey." I try to push my body away, but he doesn't budge.

"I've wanted you, Little Ballerina, since the minute I laid eyes on you." There is something dangerous about his voice, like the sharp silver blade of a knife. Phillip shoves me onto the bed with a force that overtakes me, like a giant gust of unexpected wind. His body lands on top of mine with a thump, causing me to lose my breath.

"No." I twist.

"Come on, Claire. Trust me." He smoothes my hair out of my face with one hand while holding me down with the other. His lips crush mine. I wanted him to kiss me before, but not like this. It's not supposed to be like this. I try to tell him, but his mouth is pressed so hard against mine I can't speak. I will myself to move—to stop this from happening, but I am frozen, as if stunned by a stun gun, unable to move a muscle or make a sound.

His hand slides up my short dress and in a single motion rips off my underwear, leaving me exposed and defenseless. I try again to move. But my limbs are made of stone. They are too heavy and too rigid and won't do what I ask them to do.

There is so much pressure as he forces himself inside

me.

I feel a stab of pain and fear and anxiety starting where my underwear were and shooting inward, to my very core. I cannot breathe or think, wishing I could transport my body somewhere else, anywhere else, wishing I could make this nightmare end.

There's a pounding at the door, and the pounding of my heart inside my chest, and the panting of Phillip as he moans on top of me.

"*Monsieur*, just confirming your wake up call for 6:00 a.m. It seems your phone is off the hook."

Phillip presses his hand over my mouth. I can't breathe.

"*Merci*. 6:00 a.m. is perfect. I'll make sure to fix my phone," he says, his voice sounding normal again.

With one last thrust of his body, he rolls off me and toward the phone to place the handset on the cradle. Finally my body responds. I bolt for the door, running through the hall, past the hotel employee, not looking back until I am inside my room with my door closed behind me.

14
KAT

"COACH ALVAREZ IS RUNNING LATE today, so for our morning drills, we will combine the men with the women," Coach De Luca says, in his thick voice. "To warm up, we'll begin with five laps around the field. Go!"

We take off around the orange cones marking the corners of the field. I find myself in the middle of the pack. I don't want to exert all my energy before practice, but I don't want these boys thinking they can whip past me either. I kick it up a notch and fall in stride next to a guy with buzzed, bleached-blonde hair and three unexpected long dreadlocks streaming down his shoulders.

With the thermometer around 99 degrees and about a zillion percent humidity, I'm sweating half way around the first lap.

"Scorching today," he says, wiping the sweat from his forehead with his arm.

"More fun this way, don't ya think?" I pant as the

morning sun sizzles my skin.

"You've got a strange way of having fun." He laughs and moves closer to the front of the pack.

After laps we move on to some control drills. I get paired with the boy with the dreadlocks.

Coach blows his whistle, signaling the beginning of the drill.

"Not bad," my partner says, after I maneuver through the drill and pass the ball to him. "I'm Tony."

"Kat," I say, watching him maintain perfect control of the ball. "Not bad yourself."

He taps the ball back to me. I catch it on my instep, and *whoosh* send it back to him. The sun glints on his nose. There's a sparkle there, like glitter. It could be sweat, but it's shinier.

"Love your nose ring," I say, pointing to my nose as he sends the ball my way. "I've always wanted a tiny stud on the side, just like that."

Tony nods as he passes the ball again. His pass is a bit too forceful and zips past me. I turn to retrieve it.

"My buddy did it for me. He could do yours if you want?"

"Honest?" I ask, kicking the ball back in motion.

"Sure. Find me after practice."

"Sweet." I nod.

Coach Alvarez jogs onto the field, sweaty and red in the face. The men's team follows him onto their pitch for the rest of the day.

After practice I'm guzzling my second bottle of water when Tony appears by my side. "You really want a stud, Kat?"

"Darn straight," I say, knowing full well my mama will

kill me.

"I texted my friend, and he said he'd set you up. Come on."

"You sure he won't mind? He doesn't even know me."

"C'mon."

I follow Tony to his rusty black El Camino and climb in. The upholstery is torn and the dash looks beat up, but hey, it's a car, and that's more than I have.

Tony slams his door shut, fastens his seat belt and turns the ignition. "You might want to roll down your window. I don't have AC."

"I'm already saturated in sweat. I don't think I could get any hotter." I laugh and roll down the window.

"You like the Dead?" he asks, cranking up Jerry Garcia's voice on his stereo.

"Sure." I thump my thumb ring on the console to the beat of "Uncle John's Band" as we drive through town. We don't really talk as he drives, just kind of groove to the music, which is fine with me. I replay the scrimmage we had at the end of practice today in my head.

"*Grrr!*"

"What was that for?" Tony asks.

"Did I growl out loud?" I ask.

"Yup."

"Just thinkin' 'bout how that Sarah girl got past me during scrimmage."

"Bothers you, huh?"

"Like crazy!"

"Here we go." We pull into a parking spot at an apartment building.

"Your friend lives here?"

"Yeah, he's a junior, so he can live off campus. He

works at Corner Cup to pay his rent."

"I've been meanin' to go there. Good coffee?"

"Best coffee and great hangout. Come on. We'll do your nose, and then head over there so you can see."

"Great."

Tony hops out of the car, crosses the lot and opens the door to 28J without knocking. My eyes adjust to the dimness of the small room crowded with a sagging couch draped with a Star Wars sheet, two beanbag chairs, a beat up coffee table and a tangle of electronics.

"Tony!" A tall, skinny guy with pale skin and amber-colored eyes, sporting the same short hair and a couple of random dreads as Tony, pops out of nowhere. He gives Tony five and plops into one of the bean bags, scattering an explosion of dust into the air, bringing with it the smell of stinky socks, moldy pizza and stale cigarette smoke.

Bachelor pad, I remind myself.

"Dog this is Kat." Tony points from his friend to me. "Hey, that's pretty funny."

"Dog?" I laugh. "For real?"

Dog grins a cute, boyish smile, then barks. "My real name is Douglas. Not much of a stage name. I always wear this necklace." He tugs on a chain heavy with dog tags. "Doug—dog tags—Dog. I don't know. It just stuck."

"I'm Katherine, but that's too formal and fancified for me. Kat suits me better."

"I like Kat." Tony smiles, his eyes flashing approval.

"S'up?" Dog asks Tony.

"Like I texted, man, Kat wants her nose pierced. Can you do it?"

"Sure." Dog hones in on my nose. "There's just a small fee."

"Shoot! I didn't bring my wallet. We were at soccer, and well…" I dig through my soccer bag, knowing I don't have a cent. "I'm sorry."

Dog laughs. "I don't want your money. I'm trying to get the word out about my music, so I need you to play this for your friends and bring them to see me play." Dog digs through a red plastic milk crate and grabs a CD. On the white label someone's scribbled "Dog's Howling" with a black Sharpie.

"Nice." I point to the title. "Thanks. I love music." I take the CD.

"Come over here. It gets the best light."

I pick my path carefully, trying not to step on any of the laundry or Taco Bell wrappers on the floor as I make my way to the coffee table. Tony gently positions me on the corner. I hope I don't stick here permanently.

"Okay, so not much to choose from, but I have a silver stud, this little arrow, a gold stud, or this star."

"The silver stud is perfect." I reach out and touch the tiny, slick ball carefully, like it might shock me. "Where do you play?"

Dog disappears to what I guess is the bathroom, but shouts loud enough for me to hear, "I play at Corner Cup. I work there, and I play there. I kind of live there."

"Tony says it's chillin'. Sounds like fun."

Thankfully Dog returns with a bottle of rubbing alcohol and a cotton ball. I was starting to freak a little about the less than sterile environment. The last thing I need is an infected nose. I'd get the extra long lecture from Mama if that happened. Dog wets the ball, and the entire room is overpowered by the pungent twang of alcohol. It reminds me of a doctor's office.

"Ouch!" The quick sting is like getting a shot.

"Wasn't *that* bad, was it?" Tony asks.

"I'm all right." My eyes water a little from the prick, but it was over fast. I tap my rings on my thighs like I'm drumming, willing myself not to look like a sissy.

"Great, let's get an espresso." Tony stands. Dog slings his guitar case over his shoulder.

I pick up the used cotton ball and screw the lid back on the alcohol. "In here?" I ask, motioning to where Dog got his supplies.

"Yeah, thanks."

I toss the cotton ball in the trash and look at myself in the mirror.

"Sweet! Super sweet!" I say softly. "Love the nose ring!" I say loud enough for the guys to hear. And I do. It feels freeing. Like a symbol of independence. Like a mark that tells the world I'm in college. I put the alcohol in the cabinet, assuming that's where it came from.

"I can't thank y'all enough." I hug Dog, then Tony. "I LOVE it!"

"No prob," Tony says.

"Yeah, plus remember, we had a deal." Dog looks all serious. "You've gotta get your friends all ramped up about my music. Have them check me out on YouTube and stuff."

"I swear it."

"All set?" Dog asks, already out the door.

I check the time on my phone. "Shoot. Y'all know what? I'm gonna have to skip that coffee. I should really get a move on."

"One cup of joe then you can go." Dog grins.

"I truly am craving a chai latte, y'all, but I'm drivin' home for the weekend and still need to pack. I've gotta motor."

"No worries. Next time." Dog waves.

"I'll give you a ride." Tony motions toward the door. "I'll meet you up at the Cup in a few," he tells Dog.

"Deal."

"I can walk. It's not that far."

"I need gas anyway." Tony shrugs.

"Thanks so much for the piercing, Dog. It's sweet, really. And I promise I'll bring my friends to hear you play and spread the word all over campus. You'll be famous in no time."

"Thatta girl!" Dog slaps me on the back.

"Sorry," I tell Tony, when we're back in his car. "I didn't mean to ruin your hang out time."

"No worries. I'll only have to wait about ten minutes until I get my espresso. I think I can handle it." Tony winks. "Maybe."

Tony pulls into the athletic dorm parking lot. "See ya next week at practice."

I take one last peek in the visor mirror at my nose. I feel a solid thump in my chest, like the satisfaction of the ball hitting my foot in just the right spot. "I owe you one, really, Tony. Thanks."

"You look fierce. Sarah'll never get past you again."

"Ya think?" I ask, snapping the visor shut.

"I know." Tony gives me the rock, and I pop out of the car.

15
CLAIRE

I SLIDE THE BOLT INTO place.

I walk into the bathroom and pull back the shower curtain.

I twist the hot knob all the way. I twist the cold knob a little bit of the way.

I reach behind me and unzip the zipper Phillip never bothered to touch. My new Parisian dress drops to my ankles. As it falls, I see the thin scarlet lines running from between my legs to my anklebones. I carefully remove the dress from my feet, so it won't get smeared or stained with the blood. I step into the shower.

Hot water.

Lather.

Rinse.

Shampoo.

Lather again.

Rinse again.

Shampoo again.

Lather again. Scrub harder. Scrub more.

Rinse again. Rinse off every soap sud, every drop, every trace.

Conditioner in my hair this time. Let it sit while I count to 60.

Fifty-eight. Fifty-nine. Sixty.

I'm cold, so very cold.

Twist the cold to the right, turning it off completely, allowing only hot water to stream from the showerhead.

Shivering still.

Twist the hot off. Step out onto the white bath mat. Pull a thin towel around me. Pull it tighter. Tighter. It won't go around me tight enough. It can't make me warm.

Slide my pajamas on. Socks too. Curl up in bed. Still shaking. Can't get warm. Stand up. Open closet doors. Find two extra blankets. Spread one on top of my bed, smoothing it out. Shivering. Spread the other on top of that, sliding my hand over the fuzzy top. Shaking. Walk to the window, ensuring it's latched. Walk to the door, checking the lock and the bolt.

Crawl back under the covers. Tuck them all around my body, forming a cocoon. Less cold, but still shivering.

Darkness.

Knock. Knock.

Body tenses. Freezes. Like a stone. Again.

"Claire?" Mom's voice calls me from sleep. "Claire, the door's locked."

"Sorry." A cartoon balloon rises over my head, with the word typed within it.

Pull back the covers. Stand. Walk to the door. Reach for the bolt, but pull back my hand.

Inhale. Exhale.

Peer through the peephole. It's Mom, only Mom.

Slide the bolt back and twist the lock, then slowly open the door.

"Thanks, honey." Mom hugs me. "Sorry I woke you."

No words in my throat. No words on my lips. Silently, close the door behind her and twist the lock back into its safe position. Slide the bolt back into place, walk back to my bed, pull the covers back over my body and curl my body into a ball, into itself.

"Go back to sleep," Mom whispers, kissing my forehead, which barely peeks out from under the covers. "We'll talk in the morning. Night, night."

Night, I think the word in my head, and embrace the darkness.

16
PALMER

I STEP OUT ONTO THE porch and spin for effect, letting the flippy skirt of my black dress, graze my thighs and flare around me.

"Wow!"

I beam, knowing I made the impact I'd planned, and kiss Keegan on his cheek, leaving red lip marks from the scarlet lipstick I added for a sexy stripe of color. This is our last night together before I leave for school, and I want it to be perfect.

"You don't just look good, you smell good." Keegan's warm hand wraps around mine as he leads me to his car. The extra perfume I spritzed behind my knees and ears is working its charm.

"You look quite dapper yourself." I raise my eyebrows as I swing my legs into his car. Keegan's plaid shirt looks crisp with his pleated khakis. His brown leather belt and shiny penny loafers complete his prepster look. But his unshaven face gives him an edge of cool, not too neat, very hot. I love that he got all dolled up for me.

Dinner at my favorite Italian restaurant flies by. A candle flickers in the middle of our table and glasses clink in the background. I catch myself staring at Keegan, trying to memorize every detail about him—how his eyebrows knit together when he's thinking, how his thick fingers wrap around his water glass, how he tilts his head back when he laughs. Every time I start to mention next week or this fall or college, I feel like I have a handful of pine nuts stuck in my throat. My vision blurs. Keegan changes the subject.

After Keegan pays the bill, I feel full and floaty, like I never want to leave this restaurant, this moment, this chair, the smile Keegan is giving me right now. But at the same time, the air is thick and heavy, like it's weighing down on me, sinking me deeper into my seat, not allowing me to move or breathe, like I might suffocate if I stay.

"I have a surprise for you," Keegan says, helping me out of my chair.

"I do love surprises." I sway my shoulders side to side. "What is it?"

Keegan takes my hand. We walk past the other tables, past the hostess stand and to the door. I'm about to pop with all of the intensity of the night and the possibilities of the surprise.

"What *is* it?"

"You'll see." His eyes lift upward in a smile. "Let's just say, I'm not ready for this evening to be over. I'm not ready to let you go. Not yet."

The tears are warm in my eyes. I dab them quickly, so my mascara won't smear, and try to lighten things up.

"Remember, I'm coming back next weekend. We've

gone longer than a week of not seeing each other before." I rub his fuzzy buzz cut playfully.

"I've got it marked on my calendar. But I don't want you to stop thinking about me for one minute when all those upper-class Clarkston guys start flirting with you."

"P-lease…" I laugh as I buckle up in his car. "Who would flirt with me, plus I won't be looking at any of the Clarkston guys." I kiss his cheek.

"Palmer." Keegan has his key in the ignition, but stops and looks at me before turning the car on. "You are gorgeous. Everyone will be flirting with you."

"Stop!" I smack his arm lightly, giddy with the compliments and the strange rush of excitement swirling around me. "I'm only yours."

"Don't let anyone think otherwise." He raises one eyebrow and leans forward, kissing me. His lips draw the breath out of me, and everything gets dark and swirly in my head. His hand slides up the fitted bodice of my dress. I exhale at his touch, pressing my lips harder against his.

"C'mon. We have a surprise to get to." Keegan pulls away and turns the key. He never pulls away from me. That's my job, but there's a twinkle in his eye. He's up to something.

He pulls into the parking lot of the playground where I grew up swinging, climbing and sliding. "*Ta da.*"

"Are we going to climb the monkey bars?" I ask, hoping he'll reveal his plan.

"Not exactly." He comes around to my side, opens my car door, helps me out and ushers me to the sidewalk. "Wait here a sec."

Although the playground is lit, the rest of the park is gray and shadowy. I crane my neck but can't see what he's digging out of his trunk.

Keegan appears at my side with a blanket and a gift bag. He is not a gift bag kind of guy, and I don't recall him ever getting cold. My heart beats faster than the crickets chirping in the warm night air.

"Come on," he whispers, taking my arm.

Everything feels too intense, like the match point at Wimbledon, like everything hinges on this final evening together, before I go to school. I usually love intense, live for it, really. But the pressure to make everything perfect is making it difficult for me to breathe, to speak, to move. I try to think of something goofy to say to pop the balloon of expectation before it bursts. I could jump in a swing, or make a joke about our waiter's tie, which was so skinny he could have used it as a shoelace, but Keegan is solemn and determined. It would be wrong for me to ruin this moment. So, I follow, taking little steps. My four-inch heels tap the sidewalk, echoing in the stillness of the vacated park.

"Here," he says, spreading the black and gray plaid blanket under the awning of the drooping branches of a willow tree. After some smoothing and sliding, Keegan motions for me to sit. I try to sit gracefully in heels and a mini dress, deciding legs stretched forward, crossed at the ankles is the most ladylike. I prop myself up with my hands behind my back and smile, like a model in a photo shoot. I feel glamorous. I lick my lips, waiting for Keegan to speak. Instead, he slides down next to me and starts kissing me, a desperate, needy kiss. I lean into his kisses, letting them overpower the anxiety stirring inside of me, the going-away-to-school, saying-goodbye-to-my-boyfriend jitters. We kiss like we're on a movie set, like we'll die if we stop, like without kissing each other there is no air. Keegan leans closer into me, pressing me gently to the ground. My arms are relieved to not have to prop me up anymore, to let go, to relax. His body is warm and strong and solid.

I smell the grass and his cologne and taste peppermint on his breath. His body seems to grow around mine, bigger, stronger, surrounding me, until there is not a me with Keegan on top, but an us, wound around and through each other. His hands slide everywhere and their touch taunts me. I usually swat him away, but it feels lovely, like an itch to a scratch. But just like an itch to a scratch, it's insatiable. Everywhere his hands glide I want them to touch again and again and longer and longer.

He pulls his lips away from mine for a moment, a flash second, to breathe my favorite words, "I love you, Palm."

I pull him back into a kiss unable to stand the moment our lips were apart. I refuel myself by connecting our mouths, then focus long enough to pull away and answer, "I love you too."

Then we're both immersed in each other more intensely than before. His fingers slide up my legs to my thighs and trace the edges of my panties, tickling and exciting me, but I'm so lost in our oneness, I don't consciously note what's going on. In another heartbeat, he's sliding down his pants. The sound of his zipper is like an alarm clock shaking me out of an ethereal dream.

"No!" I pull the words out of my mouth from somewhere beyond my physical self while struggling to push the magnetic force of my boyfriend off of me. I only manage to get him over to the side and Keegan leans back in, sliding his hand into the small of my back and pulling me back into him. A second ago, I would have melted back into his form, but I feel like I've wakened from a drug-induced fantasy.

"No, Keeg." I push back again, breathing a little too heavily.

"What's wrong?" His silver eyes search my face as he pushes a loose strand of hair out of my eyes.

"It's too much. Too far." I shake my head, gasping for air. I need air.

"Too much?" He gives me a light kiss on the lips. "I love you. There can't be too much. I want you, all of you, forever, Palm."

I feel disoriented, struggling to distinguish between dream and reality.

"You love me, right?" he asks, kissing me lightly again.

"Yes." That's an easy one. "Of course, I love you."

"See, there can't be too much of that." He smiles a crooked smile and pulls me back into his arms.

As inviting as they are, I know if I go back there, things will go where I can't turn back. I bite my lip hard until I can feel the pain. I turn my mind inward away from Keegan and toward the sting in my lip. Doing that, I'm able to sit.

"I can't."

"Can't what?" Keegan looks so confused, one eyebrow raised higher than the other, like he doesn't realize where we were headed, like he doesn't remember his fly is unzipped.

I'm straining to find the right words. If I say "make love" or "have sex" then I'm saying out loud the forbidden, what we mustn't do, what we were about to do. If I blow it off, maybe it will go away. Oh, please go away!

Like an answer to my plea, something inside my heart tells me this is not going away. I need to be strong.

I exhale and square my shoulders. It feels like the fog surrounding us dissolves. A chill prickles my skin, making me very aware of what I almost did.

Okay now. I could really, really, really use some strength. I beg in my head for the words and resolve I can't find.

I'm here. The voice inside, the voice that must be God, reminds me. *I'll walk you home.*

What? How could God walk me home, and what does He mean by that? Sometimes I feel like I'm getting a bad signal when I try to decipher God's intentions for me.

"Come on, Palm." Keegan's deep voice coaxes. "Here." He sits up. "I was going to wait to give you this when I dropped you off, but maybe now is better." Keegan scootches over to the base of the tree where the navy blue and red striped gift bag rests. Leave it to a guy to use navy and red stripes. He grabs the edge of the bag and eases back next to me.

"For you."

There is no tissue paper to nose through, so I take my time pulling apart the top and peeking inside. At the bottom is a small box. "*Hmmm.* What's this?" I ask.

"Open it."

The cardboard lid is snug, but wiggles off revealing a pale green heart charm made out of a smooth stone or maybe glass, embedded in funky silver wire on a sleek black cord.

"I absolutely LOVE it! Did you pick this out?" I look at him, astonished. Keegan's always been good to me, but his style rating is, well, he's a jock. This bracelet is art fair chic, my favorite color, and I have a freaky obsession with bracelets—cannot have enough!

"When you went to orientation, there was that festival my mom drags me to every year." He fastens the clasp around my wrist. "And while she was looking at earrings to send my twin cousins for their birthday, I saw this, and I knew." Keegan clears his throat, which sounds unnaturally thick with emotion. "I knew I wanted you to wear this heart every day you're at school, so you'll never forget where your heart belongs." He tips his head, folds his lips and looks down.

Keegan fighting back tears makes my eyes fill. As a hot tear slides down my cheek, I kiss him on the head. "Thank you." I shake my head as another tear falls. "Thank you for everything. It's perfect, Keeg. I mean the bracelet is beautiful. I would have totally picked it out for myself, but how you thought of it…how you picked it, well, you spoil me."

He looks up. "I'll always spoil you. Always. Now where were we?" He wraps his arms around me, and his lips work over my mouth. Shivers climb from my toes to my scalp. The heat and tug return inside me. Moments later his fingers are back at my undies, tugging at their sides.

I swat his hand away, but it comes immediately back. I swat it again. He gently takes my hand and puts it on his waist, intent on his plan.

A warm breeze stirs through the otherwise still evening.

"No, Keeg." I pull away, feeling disheveled inside and out. "We can't do this. I'm sorry. It's just not okay. I thought…" I reposition my underwear, wriggle my dress back to a respectable place, and sit up.

"You thought what?" Keegan sits, all the sweetness and sap drained from his face and replaced by a clenched jaw and dark, flat eyes. "Because *I* thought if two people loved each other and promised to always be together, they'd do anything for each other. *I* thought since you love me, you must want me like I want you. *I* thought the bracelet showed you how I feel." His voice gets rougher and scratchier with each word.

I look around. I don't know what I'm looking for, someone to explain to him? But there's no one here. Thank goodness no one's here! What if they'd seen? What were we thinking groping in a public park? Anyone could have seen us! What were we thinking, letting things go that far? What is he thinking, so angry at me? What am I thinking? Fear? Shame? Love? Anger? Hurt? The tears don't trickle now; they pour.

"I do love you!" I shout back, with so much emotion it strains my throat. "I love you so much it hurts! I love you so much, Keegan, that I couldn't think of something to get you for tonight, even though I've been looking for weeks. Because nothing seemed right, and everything seemed trite or like I was saying goodbye, which we're not." The words come out shaky between my gasps for air and my tears. "I love you so much, I've been sick to my stomach thinking about living without seeing you for days on end. So much that I haven't even packed! I'm leaving for college tomorrow, and I haven't packed, because I thought if I packed it was like admitting I was leaving."

"Great Palm." Keegan's voice is calm now, but not tame. There is a wild underbeat, like the calm crouch of a lion ready to pounce. "Turn it all back to your woes. Poor Palmer. Her life is so tough. She's going to the rich, preppy, smart school where everyone will love her. She wants to tease her boyfriend, but not take any responsibility." He stands and zips his fly, shooing me off the blanket. "You say you love me. Prove it, Palmer! Prove to me you love me!"

I tilt on my heels and almost fall, as if someone pushed me—pushed everything in me, even the words right out of me. I regain my balance, but sobs rack my stomach and mascara blurs my vision.

Keegan stares at me, like I'm a sporting event he's watching from the stands. He grabs the blanket and the bag in a giant wad.

"That's what I thought!" He throws his car keys at me. They clatter as they land by my feet. "Drive yourself home!" He turns and stomps off leaving me under the tree alone.

17
CLAIRE

"CLAIRE." MOM'S HANDS PRESS LIGHTLY on my blankets. "Who was sleepy?" she asks brightly. "I was the one up all night. Sorry again I woke you. Arnot and I just had the loveliest time." Mom sits on the side of my bed. "We spent forever on the tower. We waited until the fireworks went off again. I guess that's another hour."

The memory of Phillip kissing me on top of La Tour Eiffel brings everything rushing back.

Mom sighs, laying her hand on my enshrouded arm. "We rode the metro back to the Latin Quarter, then sat at a café and ordered espressos. You know I never drink coffee at night!" She shakes her head. "Keeps me up. So, we sat there and chatted until 2:00 a.m.! Can you believe it, your mom staying out past midnight? But it didn't seem late or crazy, it just seemed French." Mom smiles, stands and walks toward the mirror, brushing her hair.

"How about you, honey? Did you and Phillip have a nice time?"

I am frozen in my own body. How can I tell her what

happened? What exactly did happen? I mean, we definitely had sex, but I didn't want to. I didn't want to at all, and he made me. Is that Phillip having sex with me? Did I lead him on? I flirted. I let him talk me into that dress. I wore it just for him. I let him kiss me.

Whoosh. I feel the force of his body. The boxer shorts. My stomach cramps.

"Honey?" Mom turns back toward me. "Are you okay? You look white as a ghost."

"I don't f-f-feel very good," I stammer.

"Probably that wine and rich food." Mom sits back down on the bed. "I wondered if I should say something, but it seemed okay. Those *escargot* didn't sit quite right with me either." She places her hand on my forehead. "You don't have a fever."

"I think I'm going to be sick," I groan, pulling the covers back and rushing to the bathroom. I lean over the toilet, gagging, expecting to vomit, but nothing comes out.

I am empty.

Mom comes in, finding me hanging over the toilet. "Hey. You need to take it easy. Should we just rest in the hotel today, a recovery day?"

I turn my head toward Mom, fresh blouse, walking shoes on her feet. "This was supposed to be our girls' day," I moan.

"We still have tomorrow. I'm sure Arnot could find some work to do while we play. Today we can stay in, and tomorrow could be our girls' day out. Let me just text Arnot and let him know we won't be meeting him for lunch." Mom seems overly animated.

I close my eyes. I don't want Mom here, hovering over me. I'm afraid I'll say something. I'm afraid she'll know.

"You go out today. Don't waste your day on account of me. I'm fine. Just exhausted. I just want to sleep, and I don't think I could eat." I motion her toward the door.

"Maybe that would be best." Mom stands and pulls me with her. "Let's get you back in bed. I'll get you a Sprite or something. Then I'll get out of your hair and let you rest."

"Thanks." I smile meekly, relieved. I crawl back into my rumpled nest, laying my head on my pillow, thankful for its softness. Succumbing to the darkness behind my eyelids, I close my mouth and eyes and mind to the blankness of sleep.

I hear Mom unlock the door, smell her warm breath as her lips brush my cheek, feel her cool hand check my forehead again for a fever. I should move, should open my eyes, should say something, but I can't. I don't have the energy to stretch my eyelids or exercise my jaw. It is so much easier to remain still and silent.

**

BIRDS CHIRP. THE CLOCK READS 6:30 a.m. Early. For today. But what happened to yesterday? Did I sleep right through? I sigh, proud in a way for avoiding yesterday altogether. I didn't have to talk. No one could look at me. No one could ask anything. Then I remember where I am. I slept an entire day in Paris! My chest tightens, angry with myself. How could I be so stupid again?

A smell fills my nose—the scent of Phillip's hand covering my mouth. I jump out of bed and away from the memory.

I tiptoe to the bathroom and stare at the ghost in the mirror. An ache spreads over me. Tears soak my face. I shake my head, trying to shake the tears away, trying to shake what happened with Phillip away. Why did that happen? Why? Why? Why? I stomp on the cold linoleum. How could he do that to me and just disappear across the Channel? Words so harsh, so cruel, I've never uttered before, pour from my lips as I picture Phillip's smile, evil like the grin of President Snow in *The Hunger Games*.

This is my last day in Paris, the city of my dreams. I will *not* let him ruin this for me. I *will* shower and get dressed and do today. I'll be a tourist and a loving daughter, and do the things I'm supposed to do. I have to.

Out of the shower, I blow my hair straight and finish it off with Mom's flat iron. New day. New me. The memories of Phillip pressing against me sneak back into my mind. I open my eyes wider, forcing them to disappear somewhere into the part of my brain I don't use.

"Claire?" Mom blinks. The clock reads 7:45 a.m.

"Good morning." I force a smile.

"You feeling okay, sweetie?"

"Yeah, fine. I must have had a 24-hour bug. I'm great. Really." I hug Mom. "Sorry I ditched you yesterday." I say the words I'd rehearsed, praying Mom won't notice the tremble just below my voice.

"Oh sweetie, it's fine. I'm just sorry you missed a whole day, and it was a lovely day." Mom slides up to a sitting position with a goofy grin on her face.

"What did you do?" I ask, thrilled to turn the subject away from me.

While Mom fills me in on her sightseeing with Arnot, who as it turns out, canceled his meetings to be with her, I pull back the curtains and open the swinging windows, allowing the fresh French morning air to permeate the room.

On the street below, vendors chat with truck drivers delivering their orders for the day. Café owners slide chairs out onto the sidewalks. Businessmen and women shuffle down the street in suits carrying brief cases—just the same as every other morning for them. For me everything is different.

Mom babbles as she makes her bed. "I still didn't get the scoop. Did you love the Eiffel Tower? Did you and Phillip exchange phone numbers? When he gets back to the States we could double date!" She giggles.

An invisible fist punches my stomach. I have no words to describe that night, and I certainly can't tell Mom what happened, but she's watching me, waiting.

"The view from the Eiffel Tower was beautiful." I stick to the truth. "I wish I could have stayed up there forever." All true. If I were still up there, none of this would have happened.

"Wasn't it incredible?" Mom gurgles while brushing her teeth. "Let's go back tonight. Who knows when we'll get the chance to come to Paris again! We might as well do exactly what we want."

Do the things *we* want. I feel power in that, in being in control. How did I get so out of control? How did I let this happen? Why did I go into a boy's hotel room? I'm such an idiot! It didn't feel like I was doing something wrong or slutty, because that's not what I planned to do. Kiss him. Okay, I wanted that, but that was all. How did it go from wanting a kiss goodbye to him being on top of me? Why didn't I stop him? Why couldn't I stop him?

I need to regain control. That's what I'm going to do. I. Will. Be. In. Control.

Mom grabs some clothes from her suitcase. "I'm calling

Arnot."

Arnot's name makes me shudder. Arnot—Phillip—Phillip—Arnot. Same eyes, same smile. I see it now. Arnot's not a smarmier version of Phillip—just an older version. I want to tell Mom what happened, but how? She'd probably want to crack Phillip's skull. Or would she think it was my fault? Because I shouldn't have been there. I shouldn't have kissed him. I wouldn't blame her for blaming me.

What if she told Arnot? It could screw up their relationship with an elephant in the room like "your nephew had sex with my daughter." And Phillip would deny it, wouldn't he? I feel feverish, as I swallow the invisible lump lodged in my throat like a slimy snail.

Plus, if I tell Mom, it could knock her off her semi-stable feet back onto completely neurotic ground. "Where did I go wrong? I shouldn't have left you alone. I'm a terrible mother." She'll torture herself. "I can't believe you're not a virgin, after everything we've talked about. You're smarter than that." She'll lament. She might even lock herself in her room again distraught with me—distraught with the world. Last time she had a breakdown, I had to call her school and say she had swine flu. I can't go through that again. Neither can Mom. No, I have to handle this on my own. I'm going to be in control, right?

A wave of nausea floods over me, like being in control is way more than I can handle. I sink to the bed.

"Claire?" Mom asks, waving her mascara wand in the air.

"*Hmmm?*"

"He suggested Versailles, but that's almost a whole day, and I wasn't sure if you'd be up for it."

Think fast, I tell myself. All day at the palace with Mom

and Arnot sounds horrible. NO. I need time and space—a day by myself roaming around Paris. Isn't that what I've always dreamed of?

I sputter quickly, "Why don't you and Arnot do Versailles? You really want to see it, right? And then you two can get some time without your daughter tagging along." I tuck my hair behind my ears. "Hey, you never told me. You would have told me, if he'd proposed, right?"

"Not yet." Mom sighs and shrugs. "But maybe today where Kings and Queens once walked." Her voice sounds far off. "What would you do?"

"There are a million things I'd like to see. No offense, Mom, but I can't wait to stroll the streets without a chaperone."

"Are you sure?" Mom rubs her hand across my head, checking for the fever I never had. "This is our last day. You'd have to promise to keep your phone turned on, so I can find you."

"Absolutely. We'll reconnect tonight. Promise."

Mom agrees to our plan and bounds out the door like a schoolgirl with a crush, while I fight the urge to crawl back under the covers. I deliberately tug on faded jeans, a tank and a pretty pink and cream scarf I bought from a street vendor for five euro. I pull my hair into some semblance of a bun and slide on my shades. I don't want anyone to recognize me or talk to me or even look at me today, a bit like a movie star hiding from the paparazzi. I snort. Who would be looking for me? Phillip's face flashes before my eyes, and I slide it away.

Pretend it didn't happen, I remind myself. Pretend I'm a world-class ballerina, escaping my fans for a holiday in Paris. Much more fun! I nod, determined to keep the persona for the day.

I find the nearest Metro, bound down the stairs, insert my small white ticket in the slot and push through the turnstile headed to Sacre Couer. At my stop, I climb a zillion steps to get to the street. Where exactly am I? I don't see the magnificent church on a hill in any direction. My heart races. I turn around, trying to get my bearings. I don't see anyone suspicious.

I untie my scarf from my neck and wrap it around my head like a headband. I need to be smart. Ask for directions, but be careful who I trust.

"*Pardon*." I get the nerve to ask two teenage girls. "*Où est-ce que Sacre Cœur?*"

"*Montez les escaliers*," the one with the dark skin says, pointing.

I want to trust her, to climb these steps, but I'm hesitant. The last time I trusted someone everything fell apart.

But where else can I go?

I ascend to a busy street cluttered with street performers juggling bowling pins and break dancing to eighties music blaring from jam boxes. Tourists aim cameras, unfold maps, and point to the magnificent, sugar-white cathedral at the top of countless steps. Students gather, nibbling baguettes and chattering. A carousel spins ornately painted animals. Its lights flash while carnival music chimes, calling the children to play. The aromas of roasted peanuts and cotton candy waft from food stands. Musicians strum tinny acoustic guitars while groups stop to listen and drop Euro in their open cases.

The beauty, the activity, the excitement in the air suspends me. An incognito ballerina could blend into this crowd. I could lose myself here. Can I lose the memories here too? Sacre Coeur is beautiful, so much bigger and whiter than I imagined, like a palace in a fairy tale.

I pay the admittance to climb more stairs for the view. My legs step, step, step up endless skinny staircases. The narrow passage inside the church bends and curves so there's no seeing what's ahead. What if someone comes the other way? How would we ever get past one another? But other than the muffled voices of a group somewhere ahead, I see no one. Eerie? Why is no one else here? This is a major tourist attraction. Does the crowd outside know something I don't?

The ceilings and walls seem to shrink, making the stairwells shorter and narrower. There are no lights, just a dim natural glow coming from somewhere I am not. My heart jumps up and down in my chest. If someone was after me, would anyone know? Would anyone hear my screams? Would I be able to scream? There is no escape. It's a one-way climb with nowhere to turn around. I will myself to climb faster and faster to finish.

Finally, a window. A quick peek outside to see the light of day and a promise of something safer.

I promise you'll be safe.

I know this is God's voice, breaking through the chilling, jagged thoughts in my head. I've heard it before. But I don't want to hear it now. I am the one who needs to be in control.

I trudge forward as quickly as my short legs will carry me. I hate to leave the window, but at some point I must get to the top. If someone is behind me, if Phillip followed me here, I need to keep moving.

Stop being a baby, Claire, I tell myself, as I climb further and further upward. Phillip is in London. No one followed me anywhere. I feel the strain of stacks of stairs on my hamstrings.

Higher and higher I ascend. There is light, air, space, a terrace where I can see. I inhale the sunshine and the breeze and the sights before me. From here, I can see across Paris to the Eiffel Tower. I exhale in relief and in wonder. All of Paris lies before me—curvy roads, historic monuments and a collage of colors and shapes filling all the spaces in between. It's not as grand a view as I'd seen from the top of the Tower. Not the map kind of view, but a more personal, breathe it in, beautiful kind of view.

I adjust my gaze down toward the lawn of Sacre Coeur and all the people I'd seen on the steps.

Footsteps thump from somewhere below. Someone is coming up the stairs.

I can't breathe, like I'm being strangled. There is no time. Which way is down? Which way is out? Alone on this terrace anyone could do anything to me, and no one would ever know.

Thump. Thump. Thump.

They are coming, and I am trapped.

There has to be a way out. I have to find a way out.

My eyes dart frantically, finally landing on *SORTIE.* The exit sign, there all along. I grab the railing, so I don't fall down the steep incline, scampering down steps faster than I can *pas de bourre*. I strain my ears, but can't hear anything over my thundering heartbeat and the blood rushing through my head.

Down, down, down, dark, narrow passageways curving, never knowing. What if there's more than one of them? What if someone's coming up, and I'm blocked?

I alight in the main church, stunned by the bright light

and activity. I rush toward a pew crowded with praying tourists and away from the tower and the potential danger. I slide behind an older woman in a black dress, kneel and fold my hands so tightly together it hurts.

The pews are a high gloss wood, slick under my touch. I release my fingers and allow them to slip along the rail in front of me as I kneel. Looking up, I am captivated by an all-encompassing mosaic of a golden Christ with His arms outstretched to me against a lapis sky.

The tears I'd bottled up escape my eyes, leaving hot tracks against my cheeks.

How can You stretch Your arms out to me after this? After I let this happen? I ask Jesus, whose image is so overwhelmingly full of love, I know I am not worthy.

I love you. Always. And YOU did not let this happen. He did it to you, and it breaks My heart.

I look down, not able to accept the message of love. My body shakes as if a small earthquake tremors inside me. I long to believe the words in my head, but did I put them there to let myself off the hook? Could God really love me that much? Was it really not my fault?

I wipe the corners of my eyes with the trailing ends of my scarf. I gaze at the golden rays surrounding the image of Jesus, the people adoring Him, the intricately carved pillars and arches surrounding the altar. Shafts of sunlight shoot through a side window, just like the golden streams emanating from the portrait of Christ. It is a portrait of love.

I nod, wanting to believe, but wanting to hold onto the pain and the fear, because then at least I can control them. If I keep remembering what Phillip did, if I keep hating him and myself for letting this happen, then I don't have to tell anyone else. I don't have to hand this over to where I can't control what will happen next.

God, I love you, too. I really do, but I don't know what to do with all of this. I want to hand it over to you, but I can't.

I nod, realizing the truth. I don't want God to see, even though He already knows. It's so dirty and ugly and embarrassing and horrifying. I did everything wrong. And I have to pay for that.

I stand up and walk out of the church, my boots echoing on the marble floors. Other tourists mill in and out of the basilica, oblivious to my conversation with God, oblivious to what has happened to me. I'd like to keep it that way. What would they think? Wine? Short skirt? Kissing? I was totally asking for it. That's what they'd say.

No one has to know. Then it's like it didn't happen, right? I'm still a virgin. I went to Paris with my mom. We went out to dinner. We saw the Eiffel Tower. Phillip took me home on the metro. We said goodbye, nice knowing you, and I went into my room, where I nodded off to sleep from too much wine and a late night. End of story.

I picture that scenario, the edited one, in my head, replacing my memories with each clop of my cowboy boots. That could have happened. Phillip's not going to tell anyone what he did. That would be insane. So, it's like the tree in the forest line. "If a boy has sex with a girl in a hotel room, and no one knows about it, did it really happen?"

As I reach the door, I feel a yank. This force tugs me. I flip around against my will and see Christ with His arms outstretched. His arms are so wide and so strong, like they could take me in and wrap around me and keep me safe from the entire world, but I can't walk forward. I don't deserve to. I am numb through and through.

No words this time. I've pushed God far enough away that either I can't hear Him, or He's done with me. I don't blame Him.

I shiver. I shake my head, and step outside.

18
HANNAH

I STOP AS ABRUPTLY AS a bird crashing into a window, maybe in as much pain as a crumpled sparrow. This is not like the quad they showed us at orientation. Not even close.

Tan linoleum floors lay stark without a thread of carpet. Naked windows, make me feel exposed. A sickly yellowish hue, definitely not cream, the opposite of lemon, mutes the walls. The pungent scent of Clorox lingers, as the only sign housekeeping, or anyone else for that matter, has been here since 1972. Two beaten-up wooden desks are stacked against the far wall, along with two metal-framed beds that could easily pass as cots. Mom, Dad, Sammie and Owen are all backed up behind me, laden with crates and comforters and carpet.

"No," I whisper.

"Come on, Hannah. This carpet is going to throw my back out," Dad urges.

"I really have to pee!" Owen shouts.

I step into the room, letting them pass. Mom stands next

to me and exhales. "It's fine." She pats her hair. "We can fix this in a jiffy. It just needs a splash of color."

"I can't live here. This isn't what it looked like. This isn't what I planned." Tears choke my voice. "I've been dreaming of our dorm room since orientation. It was going to be amazing, but it's awful. It looks like a prison cell."

"Where do you want the carpet?" Dad asks, but I don't answer, because I don't want the carpet in here. I don't want to live here.

I step back into the corridor and take deep breaths. I was so psyched to be the first one here. We got an early start, because my folks need to get back for their weekly visit and grocery drop to Grampa. But now, the lack of roommates adds to the starkness of the room. Mom follows me, puts her hand on my back and escorts me back into the room. "She wants it in here, right dear?" Mom over smiles. "This is going to be their little family room—so cute."

"So *not* cute."

"If their bedroom's in there," Sammie peeks in the adjoining room, "then why are half the beds out here?"

"I don't know." I shake my head, lips trembling.

"They probably thought you would use it like two doubles." Dad sets the large roll of rug we bought at the Carpet Shack down with a plop. "Look alive, folks. We have furniture to move."

Mom, Dad, Sammie, and I grab ends of beds and desks and situate all the beds in one room and all the desks in the other. Meanwhile, I direct Owen to carry my crate of toiletries and towels to the bathroom and Sammie to plop my bedding down on one of the bunks. I go over the checklist of things I was going to do to get the room looking worthy of Pinterest. Focusing on putting things in their proper place helps a little. Dad covering the hideous floor with the coffee-colored rug helps even more.

"It's hot in here." Sammie puts her hands on her little hips.

"Duh, it's summer!" Owen shoves her, and they get into a major pushing match, which gives me a minute to escape to the bathroom—which is equally awful, maybe worse.

"Gag!" I say. "Gag!" I say even louder, needing someone to change this, to make me less appalled. We don't even have soap in here yet, which makes me wonder how Owen washed his hands.

"Dad, could you help me with the shower curtain?" I ask, coming back into the main room.

"Sure, just a sec." His back is to me as he fiddles with our window air conditioning unit. I dig in my purse for some raspberry scented hand sanitizer, adding to my mental list to find the soap.

Brrruuummmm. Dad brings the AC to life, blasting cold air and a musty cloud into the room.

"You'll need to light a candle, dear." Mom waves her hand in front of her nose.

"We're not allowed to have fire in the dorm." I wince, wishing for the sweet scent of a candle—wishing for home.

"Oh." Mom shrugs.

An hour and a half passes unloading the van, loading my room, heaving, lugging, tugging, sliding, and switching. The room looks better, a little, but I still hate it.

"We need to get back to Columbus and Grampa's." Dad clears his throat. Grampa gets a little feisty sometimes.

Sammie pulls out a CD and hands it to me. "It's all our favorite songs." She looks away, hiding her tears.

Owen hands me a picture frame with a picture of the

two of us at the beach standing next to the sandcastle we made. "So you don't forget what I look like." He cries, rubbing his fists against his eyes.

"Oh, O." I pull him tight, Sammie too. We all stand there for a moment blubbering. I didn't see this coming. I thought I'd be so excited to be free of Thing 1 and Thing 2. Truth is, I'm going to miss them like crazy. They've been with me every day for forever, and now they won't be.

"We'll see Hannah soon." Dad ruffles all of our heads. "We don't live that far away."

"Make sure you Skype." Mom dabs her eyes. "My little girl. At college."

"Mom," I groan, hugging her. "I'd just stopped crying." The tears spill again. Mom kisses my forehead and ushers Sammie and Owen out the door.

Dad puts his hands on my shoulders. "I'm so proud of you, Hannah Banana."

The banana part makes me smile, through the streaming tears.

"You've always made me proud. Now is your chance to be whatever it is you want to be. Spread your wings, little girl. I'll be expecting great things." Dad's deep voice wavers a little. "And keep running. I want you to still keep pace with me when you come home." He hugs me then disappears.

As my family leaves, I want to rush after them, to jump in their car and go back home to my pretty room and my clean bathroom. But I know I can't. Instead, I rush to the bathroom to wash my face, warm and wet with tears. My new fluffy purple towel feels soft on my skin, slightly softening the pang in my heart.

Stop! I tell myself. Crying is over. I wanted this. I open my Notes App. The list gives me something to look at other than our van driving away. Hello, I'm in my dorm. This is *my* towel in *my* bathroom of *my* college dorm. And the towel looks perfectly darling with the shower curtain that matches the polka dot bedding Kat and Palmer picked out. Absolutely gorge! Well, almost. It will look gorgeous once Palmer's, Kat's and Claire's towels hang alongside it.

I pull my washcloth out of the crate and uncover a bottle of foamy soap with a summer breeze scent. See— things are coming together. They can. They will. They have to.

I unpack and check things off my list. It's 12:38 p.m. Unpacking was tiring, but now I'm ready for fun and food. Where are they already?"

Palmer hadn't packed as of yesterday, so who knows when she'll get here. It's so hard to plan with her. Kat's parents are going to meet her here sometime after 3 p.m. to move her stuff from the athletic dorm. And Claire? None of us have heard from her except one quick text this morning saying:

I'M BACK FROM PARIS. CAN'T WAIT FOR CLARKSTON.

So, she's totally up in the air, which makes me skeptical. Looks like I'm on my own. Still, I've got to get out of this room before the hideous walls swallow me whole.

Stuffing my phone, Clarkston ID, and a twenty-dollar bill into the pocket of my jean shorts, I turn out the lights, ready to hit campus. With my hand on the doorknob, I flip the lights back on, give myself a spritz of perfume, pinch my cheeks, and tie a scarf around my head like a headband à la Claire to keep my temperamental waves from my face. Finally presentable enough in case I bump into any cute boys, and I do hope I run into cute boys—lots of them—I let the door close behind me.

The corridor buzzes with parents and crates and nervous freshman. I meander through them, thankful my stuff is already moved in.

"Hi." I smile to a red-head with a long French braid walking past. She raises her eyebrows and keeps walking.

So, she's not going to be one of my new best friends.

Near the exit I side step a hulking football player type carrying a giant carpet roll, but not looking where he's going, because he's too busy eyeing a cute blonde prancing down the hall.

As I avoid being hit by floor covering, I bump into a stocky guy with dark blonde curls and short, distinct sideburns, who also looks like he's trying to avoid the carpet quarterback. I love sideburns!

"Careful," he warns in a deep voice.

So grateful for my last minute primp as I left our room.

"Sorry," I say and take two steps back. "It's crazy in here. Is this the door to the quad or to the street?" I point in the direction I'm walking, pretty sure of where I'm going.

"Street. Way crazy! You going somewhere?"

"I've been unpacking for hours, and I'm starving. I need to find some lunch."

"You and me both." He opens the door for me and smiles, his eyebrows veeing together—totally endearing. "I'm A.J."

He has a cool initially name? I knew I was going to love college!

"I'm Hannah." We fall into stride. "Have you eaten downtown yet? I was planning on bagels, because I've been craving one of those everything bagels with turkey and veggie cream cheese ever since orientation."

"My Dad and I went to the burger joint at orientation, which was good, but I haven't tried bagels yet. Let's do it." I am suddenly thankful my roommates haven't shown up yet.

"Do you have any roommates?"

It's like he read my mind. I must look like a loner headed downtown solo. Hopefully loner doesn't translate to loser. But I guess A.J.'s alone too. "Yeah. There are four of us, but the rest of the girls aren't here yet. How about you?"

"Okay. Kind of weird. Me, too," he says.

"Did you know any of them?" I ask, the August heat scorching my skin. I should have put on sunscreen.

"One guy, Danny, is my buddy from high school. We're from Detroit. The other two went to high school together too, somewhere near Indianapolis. We all met at orientation, and it just seemed more fun to have a bunch of us to throw the ball around or play cards, whatever."

"Oh, how super fun." How super fun it would be if we all paired up with each other—four of us, four of them! I guess Palmer's out, because of Keegan. I don't know about Kat. Claire said she doesn't have a boyfriend. Triple or double dating would work too.

"How about your roommates?" He asks.

"Kind of the same and kind of not." We pause at the crosswalk and continue when the light blinks WALK. "My best friend ever, Palmer, is one of them. Then there's this girl, Kat, who just transferred to our high school this past year. So we kind of know her, but not really, but she's really cool and plays soccer for Clarkston. And then there's Claire. None of us knew her before, but I met her at orientation. We totally hit it off. She's been in Paris, and we've barely heard from her, so I'm a little worried about her. Anyway, that's

147

us."

We're on Main Street now, lined with pizza shops, sushi bars, boutiques, and ATM machines. It's jammed with parents and kids swarming in and out of the bookstore. It's like all of Clarkston is pulsing with adrenaline.

"The bagel shop's just down here." I feel savvy pointing the way past the little public square and the gazebo.

Bagels-R-Us has a chalkboard behind the counter with handwritten bagel sandwiches and specials written in pinks, purples, greens and yellows. Three workers with multiple piercings and tattoos slice, toast and wrap bagels topped with everything from bananas to banana peppers in foil. A.J. and I fall in line as the smell of fresh baked bread and melting cheese taunt my hungry stomach. I want to pinch myself. A few hours ago I was crying in my ugly bathroom, but just like that I'm standing in line at an ultra hip bagel shop with an adorable college guy.

19
KAT

"HEY Y'ALL!" I ANNOUNCE, LUGGING my duffle bags, as heavy and bulky as the equipment bags our team drags to away games, into the room. Alex is two steps behind me, carrying a cardboard box containing everything I shoved from my bed—pillow, my new comforter, and even my favorite teddy bear, Cooper. My folks are in the rear with more gear.

Here I go again. I wonder how many times I'll move in my lifetime. I'd just gotten settled in the athletic dorm. Kind of.

Hannah rockets out of her seat. "Kat! I'm so excited you're here! I was absolutely dying waiting for you! I've been here since this morning and unpacked and grabbed lunch." She hugs me, like we're long lost sisters, puts her lips right against my ear, so only I can hear. "And I met a guy."

Man, this girl can talk.

"Wow. All I've done is kicked the ball around and forced my family to act as pack mules." I return her hug and drop my duffels. With Hannah's stuff, it already it looks much less institutional than my washed out athletic dorm. The rich, dark brown carpet, the white board hanging on the door and knick-knacks here and there make this room look like somewhere I could stash my cleats for a while.

"What time did you get here?" I ask Hannah.

Before she answers, Alex whinnies like a mule. "Master mule driver, where can I set down your belongings? It's been such a long journey, and my back is tired."

"You must be Aquaman." Hannah giggles. "I'm Hannah, and I love your Southern accent."

"This is my brother, Alex, posing as a beast of burden." I grin. "And my Mama and Daddy."

"It's a pleasure to meet you." Daddy shakes Hannah's hand.

"Hello, sugar." Mama hugs Hannah. "The room is darlin'. Like the Ritz compared to that athletic dorm you've been staying in, dear. Where will we put that futon? It's next in, I'm afraid."

"Hello. Hello!" Palmer's unmistakable prom queen voice chirps from behind.

"Looks like the gang's all here." Her mom charges forward, placing a lamp right in the middle of someone's desk. I guess she's claiming it for Palmer.

"We could have sprung for the more expensive room," Palmer's dad mumbles, scanning our suite.

Her parents are as beautiful and dramatic as Palmer, only more over the top like television characters. Palmer strides in like she's working the runway, all perfect steps and swivels. The only thing she's carrying, besides her Burberry purse, is a vase of brightly colored zinnias. "Home sweet home." She flashes her movie star smile and hands them to Hannah. "Everything looks great, Han. Nothing like flowers to give a touch of class."

Daddy and Alex go back to the U-Haul under Mama's direction to get the futon.

"Kat!" Palmer squeals, squeezing me. She smells like a rose garden—no lie—not like perfume, but like someone's rubbed flowers against her skin. "This is going to be so perfect!"

"Any word from Claire?" Hannah asks.

"Not to me." I say.

Palmer stacks a handful of books on a ledge. "I haven't heard a peep from her. Not one. I hope she's okay."

"She'll be here. She has to be. She seemed so sweet at orientation. I promise." Hannah chomps fiercely on a piece of gum.

A crowded procession of family members, the futon, beanbag chairs, curtains, hanging clothes, and beauty supplies squeezes in and out of the door for the next hour and a half. I sneak laughs, whisper comments and exchange eye rolls with Palmer and Hannah, like long lost sisters as our families grumble about how much stuff we have, how small our room is, and how hot it is outside. I selfishly want our families, as charming as they are, to scram, so we can get down to being roommates. I didn't expect to be this excited. I hadn't thought of our situation much. I've been so focused on soccer, on proving myself there. But it hits me—I'll be living with these girls all year.

When there's nothing else for Alex and my folks to do, they announce they're headed home.

"Thanks, Mama." I hug her. She holds me and hums a

little song she used to sing to me when she laid me down as a little girl. "Love you, darlin'," she whispers, pulling away and darting out the door. My throat clogs with emotion.

Daddy's next. "Sugar, remember, we're not that far away if you need something, really need something. We're family and we'll always stick together. Study hard. We'll see you at that first home game." He gives me a quick squeeze, then follows Mama to the corridor and takes her hand.

Maybe it's because I've been training at school during the week and going home on weekends, but I kept thinking I'd see my family this weekend and the weekend after that. But it's different this time. Saying goodbye is harder than I thought. Throughout all our moves, we've always stuck together. Until now.

Alex sticks his hands under my armpits and lifts me in the air. I laugh, thankful for his light mood. "Hang tough, girl. Don't kiss any boys."

"Words to live by."

"Love you, sis," Alex says. I know he means it. We just rarely say it.

"Love you too, bro." I give him a bear hug, not wanting to let go, but he breaks away.

"*Adios*, y'all. Take care of my sister, all right?" Alex bows and follows Mama and Daddy out to the curb. I fan my face, hoping the tears trapped in the corners of my eyes will evaporate.

Palmer's family leaves too. Soon everyone's out the door, and our crowded room feels more like we can actually fit in here.

"Your brother is so hot!" Hannah squeals.

I snort.

"It's all right." Palmer puts her arm around me.

"Hannah thinks every boy without a serious acne problem over the height of 5'3" is 'so hot.'"

Hannah grabs a sweatshirt off a beanbag and snaps it at Palmer.

"Nice to have our room to ourselves, girls." I dive onto my bottom bunk.

"Sorry about my mom." Palmer slides off her heels. "She tries not to get emotional, so she just gets bossy instead."

"That's all right," I say. Her mom is overbearing. "My daddy said about three words. I think all the polka dots and people flustered him a bit. He's really not rude. I promise."

Hannah plops down next to me, examining the poster of the 2012 US Women's Olympic Soccer Team I've hung from the bottom of her bed, which is the ceiling of mine. "Hey, I watched some of that on TV. Didn't they win a medal?"

"Gold." I nod sitting up. "Those women are so beast. Alex Morgan is my hero."

"Kat!" Hannah squeals. "Did you get your nose pierced?"

"Yup. You like?" I turn my head side to side to show off my sparkle.

"Very chic." Palmer approves.

"Really? 'Cause I love it, but when Alex saw it, he sang to the tune of Rudolph, 'Kat Wiley, the soccer player, had a very shiny nose.' And Mama gave me a lecture about looking like 'a tramp.'"

"It's small and has flair, and it's totally not trampy." Palmer tilts her head and smiles.

"Thanks." I slide my thumb ring up and down. I didn't care what my folks thought, but it feels good knowing

LAURA L. SMITH

Hannah and Palmer like it. I don't know why.

"When did you get it done?" Hannah leans against me.

"This guy on the men's team, Tony, has his nose pierced. I told him I liked it at. So, after practice Tony took me to his friend's apartment and *pop*! I snap my fingers. His friend, whose name is Dog, no lie, pierced my nose."

"Dog?" Palmer asks.

"You've already been hanging out with cool guys in apartments and haven't introduced us?" Hannah fake pouts.

A snort escapes my nose. "When would I have introduced y'all?"

20
PALMER

THE WHIRR OF COFFEE BEANS grinding, mix with the twangs of a guitar being tuned by Kat's friend, Dog. Hundreds of voices mingle together. This place has so much personality. It's so college. I totally imagine myself camping out with my laptop here and writing for hours on end while sipping lattes. How totally artsy!

A punk-looking guy waves from the stage. "Kat!"

"That's Tony," she shouts to be heard over the crowd. I follow her lead, holding Claire's hand. Claire finally arrived about an hour ago, like a stray kitten with only one trunk and a nervous mom. Even though I'd never met her, I immediately claimed her as my own. She's beautiful and has incredible style, and clearly needs someone to lean on. After what happened with Keegan, it feels good to have someone who seems to need me. I grip her tiny hand in mine, weaving through a maze of chairs, tables and sofas to the edge of the stage.

Tony gives Kat five. "We saved you some seats." He nods toward a cluster of furniture consisting of a giant orange velvet couch pushed alongside a mustard colored armchair and a brown wooden bench.

I sink into the couch and can't resist rubbing my hands up and down the fuzzy fabric. I pull Claire next to me. "Isn't this so soft?" I want to get to know her. She seems sweet, but so shy. It must be the hardest for her. We all knew each other, at least a little before today. And we were all moved in when she showed up. I want her to feel like one of us, because she is.

"Doesn't it look like Central Perk, that coffee shop in the *Friends* reruns?" I ask her.

She nods. "I think I could hang out here. A lot."

Maybe she's starting to relax. She unwinds a paisley printed scarf from her neck and ties it around her waist.

"OhmygoshIlovethisplace!" Hannah squeals.

"I know, right?" Kat nods, tapping her rings on the table to the music blaring over the speakers.

"It is sooooo college," I say.

"This is Hannah and Palmer and Claire, my roommates," Kat says. "And this is Tony."

"Hey." Tony tilts his head.

"Nice to meet you." I shake Tony's hand, which has a soccer ball tattoo branded on his wrist. Claire scoots closer to me and turns her gaze to Kat's friend, Dog, plugging in his amp.

"Thanks so much for inviting us. It is way cool to see a concert downtown before classes even start." Hannah glows with perma-grin on her face.

Dog taps on the mic. "Testing. Testing. One. Two. Three."

"Kat? How lucky is this?" Nicholas McMillan, a redheaded guy who went to our high school, slides between Kat and Tony, practically pushing Tony off the couch.

"Hey, Nicholas. I didn't even know you went to Clarkston." I wave from across the table. I don't know much about him, but he's clearly crushing on Kat.

"Hi, Palmer. Yup, I live in Brackman Hall." He leans into Kat, and I overhear him whisper, "I swear fate keeps bringing us together. You can thank me later for saving you from these freaks." He motions to Tony and Dog.

This is good stuff! It's like a soap opera with no remote, but who would want to change channels? Sadly, I can't hear her answer.

"I'm going to grab the first round of drinks before the show starts. We can get food when he breaks. What's your poison?" I stand and gather everyone's orders. As I take a step away from the table, Claire's eyes look panicked. Hannah's chatting intently with one of Tony's friends and Kat's sandwiched between two boys. "I'll be right back." I squeeze Claire's arm.

As I stand in line for coffees, Dog starts a set of lovely acoustic songs like Simon and Garfunkel and the Beatles and Elton John, reminiscent of songs my parents play at dinner parties, but with an edgier groove. As I wait, the music fills me, swells inside me. By the time I have my order, I'm feeling melancholy. I make my way back to our table and pass out drinks—a chai for Kat, Hannah gets Corner Cups' version of a Frappuccino, they call it the Frothichino or something like that, and I hand Claire a café au lait. I ordered a mocha to lift my mood.

Every love song lyric reminds me of Keegan—how we were, how we are, what we should or could be. I suddenly feel like I might crumble. Note to self: *do not listen to the Beatles when standing alone*. I have to stay pulled together in front of my friends. This is my first day of college. I'm supposed to be ecstatic. Everyone, including little Claire, seems mesmerized by the music, so I sneak toward the bathrooms and out a side exit to get hold of myself.

The garbage from the nearby dumpster rots in the summer evening heat. *Eww*. I can't stand out here long.

I check my phone, like it's a magic eight ball about to predict my future. One text from him.

I CHANGED MY FB STATUS. NEED TO TALK ABOUT NXT WKEND.

My fingers fly, switching me out of text mode and into my Facebook app. I scroll down and click Keegan. For three years his status has read, "In a relationship with Palmer Ruscilli." Not anymore. The two words pierce my heart: "It's Complicated."

What in the universe does that mean? Is he breaking up over Facebook? Pathetic! Is he just trying to freak me out? Because it's working.

I start to call him, but push the home button before my phone dials. I pace back and forth in front of Corner Cup's side window. I won't give Keegan the satisfaction of knowing he's freaking me out. He knew I was moving to school today. He knew what a big deal it is. Everything was so perfect, and now it's so not. I stomp the ground, my heel clacking against the pavement.

"Jerk!" I yell.

A guy crossing the street glares at me.

"Not you!" I scream. "My boyfriend!"

"Sorry, sweetie." He keeps walking with his friends. "If he's really a jerk, you could come to Tipsy Toads with me. I'll buy you a beer." His friends laugh and nudge him.

"In your dreams!" I roll my eyes. Last thing I need. And is there really a bar named Tipsy Toads?

I take a sip of warm, chocolaty mocha and another and another, looking for answers and comfort in a cup of brewed beans. The bracelet Keegan gave me last night (was it just last night?!) slides back and forth on my wrist each time I tip my cup. Why did he tell me how much he loved me if he didn't mean it?

He walked away with me standing under that tree with tears streaming down my face and his keys at my feet. We were going to get married. We were going to live in Howard Park, that darling little neighborhood where old wooden houses with narrow yards and front porches are being renovated. Our kids were going to be adorable, all three of them! My cheeks tingle and the corners of my eyes feel heavy. I exhale deeply, take another sip of mocha, and shake our plans from my head.

When I woke up this morning, it was a frantic, delirious packing session and then two and a half hours in the car to Clarkston, which gave me way too much time to think. No way Keegan went out last night planning to break up with me. He spent a fortune treating me to my favorite restaurant. He got dressed up. He bought me jewelry. He had plans of sealing the deal, of making things official, of taking us to another level. Part of me was freaked he might propose. Hello? We're still only eighteen. Maybe that would have been better.

Not really.

Should I have slept with him? Would that have proved

LAURA L. SMITH

to Keegan how much I love him? I bite my lip, and wipe away tears quickly and carefully with the back of my hand. I'll be furious if my mascara smears on top of everything else.

"Planning on going in anytime soon?" a guy with a bad Justin Bieber haircut asks. "Or headed out?" He motions to my cup emblazoned with Corner Cup's logo and then to the door, which I'm clearly blocking.

I shake my head and any renegade tears while stepping aside. "Sorry. Just taking a breather."

"Music that bad?"

I steady my voice. "Actually, the music is great. I was just checking my phone." I flash a smile, reassuring shag boy and myself everything is a-okay.

"Did you at least get the text you wanted?"

I shake my head, realizing I'm still holding onto my phone like Dumbo grasping his magic feather. I quickly slide it into my Burberry clutch, disposing of the evidence.

"I'm Zach. I heard the coffee here's pretty good, although not as good as Starbucks. When I'm at home, I get Starbucks every day. Like all the baristas know me and everything." He opens the door. I start to walk through, but he kind of pushes his way ahead.

"Palmer," I say.

"With or without you…" Dog belts out the refrain of U2's ballad.

I sing along to the U2 lyrics, thinking of Keegan and how I don't know if it's better for me to have him in my life or not.

"You like U2?" Zach shifts his weight awkwardly, and his arms struggle to find a resting spot.

"My parents do." I search for an escape route away

from this guy and back to my friends. "It's osmosis."

Dog finishes his song and everyone claps. I thump my hands together the best I can while holding my cup.

"There you are." Hannah appears at my side. Rescued. "Everything okay?"

"I'm fine."

Although I'm far from fine, I will make myself be. I have to.

"Oh my gosh!" Zach's jaw drops, ogling Hannah. "You're the gorgeous girl from orientation!"

Hannah's eyes widen as she tries to place Zach's face. I try to help her out. "Zach, this is my best friend and roommate, Hannah. Hannah, this is Zach."

"You look like Leighton Meester." Zach looks like he's drunk on love potion. "You know, when her hair was longer."

"That's me." Hannah blushes through her freckles.

Please don't tell me she's going to flirt with this dork.

"I can't believe I'm seeing you here. In person. Definitely my lucky day." Zach nods furiously.

"Nice to meet you, Zach. We'll see you around." I can't stand another second of his chitchat, although I should be grateful to Zach. His annoyingness made me forget about my wallowing. I hook Hannah's arm around mine and do an about face.

Zach grins until his gums show and waves in big jerky motions. "I was just getting a cup to go. See ya around, Palmer." He nods so far it's almost a bow. "Nice to officially meet you, Hannah. I hope I'll be seeing lots more of you."

"Have a good night."

"Gag!" I laugh, as soon as we're out of earshot.

"He's not that bad. He's kind of sweet. He did say I

looked like a celeb." Hannah tilts her head against my shoulder. "I was worried about you. You didn't seem completely 100% Palmer, you know? So, I came to check on you, and I find you flirting with a freshman?" Hannah gives me a look. "Then I knew there was really something wrong!" She laughs.

"I was so not flirting. Please! I'm all right." I say it, but I see Keegan's face in my mind, his gray eyes looking disappointed in me. I bite my tongue to fight off a return of the tears, and shake my head violently back and forth. "Keegan and I are fighting."

"What?" Hannah asks.

I bury my face on her shoulder. "Oh, Han. What am I gonna do?"

21
CLAIRE

"IF I DIDN'T KNOW BETTER, I'd say you were avoiding us, Claire Bear." Palmer winks.

Spot on, sister. I think, hoping the flush of my cheeks isn't as visible as it feels. I try to cover it up by winking back at Palmer. Winking is so not my thing. It just makes me blush a deeper shade of pink.

How did she know, anyway? I hate errands, but today they offered a safety net between me and the inevitable questions of my roommates. It was a complete stroke of luck last night that their interrogation about Paris got interrupted by Kat's text from Tony inviting us to Corner Cup. The coffee shop was fun and mellow and I didn't have to talk because of the music. We got back late, and we were all wiped from moving, so we crashed pretty hard and fast.

"We were just trying to pick out which game to play." Hannah waves a Wii remote in her hand. "We have Mario Kart and Basketball. Kat voted for FIFA Soccer, but none of us thought that would be fair." She elbows Kat and grins.

Kat shrugs and bats her eyelashes in a perfect Scarlett O'Hara impression.

"Do you have Just Dance?" I ask.

"Just Dance 4, baby." Palmer digs for the disc. I never expected she would be the roommate I'd connect with. I didn't know her at all, and everyone talking about how beautiful she is completely intimidated me. But she just saved me for like the hundredth time since yesterday.

Dancing is perfect. I was really nervous about how I'd fit in with these girls, but the music energizes me, and I don't need to talk. We laugh our way through the They Might Be Giants song, "Istanbul," and we jam song after song until my heart races so fast I feel like I'll explode.

"You dominated." Hannah plops down crisscross beside me.

"I call foul." Kat taps me on the head. "Dancin' against Claire is no different than playin' soccer with me."

"You're like scary good." Palmer sips her water. "So, Claire, you never did share your European romance with us. If I remember correctly, there was a text about a boy." She sits next to me on the futon.

I freeze.

"Yeah," Hannah chimes in. "It was like all communication with you was cut off mid-trip. We want details, girlie."

My brain flies through their questions, but I can't make any sound come from my mouth. I shake my head and look down. *Please stop talking about this. Please.*

"So…cute boy. How'd it all start?" Hannah asks, oblivious to my being on a verge of a breakdown. "How'd you meet him?"

I could use a distraction. Everyone's phones buzz 24/7. Why are they all silent now? I have to talk. They all must think I'm a nutjob already. I have to say something.

"I met Phillip first thing," I say quietly. How I met him seems safe enough. "He was there with his uncle, Arnot, who's my mom's boyfriend. They both picked us up from the airport." I try to focus on the facts, not the feelings. The feelings are what screw me up. I remember how wowed I was when I first saw Phillip.

"And then what?" Kat asks, twirling her thumb ring.

"And then..." I sigh and shift my weight. "And then loads of things. And then, Paris was amazing. And then, he was so easy to talk to, and handsome and mature. He's a junior. Studying in England." I pause to stop my voice from shaking.

"Swoon!" Hannah says. "England? No wonder you fell for him."

I look at her. She's all gaga and grins. Hannah doesn't get it.

"Come on. Don't stop there," Palmer urges. "We want deets."

I don't know how to keep going. If I say anymore, if I say what happened next, I'll unravel. If I don't say anything else, it will get stuck in me, eating away at my insides. I inhale and try to ignore the wetness welling in the corners of my eyes. "I didn't try to fall for him. I thought he was too old and too experienced and too hot to even notice me. But the four of us, Mom and Arnot and Phillip and me did everything together. It was just natural to hang out with Phillip while Mom and Arnot were all lovey-dovey. It was nice to have someone to talk with at dinner and to walk down the streets with—someone who wasn't in their mid-forties." I half-laugh and move my hair from one shoulder to the other, but in that motion a tear escapes, startling me as it pricks my cheek.

"Claire?" Kat touches my arm.

"Something horrible happened," I whisper, barely able to make out the words, but feeling them pushing their way out of my mouth.

"What happened, honey?" Palmer smoothes my hair, like my mom did when I was little, before the divorce, when she took care of me, like I wish she still did.

"It's about the boy," I sputter. "He did something, but I think it was my fault."

"What did he *do*?" Kat asks.

"He had sex with me." The words finally escape, and I exhale a long, deep, stale breath that has been trapped for days. I peer at Palmer, searching for condemnation or disgust, but she looks confused and worried.

"Does your mom know?" Hannah asks.

I shake my head.

"Does anyone know?" Palmer asks.

I shake my head again, saltwater stinging my eyes and skin as it slips across my face.

"Did you want to? Did you like him?" Hannah asks, but her voice is more curious than callous.

"No. Yes." My body trembles so much I think I might fall off the couch.

"It's okay, darlin'." Kat rubs my leg.

"I didn't want to. I wanted to kiss him. He was handsome and smart and mature, like a fairytale prince, but then…" My throat is too thick for any more words. The thickness explodes in sobs.

"Oh my gosh, Claire! What did you do? Did you kick

him? Didn't anyone hear you screaming?" Hannah's voice pierces my sobs.

Kick him? Scream? I didn't kick. I didn't scream. I didn't think of those things? I didn't do those things. I couldn't move. I couldn't speak. I couldn't figure out what he was doing or why. My mind returns to the hotel bed, like a rabbit in a trap, afraid to move, unable to escape. I shake my head.

"You didn't kick that boy where it counts?" Kat asks. "I would've kicked him so hard all of Paris would've heard him holler!"

"I couldn't." Words tumble out with my tears. "I was just there, and I couldn't, and I didn't." Another sob chokes me. I shake my head and sniff, pushing the hysterics away.

"Did he hurt you?" Palmer asks, her voice so low in my ear I can barely hear her.

"I don't know."

"How did it happen?" Hannah's on the other side of me now.

I look up and shake my head at the ceiling, trying to get enough air to speak. "I liked him. We got dressed up and went out to dinner. We drank wine. We kissed." I exhale and twist up my mouth. "What was I thinking?" My right leg bounces up and down across my left leg. Up and down. Up and down. "I didn't want to, but he pushed me down on his bed. He was heavy and strong. I said no, but he wouldn't listen and did it anyway. I told him no." As I exhale, my body shakes with the sobs that have been hiding inside since that night in Paris. Tears stream hot and violent down my face.

I rock back and forth with Palmer and Hannah and Kat holding me, stroking my hair and whispering again and again, "It's okay. It's gonna be okay."

"What a freakin' jerk!" Palmer says, like she's spitting out venom.

"He raped you," Kat says.

R-A-P-E! The word echoes in my brain. Rape. Rape. Rape. I hadn't thought of a word for the horrible thing that happened, but now it hits me. I was raped.

"Rape?" I squeak.

"Claire, darlin', if you said no and he did it anyway, that's rape."

"But he didn't jump out of the bushes or have a knife. I liked him. I am so freaking stupid. I liked him." The tears roll again.

"Are you okay?" Hannah asks, holding my shoulders square. "Did you see a doctor?"

My heart feels like it's in a vise. What else have I screwed up? "A doctor?"

"Yeah, a doctor to get proof he raped you. They have rape kits. I learned all about it in my health class. They can make sure you aren't really hurt."

Palmer looks deep in my eyes, searching for something. "We know that monster hurt you, but physically are you okay, ya know?" She sucks in her lips, rubbing them back and forth. "You want to make sure you're not pregnant."

My hand flies over my mouth. My heart pounds louder than Dog's electric guitar through the sound system last night. "Pregnant! Oh my gosh! I was in France. I didn't know where to find a doctor. I never even thought about it. Not once. A doctor?" I could hit myself for being so incredibly stupid. "Pregnant? What if I am?"

"It's okay," Kat says. "We'll get you a test. We don't need a doctor for that."

"Right. I'll buzz over to that little drugstore in the student union right now. You can take it here." Hannah stands.

Before I'm done washing my face and changing into my pajamas, Hannah's back. She's here sooner than I'd hoped. I don't really want to take this test. I don't really want to know the answer.

"Here, Claire." Hannah pulls an EPT box out of her purse. "I think you just take it out of the wrapper and pee on it."

My hand shakes as I take the box from Hannah's warm hand.

"Do you want me to come in with you?" Palmer asks. No one's taken care of me in so long, I don't know how to react. Palmer would come in and watch me pee if it would help me. I know she means it. Somehow, even her offering is enough.

"No." I shake my head. "I'll be out in a minute." I close the door to our bathroom with all of our towels hanging together like we're a family, like we always have been. Pregnancy tests are supposed to be for bad girls who get around. Am I one of those girls? Did they plan on being roommates with a girl like me?

Three minutes later, Hannah, Kat and Palmer all hold my hands as we check the results together: NOT PREGNANT–the stick actually reads those words. Not a lot of room for error, but a lot of room for relief.

"Thank the Lord!" Kat yells. "Now what?"

"What do you want to do next?" Hannah asks. "Do you want to see a counselor?"

"I d-d-don't. I don't know. I'm still trying to wrap my head around the word 'rape,' and the fact that I could have been pregnant, and that I'm not pregnant, let alone what I'm supposed to do next. I don't think I'm ready for next."

"We could set up an appointment. I'm pretty sure I read something about it on the school website," Hannah says.

"Can we do nothing?" I ask.

"Nothing?" Palmer snaps. "We need to report this guy! Press charges! Don't you want him arrested, Claire?"

"No!" I shout. I shiver at the strength of my voice. "I can't go through all that court stuff ever again. I had to do it when my parents got divorced." For all the years I've kept to myself, this is like my tell-all show, like a *Behind the Music* special on VH1. I wouldn't have spouted out this too, on top of the Phillip stuff, but I can't ever go to court. "The divorce took over two years. I was dragged to the witness stand. I was terrified, and the attorney made me feel even smaller and more foolish than I was. I just can't."

"Hey, it's all right," Palmer says, slipping next to me. "You okay?"

I shake my head. "Definitely not okay."

"You don't have to be, you know." She puts her arm around me. "We'll take care of you."

22
HANNAH

DESPITE WAKING UP AT FIVE, I find myself rushing as seven rolls around. Writing a to-do list, scribbling happy-first-day-of-school notes for my roomies and brewing a pot of coffee took more time than I thought. Plus, I chatted with Kat before she headed off to her first of two soccer practices for the day.

Palmer helps with my hair, and we quickly grab blueberry muffins at the dining hall, along with a second cup of coffee. I leave a note on the dry erase board for Claire, who's still out for the count, saying, "Roomie dinner at 6:00 ☺." It's already warm this morning, as Palmer's and my sandals click against the sidewalks across campus. With each tap of our shoes, my heart beats eight or nine times. My brain is on overload, drinking in the other groggy students ambling to their eight o'clocks, trying to pick up snatches of their conversations, memorizing what kind of book bags people carry, noting what type of sunglasses they wear. Outside of my building, next to a wooden sandwich board promoting an upcoming speaker, Palmer squeezes me. "Here we go." She kisses my cheek. "Wish me luck!"

"Good luck." I hug her.

"Good luck, back."

Palmer heads the other direction to her class. I enter the imposing brick building, and my stomach flutters like I ate birds' wings instead of muffins for breakfast. I've been at Clarkston for a few days, and we've been decorating our room and buying books, but this is it, really it. This is where college officially begins.

Inside smells like fresh scrubbed floors and windows. Students bustle back and forth across the lobby. I follow the directional signs to find my classroom #140 and walk into the fluorescently lit lecture hall. Half the seats tiered in semicircular rows around a large screen are already full. I scan the room to find a seat. Then, really?

My heart stops for a second, then beats at super human speed. I spot A.J., my favorite boy on campus, with ruffled curls, yawning in the third row. I can barely resist running over to him and fluffing my fingers through his mussed up hair.

There's a seat behind him, and I hone in on the best path to get there. Okay, I'm maybe the luckiest girl on the planet. Perspiration pricks under my arms. I squeeze them close to my sides and exhale, thankful I spritzed Forever Sunshine on my pulse points as I left the room.

I'm almost to him. What should I say? I run my tongue over my teeth, making sure no lip gloss is stuck on my smile. I tuck my hair behind my ears and motor down the aisle right behind A.J.

"Excuse me," I say, wiggling behind other students in their seats.

"Hannah! Wow, how lucky is this? It's like fate or something!"

Oh no! Zach from the coffee shop, apparently also from summer orientation, is waving frantically at me, almost flailing, in the seat right next to where I was headed.

"Hi, Zach." I smile, setting my books down. I don't want him to think I was coming to sit next to him, but it would be so awkward if I backed up and went down another aisle now, and I so want to talk to A.J. But I don't want A.J. to think I'd planned on sitting next to Zach. How am I going to convey all of this in the three minutes before class starts?

"I didn't know you were taking Botany. Are you a science major? No, let me guess, pre-med? Because I thought about pre-med. I mean, I had the SATs to totally glide through that program, but I decided to go into paper science." Zach leans a little too close, encasing me in a cloud of his heavy cologne.

"Actually, I'm an Elementary Ed major. This is just my required life science class." I try to be polite, while figuring out how to say good morning to dream boy. When Zach takes a breath, presumably fueling up to ask a zillion more questions at rapid speed, I lean forward and tap A.J. on the shoulder.

"Hey."

"Hannah, how's it goin'?" He turns and gives me a crooked smile.

Sigh. He's even cuter than I remembered, and that hushed voice makes me want to snuggle up close so he can whisper in my ear.

"So far, so good." I want to say something witty about how we're just getting started, first day of school and all, when Zach reaches his hand out and interrupts my flirt.

"I'm Zach. I'm from Dayton. You're A.J.?"

"Yeah. Nice to meet you." A.J. reaches out his hand and shakes Zach's. I'd love to get in on that handshaking action. Well, I'd prefer handholding, but it would be a start.

"So how do you know Hannah? Isn't she great? We met way back at orientation and keep connecting ever since."

Zach acts like he's known me forever, which is a little weird and not at all the message I'm trying to send to either of these boys. Maybe Palmer was right to say he's a dork. I feel trapped. How can I regain control of this conversation? I just want Zach to dissolve. Do we do experiments in botany?

"We're in the same dorm." I nod toward A.J.

Before this conversation can get any more awkward, a woman at the front of the classroom with short, peppery-gray hair announces, "Welcome to Botany 121."

I sit back and pull out a notebook. Thank goodness that convo's over, but I didn't get much of a chat with A.J., at all. For the next hour I can focus on class, and the back of A.J.'s head.

23
CLAIRE

"BLUE MONDAY" BY NEW ORDER plays from my alarm clock radio.

D.J. humor.

"*How does it feel to treat me like you do?*" the 80's band drones. Nothing like being fully immersed in my nightmare from the moment I wake up. I hit snooze, groan and roll back over. I pull up my covers. I switch sides. I move my pillow.

Ugh!

Stinkin' Monday. Crummy first day of classes. No way I can go back to sleep, but I can lie here a minute with my eyes closed before I have to face the world, ready or not.

Do I look like I've had sex? Do I have that dirty girl look about me? Those girls always look pretty in an oddly appealing, spicy MTV kind of way, but they also look a little mussed. Their eyeliner is smeared, they have bed head, their skirts are hiked up, and their shirts are wrinkled. And it's not a big deal if the nerdy, braniac girl's shirt is wrinkled. It just looks like she was too busy studying to iron it. But these girls, when their shirts are wrinkled, well, it looks like they've been doing something that wrinkled them.

I don't want to look like one of those girls.

The music starts again.

Slam! I hit my hand against my alarm clock, telling it to shut up, telling it I will not have that look!

I peek out of my cave and see three empty bunks. All of my roommates are gone. I forget when they have class, but I think it was earlier than me, thankfully.

I pull a T-shirt and jeans out of the drawer where I shoved a handful of clothes yesterday. I dig into my scarf crate and find one with deep purple, sapphire blue, and emerald green flowers dotting the silk. Tying it around my neck with shaky fingers, I feel more protected, covered. I pull my hair in a low side ponytail and apply one coat of mascara and mauve lip gloss.

"Ready, set, go."

What about me? God asks.

I usually spend a few minutes in the morning in a devotion—something that will get me on the right track for the day. I was so busy at first in Paris, and then, well then, I pushed God so far away. I don't want to listen to Him. I'm sure He doesn't want to hear from me, but I feel so fidgety this morning. I need to do something. Opening up to my roommates helped the rawness last night, like the stitches I got in my thumb when I was nine. The stitches held me together, even as the wound ached and swelled and itched for what seemed like weeks. Saying out loud what happened, having Palmer, Kat and Hannah know what happened are the needle and thread that will keep me from falling apart. But it still hurts, aches, swells, itches inside me. I need more.

You need me.

I reach under my pillow for my Bible, a pen and the spiral notebook I use to jot down thoughts. I sit down on the edge of my bed, resigned to just read the words. I don't need to listen to them, just use them to replace the ugly thoughts in my head.

"My response is to get down on my knees before the Father, this magnificent Father who parcels out all heaven and earth. I ask him to strengthen you by his spirit, not a brute strength, but a glorious inner strength, that Christ will live in you as you open the door and invite him in."
Ephesians 3:14–17a (MSG).

Really, God? I've been trying to stay away from You–from all of this–and the advice I get this morning is to get down on my knees and ask You to strengthen me? I feel so weak, God. Phillip stole my strength. He overtook me. I didn't know what to do. I didn't fight back. I'm so sorry I didn't fight back. I don't want this to be a part of who I am. I don't. I want to go back to just being Claire, not Claire who was raped, but the Claire I was before I was raped. But I wake up and it's Monday. I'm at college, and it is still here. It will always be here. It's become a part of who I am.

Claire, I can strengthen your spirit. Invite Me back in. I want to help. I love you.

I'm caught off guard. I didn't expect Him to claim love. I expected Him, almost wanted Him, to condemn me, to yell at me, but He does the opposite.

I love you.

The voice tugs at my heart again. And I know it's God, and not me putting the words in my head, because I would never dare to believe He loves me after what happened.

The sobs rack my body.

God, You've always been in me, and somehow I still feel You there, even though I've pushed You away. I just don't want to talk about this. I want to get past it. I want to move on. I thought a fresh start, new friends, new school would erase it all, like a text I could delete off my phone. But it's still here. It's still in my heart, and it still hurts. I can't make it go away, and I just want to make it go away. I'm so scared, God. Please help me!

I'll help you be strong. You can do this. Together we can do this. You can do all things through Me. I give you your strength. It might not be easy. But it is possible.

My heart beats a little slower. My shoulders relax a little. Not all at once, not completely, but as I sit and talk with God, my shaking stops. I don't feel powerful or energized, but I feel calmer, and warmer and safer, like I can walk out of this room and make it through my first class. Okay. Okay. I can do this.

I wash my face with cold water, freezing the heat of shame and fear, at least for now. I pat my skin dry with a fluffy lime green towel–part of Hannah's grand plan to color coordinate–and vow to start over. Start over with my make-up and with my approach for this day. I can do this. I will do this.

24
KAT

HEARD YOU & NICHOLAS HUNG OUT & HAD COFFEE – HOW'D THAT GO? HE SAID YOU WERE W/SOME SCRAPPY DUDE – YOU OK?

Super. Now everything I do gets back to my brother? And Nicholas has no right judging Tony. He has been great to my friends and me. Not to mention he's fierce on the fields. *Grrr.* I grip my phone tightly.

GREAT TO HEAR FROM YOU, BRO. DID SEE NIC. COOL MUSIC @ COFFEE SHOP & TONY IS NOT SCRAPPY. HE'S THE STAR OF THE MEN'S SOCCER TEAM

Zippp. I get an immediate reply.

SOUNDS LIKE YOU'RE BUSY BREAKIN BOYS' HEARTS LOL – JUST BUSY KICKIN THE BALL. MISS YOU

U 2

I open our door and hear Dog's CD playing on the jam box.

"Y'all really like Dog's music? I wasn't just forcin' it on you?" I kick off my slides and plop down onto the futon.

"Love it!" Palmer shouts from her desk.

"Have you seen Claire?" Hannah turns away from Fashion TV.

I shake my head and curl my feet under my legs.

"Did you hear from her today?" Palmer's painting her nails a deep wine color. "We left before she woke up and now she's gone. She didn't leave a note or answer any of our texts."

"I'm sure she's fine. I just checked my phone like three seconds ago." I hold up my orange case. "*Umm.* Thanks for the sweet texts, by the way."

"I wasn't complaining about *you* not answering." Palmer puts down her bottle of polish and waves her hands around. "No offense, but we figured you'd be all right. I'm worried about Claire. She seems really fragile."

"I've never seen you so worried about anyone, except your cat." Hannah clicks off the TV. "What's with that?"

"For the record, she reminds me a lot of Thunder, who I might add I'm missing like crazy, AND I was watching that!" Palmer barks. "The countdown to fashion week is critical to my future as a fashion journalist. Claire's just so cute and tiny. I want to scoop her up and give her a cuddle."

Hannah tosses her the remote. "Sorry, Palm. I just can't believe Claire was raped and that she hadn't taken a pregnancy test or gone to a doctor or a counselor and didn't even tell her mom! Can you imagine? It all seems insane to me, and a little irresponsible. I'd be a wreck, with all that stuff buzzing around my head." Hannah swats at imaginary bugs. "Why didn't she tell anyone or do anything?"

"It sounds downright awful." I shake my head.

"On a lighter note…" Hannah sits down next to me. "Tell us about Nicholas."

"Nicholas?" I remember Alex's text and feel a bit annoyed.

"Yes. Nicholas. Palm and I know him from school a little, but we didn't know you two were so tight."

"He's my brother's best friend. That's all." I shrug. "He's over at our house all the time. They swim together during the summer. Nicest guy you ever would meet."

"Super nice guy who seems super into you." Palmer smiles devilishly.

"It's not like that," I say, but my cheeks get warm.

"For real, Kat?" Palmer asks. "He was practically glowing when he sat next to you last night at Corner Cup. Not to mention he glared at Tony the entire time."

"True." Hannah nods like a bobble head. "He even interrogated me while you were in the bathroom about who Tony was and what we really knew about him. He tried to hint around that Tony's not the kind of guy he'd want any of his sisters to hang out with."

"Great." I drum my thumbs.

"Cry me a river. You act like it's a bad thing to have a couple of guys fighting for you." Hannah sighs.

"I just want to know which one you're going to choose." Palmer raises her eyebrows. "It would make a great plot for a movie."

I cover my face with my hands. "I don't want to like either one of them. It's all way too complicated. Nicholas is like family. I know he'd do anything for me, but since he and Alex hang out it would be weirder than weird." I come out from hiding behind my hands. "And Tony is like Nicholas's polar opposite. He's all cool and laid back and reckless, which is totally fun. When it comes to soccer, he's a beast, which I LOVE."

"Sounds like bad boy Tony is winning." Palmer waves her nail polish brush like a magic wand in my direction.

"I am a bit smitten by his soccer moves, and his life is so different than mine. So casual, ya know?"

"*Ooohh*! I knew there was romance at our table last night. I am so jealous!" Hannah squeals.

"P-lease!" I shake my head, feeling myself get redder and redder by the second. "Tony would never go for a girl like me. He's way out of my league. Not to mention, he's not exactly the kind of boy I'd take home to Mama."

"Why not?" Hannah asks, which is a good question. I don't have a good comeback. Why couldn't I date Tony? Who am I to judge him, just because he has dreadlocks and a messy apartment? That would be like what Nicholas and Alex are doing.

WANNA MEET ME AT CORNER CUP FOR A SHOT?

"Speak of the devil." I grin, reading Tony's text.

"Which devil is that?" Hannah peeks at my phone.

"Tony—askin' if I want to meet him for a shot! I told y'all I couldn't bring him home to Mama."

"What kind of shot are we talking about?" Palmer puckers her lips.

"I'm about to find out."

A SHOT? I type back.
ESPRESSO. YOU COMING?

I snort. "Espresso. Funny."
"So, he's not so bad." Palmer laughs. "Oh well."
TOO LATE IN THE DAY FOR ME TO DO SHOTS ☺. I'LL
COME BY FOR A FEW MINS – STILL NEED TO EAT & ANOTHER
PRACTICE. YOU THERE YET?
ME, TOO. ON MY WAY. SEE YOU THERE.
K

"Looks like I'm headed to Corner Cup. Y'all wanna
join me?"
"And rain on your parade?" Palmer pats my knee,
carefully keeping her fingers splayed to avoid smudging her
nails. "No thanks, I'm going to wait here and see if Claire
comes back."
"Better stay put. I have four more chapters of Psych to
read." Hannah holds up her textbook. "Will you come back
for dinner, though?" Her eyes plead. It's cute how she wants
us all to be like a family, and really nice she keeps including
all of us. I was nervous she and Palmer would pair off, but it
hasn't been like that. Maybe I shouldn't leave.
"Do y'all think I should wait for Claire, too?"
"We've got it covered." Hannah shoos me out the door.
"Let me live vicariously through you. You'll see Claire at
dinner."
I check my watch. "Right. I'll be back, and we'll all eat
together. And text me if y'all hear from Claire."
Another text vibrates in my pocket.

WANT TO MEET AT THE LIBRARY TO SHARE 1ST DAY

STORIES AND MAYBE STUDY?

"*Ahhh*!" I moan, holding up my phone. "It's Nicholas. He wants to study. What am I gonna do?"

"What do you want to do?" Palmer asks, applying a second coat on her nails.

"Roar!" I sink back into the futon. "I already told Tony I'd meet him, but I don't want to hurt Nicolas's feelings."

"Just tell him the truth." Palmer makes an even shiny stroke. "Tell Nicholas you'd love to, but you can't right now. Keep your promise to Tony, and you'll know you did the honest thing."

"Or…" Hannah pops open a Diet Coke. "Tell one of them *I'll* meet them, and you meet the other one. And we're all happy." She laughs her sweet, welcoming laugh, which makes me blow out my stress in a giant exhale and laugh with her.

"Right."

I text Nicholas back, explaining I'd love to another time, like maybe tomorrow, and head out the door.

My brain races the entire ten-minute walk to Corner Cup. What would Alex say if he knew I was ditching Nicholas? What would he think about Tony if he met him face to face? Does Tony really like me like me, or is he just palling around? Do I even want him to like me? Well, sort of, definitely, well, what would that mean? I think everyone's right that Nicholas is interested in me, but why me? Doesn't he know that could mess everything up?

In my head my cleat taps a soccer ball. I picture myself setting up for a penalty kick, running straight on at the ball, so the goalie won't be able to anticipate which way I'll shoot. I pretend to shoot left, and there's Tony, leaning against the back of the goal. I take another imaginary kick, this time to the right. Nicholas is holding out a rose to me.

Focus, I tell myself. I switch to mentally dribbling the ball foot to foot, back and forth. When I get to the door of Corner Cup, I haven't solved for anything, but I'm less wound up.

"Kat." Tony leans against one of the big front windows of the café. He holds a cigarette.

"Hey." Okay, I didn't know he smoked. Not a huge deal. Just didn't know.

"Want a hit?" he asks, holding out a bumpy, hand-rolled cigarette.

"No thanks." I shake my head. "I need every ounce of breathing capacity available after the sprints Coach made me do this mornin'." I force out a laugh.

"You ever tried K2?" He takes a puff and lowers his hand.

"Isn't K2 a killer high mountain?"

"You got it." Tony laughs a little too loudly. "It's a killer high all right. Only it's legal."

I shake my head confused. He's not making sense. Is Tony getting stoned? So. Not. Cool.

"It's a kind of incense. You can buy it almost anywhere." Tony holds up his cigarette again. "But instead of burning it, you smoke it." He sucks in another big breath from his cig. "Nice." He exhales. "You should try. Totally legit, and as far as your lungs go, I've seen you sprint. You're the fastest girl on the team. By far." He exhales a long trail of smoke. "One hit will not do a thing to those pretty lungs of yours."

I stare at the glowing end of his cigarette, unable to think up a witty response, or any response for that matter. I

don't want to sound like a prude, but I am so not prepared
for this. Not prepared for Tony to be here by himself waiting
for me, like in my vision of him by the soccer net. Not
prepared for him to be smoking, let alone smoking this crazy
K2 stuff. I am not prepared for him to have said I'm the
fastest on the team or for him to call me pretty, even if he
was talking about my lungs, which is a little strange.

"You okay, Kat?" Tony asks, but it's like he's in slow
motion. Why didn't I study with Nicholas or stay home with
the girls?

"I'm fine." I lie. "I just have a lot of readin' to do
tonight, and I'm not sure when it's gonna get done." I point
to my backpack. "I'm gonna head inside, grab a sweet tea
and plow through a chapter or two. Wanna join me?"

"Sure." Tony nods, not looking offended I didn't try
climbing his mountain. "Go ahead. I'm just going to finish
this." He waves his K2. "I'll be in in a few."

I nod nervously, a thick prickle scratching my throat.
Inside Corner Cup, the heavy scent of dark coffee makes me
long for the largest, strongest brew they serve. But, just like I
would never smoke, I'd never drink that much caffeine in the
afternoon. It's stupid if I'm going to train to go pro. There
are some things I would never subject my body to. Too
risky. I order a sweet tea. The girl with a pierced lip looks at
me like I have three heads, so I settle for an iced tea and a
handful of sugar packets.

25
PALMER

I HATE THE WAY MY face feels as it scrunches and contorts. It must look hideous. A rush of heat pours through my body like I've swallowed lava. My lips puff out as I rock back and forth in my sandals. "How could you not call?" I whisper to Keegan, wherever he is. Tears sting my eyes. "How could you not care?"

I try to swallow the baseball-sized lump in my throat, but another one appears. I try to swallow the second lump, but it pushes out of my throat in a sob as the tears explode. I let my body collapse against the door of the bathroom and slide down onto the fuzzy bathmat.

"You okay?" Hannah asks, from behind the door.

I creak open the door and tilt my head, so she can see what a mess I am.

"What's wrong, sweetie?" she coos like Florence Nightingale, ready to save the day with a bandage. Only there's not a bandage big enough for this.

"Keegan didn't call – not once - all day. I miss him, and I thought, you know…" I gasp for air between sobs. "I thought it was going to be so different."

Hannah sits down next to me on the floor and wraps her arms around me. "Did you think college was going to be different?" Hannah speaks slowly and smoothly, holding me tightly so all those swirly feelings can't take over.

"It's not that." I pull back, so she can see I'm telling the truth. "I love Clarkston," I sigh. "I love you! And Claire and Kat are sweethearts. I know we're going to be the best of friends forever. It's almost too good to be true, how it all worked out with the four of us." I sniffle.

"It is definitely divine intervention." Hannah smiles, showing her dimples. "There's no way we could all be like long lost sisters unless God intended for us to find each other." Hannah taps my knee. "So if it's not about us, it's all about Keegan?"

I nod. "I know. I know God's in all of this, right? He's in everything. But, Han, where is He in what's going on with me and Keeg?"

I can't believe I've questioned God out loud. It seems sacrilegious. I'm not supposed to question God, but I don't understand. It's what I've been wondering since Keegan left me in the park. If God wanted me to wait, and I waited, then why do I feel physical burning, seething pain that steals my breath right out of my chest? I feel like my heart is ripping in two, like there's someone tearing it to pieces.

"I don't know." Hannah shakes her head.

We're quiet for a couple of minutes while I wonder how evil it is to question God. But I don't understand. I want to, but I don't. I dare Him in my mind, *Where are You God? Why did You do this?*

"I know you love Keegan." Hannah rubs my leg. "And Keegan's great. I mean we've all been hanging out together forever. But what if…" Hannah's voice trails off as her finger traces an S pattern on the skirt of my sundress.

"What if what?"

"What if he's not THE one?" Hannah whispers.

"How can you say that?"

She sighs, and I feel her breath against my shoulder. "I mean, what if God has someone even better than Keegan picked out for you? Or what if Keegan IS the one, but you guys aren't supposed to get married for a while, so you can experience all the fun of Clarkston? Or maybe there's something else we can't even imagine. Maybe you need a break from Keegan to dive into your writing. Who knows?" Hannah's eyes look hopeful.

I wish I felt her hope. "I don't want a break! I don't want someone else. I just want Keegan." I spit out the words at Hannah as if she's to blame. An ache from the top of my nose spreads across my brow line as the tears spill again.

Hannah rubs my back. Her hand rubs up and down my back in a rhythm. My mind flashes to a movie montage of Keegan's droopy eyes turning upward, his warm lips on mine, and countless nights on the phone listening to his voice as I fall asleep. I feel his hand swinging mine back and forth as we walk down the hallways at school. I hear the sound of his kooky laugh, which always gets me laughing.

"Have you journaled about it?" Hannah asks. Hannah, my mom and my sister are probably the only people who know I sort through my thoughts in my journal. Not even Keegan knows. I wonder why I've never told him.

"No," I admit. I've been running from class to class to meeting to meal. I haven't had time. I haven't *made* time.

189

"You could call him, you know."

I could call *him*.

"I don't want to give him the satisfaction. Plus, what would I say?" I ask, listening to the *drip drip* of our ancient showerhead.

"You could tell him you miss him."

I do miss him.

"And give him the upper hand? Not after how he left me." Rage beats against my ribs, and then insecurity dances around it. "What if he doesn't want to talk to me? Cause he might not."

"How will you know if you don't call?" Hannah stops the soothing pattern her hand was making. "He's crazy about you, Palmer. Always has been. He always has his eyes on you in the cafeteria, at a party, in class, at youth group. His pressuring you was wrong. He's gotta know that."

"Was it really?" I ask. "Was it really so wrong? We love each other. Isn't that why God created sex? For people who love each other? It's not like it would be a fling!"

"It wouldn't be a fling, but you're not married." Hannah's voice sounds thin.

I love Hannah, but she's never been in love. She's never even had a boyfriend for more than two weeks. There's no way she can understand what I'm feeling. She can't. It's not as easy as all that. I shake my head.

"Hey." Hannah's hand is on my arm now. "We're not going to dinner for an hour. You could journal or call him, or maybe both." She stands and softly walks out of the bathroom, giving me the space to decide.

I could call him now. Maybe Hannah understands a little.

I feel the weight of my phone in my hand. My thumb

instinctively slides across the screen, scrolling to favorites. The top of the list is Keegan.

"Hey, Palm." His deep voice rolls into my ear and through me. The pain in my heart tugs toward the phone.

"I miss you." I choke out the words.

"I miss you, too." His voice beckons, like a way out of my pain and anxiety and confusion. Why was I so weirded out? We had a fight. We've had them before. We're both stubborn. We just need to talk through this. He missed me, too. We can work it out.

"Palm?"

"Hey. I just…it was my first day of classes."

"Yeah. I know."

Now that I have him on the phone, it's like the other night never happened. Like everything is normal. "I think everything went all right." I spin into a description of my classes and professors, and how much fun I'm having with Han and Kat and Claire. It becomes a normal conversation, like I would have had with him last week. All the details of the last three days, from my clothes not fitting into my itty bitty dorm closet, to the frozen yogurt machines in the dining hall, take shape and feel sorted when I tell them to Keegan.

"So you're busy." He pauses, a long hollow emptiness on the other side of the phone. Even though we're miles away, I can see the expression on his face as if he's asking a loaded question.

I answer quickly to avoid the real issue. "I like my classes, but I really miss you." It's no use. I blink, trying to avert more tears. "I don't know what happened the other night, but it was all screwed up." I try to catch my breath. The bathroom seems to be getting tinier and tinier, limiting my grasp for words.

"You can say that again." Keegan's voice has an edge, like he's mad all over again.

"I don't know what went wrong, Keeg. Everything was perfect." I look down to my wrist. "I'm wearing the bracelet. I haven't taken it off." I slide the cord between my fingers, like I have so many times over the last few days.

"You like it, really?" I imagine Keegan's eyes lifting upward. He wants me to like it. He does care, but does he care enough? What does he want from me? What will it take to make things right?

"I love it. I love you." I practically beg for his response.

"I love you, too."

I lean back into the door. I really needed to hear him say it. It's all I've longed to hear for the last few days. So why is there an eerie vibe coming through the phone? Even his statement of love seemed to end in a question mark.

"Then why did it go so badly?" I explode with the emotions I've been trying to keep in check ever since the night in the park. "You left me in that park, Keegan! You changed your Facebook status! Why did you treat me like that? What went wrong?"

"I'll tell you what went wrong!" His voice is no longer smooth, but it bellows. "You slapped me across the face."

"I didn't slap you!" I thought about it at the park, but I didn't do it.

"I pledged my love for you, practically proposed there under the tree, and you said no. Like none of it mattered. You might as well have slapped me across both cheeks, like I was some kind of pervert or something." His voice shakes now, like he might be crying. Blast it! I didn't want to make Keegan cry.

"I pledged my love too. I just didn't…we just

192

shouldn't…I can't…"

"Can't show me you love me?"

I feel like someone's removed my heart. Empty. Hollow. I hate this. We love each other. What if Keegan's right and I'm wrong? What if making love would be the ultimate reflection of our love, the cement of our relationship?

"I love you," I whisper.

"I love you, too."

He can't be a jerk. Right? His feelings were hurt. He didn't handle it well, but maybe I didn't either. He loves me and wants us to be together.

"I wish I could see you right now," I say, without thinking, aching to wipe his tears, to kiss him and let him know I mean what I say. I need to feel his arms wrapped around me, comforting me, soothing all my stupid insecurities. This over the phone stuff sucks.

"Come home this weekend."

"You still want me to?" I sit up from my slouch.

"That was the plan, wasn't it?" Keegan sounds less angry, and more like the boy I fell in love with.

"That was the plan."

"Then come."

"Of course." My words are thick, draining my body.

"I'll see you Friday." Keegan half-laughs, which allows me to breathe.

And just like that, it's settled. I'll go home as planned. I'll see Keegan. We'll talk face to face and sort this out. We still love each other. What could be complicated about that?

26
CLAIRE

AFTER DINNER WITH MY ROOMIES, playing Euchre, attacking and bemoaning our homework and sharing stories, I'm tired and talked out. I snuggle under my cozy comforter. Hannah's parents bought matching ones for each of us. I think I'm the only one still awake. The ticking of a battery-powered clock mounted on the wall keeps me up.

Tick tick tick.

I think over my day, my strength and resolve swung back and forth like a pendulum. I played the undercover game I invented when I went to Sacre Coeur. I walked to and from classes hidden beneath my Jackie-O frames. I only jumped once, when that guy I didn't know with dark hair, like Phillip's, said, "Hi".

I spent my time in class trying to memorize the *passé parfait* verb conjugations in French and the logarithmic equations in Calc. My head whirred, focusing and refocusing. What if I could spot life, like I spot my turns in ballet, picking one place to focus my gaze so I don't get dizzy?

I tap my leg to the beat of the ticks of the clock.

Tap tap tap.

After class I freaked out in the bathroom. Feeling temporarily safe inside my stall, until the door rattled. I froze behind the wooden door, wondering who was out there and what they wanted?

"Sorry," the girl with the New Jersey accent said when she realized the stall was occupied.

How long am I going to live with this fear? How can I keep the calmness I felt this morning? Why can't I hang onto it? *Strengthen me by His spirit*—that's what Paul said to the Ephesians, right?

I want to reinvent myself like a dancer in a new role. I want to switch from being Sleeping Beauty under the sorceress's evil spell to being Clara in the *Nutcracker*, bravely standing up to the evil Mouse King and throwing my shoe at him, taking him down. Can I do that?

What if I'd thrown a shoe at Phillip? Or kicked him? Or even screamed, like Hannah said? No, that night I was much more like Sleeping Beauty, in a hazy trance, lured to the spinning wheel unable to stop myself from being pricked, unable to control the consequences.

"Hurry, hurry, you're late!" Hannah mumbles from her bed. She must talk in her sleep. I wonder who she's talking to in her dream. Probably me, I snort.

Longing for sleep, I count the ticks like sheep – one, two, three.

Just as I'm sinking into they rhythm of the clock, the methodical tick is interrupted by a loud creak.

My chest tightens. My eyes pop open. All I can see is

darkness. I hold perfectly still. Is someone coming? I hold my breath.

Thud.

I feel the opposite of safe, like everyone and everything is coming to get me. It's that same horrified feeling I had as a little girl right after Dad moved out. I'd hear something in the middle of the night and imagine the boogey man had decided to attack. For over a year, I'd snuck into Mom's bed. She always let me crawl in next to her.

No one ever broke in. There were no real monsters. At least not the kind I'd imagined as a girl.

It's silent again except for the ticking of the clock. I allow myself to breathe. Maybe it's nothing. I squeeze my eyes shut, hoping it's nothing.

My mind flutters until my breathing relaxes and the sleep I fought so hard to avoid takes over my exhausted body.

27
HANNAH

I PLANNED IT PERFECTLY. I'M here ten minutes before class starts, so I can sit in the row A.J. sat in on Monday. The only problem is if Zach ends up near us again. How am I going to sit next to A.J. without Zach sitting next to me? Dang it! I thought I had it all figured out last night. I take a step forward, and then hesitate in the aisle. Which would be worse? Not seeing A.J. or Zach jabbering and ruining the whole thing? More students spill into the classroom. I don't want to be standing here like an idiot when either of them gets here.

I turn around, leave the classroom and hide in the ladies room. If I stay here until class starts, I could end up sitting next to a bunch of strangers in the back row. I push my bangs out of my eyes and pout. I woke up early to pick the perfect outfit and straighten my hair. Now it seems pointless.

I chomp my gum furiously. I want to see him. Okay, time to get a move on.

My skirt rustles as I make my way toward the lecture hall. It's about five minutes until show time and still not many seats are filled. I head in the general area where the three of us sat last time, but when I hear Zach chattering from behind, I immediately turn toward the other side of the room hoping he won't follow me. I slide into the middle of the front row on the right, so I'll be harder to get to, and lower my Vera Bradley bag to the ground. My head lowers with it. Keeping my head down, I take longer than I should searching for my notebook and pen, I hold my breath, hoping Zach might not see me. I keep my eyes glued forward as I sit up and get situated. I cannot make eye contact with him. The clock in the front of the room reads one minute until class begins.

Dr. Gillespie walks to the front of the room and begins an hour monologue on photosynthesis.

Zach either didn't see me or couldn't get to me, or maybe I'm taking too much credit for him liking me. Maybe A.J. didn't see me, couldn't get to me, or has no interest in sitting next to me. Or maybe he's absent. I try to focus on light and plants, but my mind keeps drifting to A.J. Is he back there? Can he see me? Does he like my hair like this? What's he wearing today? Will I see him after class? What if we were study partners? I glance casually to the back of the room. I see Zach in a Clarkston T-shirt that looks a little too brand new, like it still has creases in it from being folded on the student bookstore shelf.

I can't find A.J. without being obvious. I hope he's back there, wondering about me like I'm wondering about him. I doodle on the edges of my notebook an "A" that I turn into a flower. I doodle a "J" and morph it into a leaf.

After what seems like nine hours of listening to the

monotonous voice of my professor, class is dismissed. Swivel chairs squeak. Books slam. Feet shuffle toward the door. I frantically search the other students for the right color hair, the right height, the right build. I scan heads and shoulders and book bags.

There he is. My eyebrows jump. I'm afraid my feet might have jumped a little, too. He's such a hottie, even from behind.

I need to time this perfectly.

I speed up my pace until I'm right behind A.J. It's like he senses my presence. He turns and flashes a crooked smile. "Hannah, I thought I saw you up front today, but your hair looks different or something."

Oh my gosh! He's talking to me, and he noticed my hair! I laugh nervously, but hope it's coming across as friendly. "I straightened it for fun."

"Nice."

"Thanks." My lips might crack from stretching into such a huge smile. "So," I say, changing the subject. "A test already next week? That seems really fast. How many chapters did she say it's over?"

"Too many," he says. "Everyone in this class is just taking it to fill a requirement, right? She can't believe for a second any of us cares about plant reproduction."

He's so cute. I think I stop breathing.

"We should study together."

Now I actually can't breathe. I clutch the soft shoulder strap of my bag tightly trying to balance myself. He just asked me to study with him!

"Sure." I finally remember to answer.

"You headed back to the dorm?" A.J. tips his head toward the sidewalk leading home.

"No, I have another class." I frown. *Why do I have to have another stupid class? I could walk home with him and amplify this electrical current zooming between us.*

"Well…" A.J. shoves his hands in his pockets, like he's about to say something, maybe something spectacular. "I don't have another class till eleven, so I'll catch ya later."

Sigh. That's it?

I'm not ready to pull away from this tingling static. I want to do the opposite. I want to lean into it. "When do you want to start studying for the test? Should we meet in the study room in the dorm's basement?"

"Sure, the basement works. Next class we'll figure it out."

Just as I'm about to smile and do a half spin and walk into the sun in an elegant goodbye, an adorable redhead rushes toward us.

"Hey, babe." She slides her arm in A.J.'s.

"Mags." He gives her a sideways grin. I love that grin of his.

"I don't have class again until noon, and my roommate has classes all day…" she purrs at him, clearly oblivious to the fact that he was chatting with me.

"Maggie, this is Hannah. Hannah, this is my girlfriend, Maggie."

Open chest. Insert knife.

"Girlfriend?"

Did I say that out loud? I hope I just said it to myself. How could he possibly have a girlfriend? He just invited *me* to study with him. He went to get bagels with *me*. I am not imagining this. What is it with every boy I have a decent conversation with being involved with someone else? Who is she, and does she know how flirty he is?

"Hey." Maggie snarls. Maybe she's part cat. "Nice to meet you and see you later, Harriet. B-bye." She turns A.J. the other direction, leaving me standing here nodding.

Harriet! There's no way she thought he said my name was Harriet! That's like an old lady's name. My stomach feels like I skipped breakfast, even though I didn't. I don't want him to sneak off with her. It's so not fair. I want him to walk arm and arm with *me*. I could be A.J.'s girlfriend. We could study and laugh and get bagels every day.

"See you later, Hannah."

Unable to answer or hold my fake smile another second, I take off toward my next class. Why does this always happen to me? Why am I a human boy repellent?

28
CLAIRE

"AND *PLIÉ* AND UP." THE ballet instructor uses her voice to tap out the rhythm of the piano. I know I only took a couple of weeks off dance, but I've missed the smell of resin and the smooth wood floors. I concentrate on an invisible string pulling from inside my body, upward from my bellybutton to the ceiling, downward from my bellybutton to the floor, my core perfectly balanced as I lengthen my torso while bending my knees outward. The dance studio is where I feel most balanced, most in control.

"And grand *plié*, slow-ly up." Ms. Kladinski's bio on the Clarkston website said she used to dance with the Russian ballet, but fell in love with an American soldier and defected to the States approximately a million years ago. How romantic is that? We're in the first ten minutes of my first class, and I can already tell she is strict and fabulous.

"Other side, ladies." Her accent is thick, even after all these years in the States.

Another dancer, whose nametag reads Ashley, asks, "Aren't you hot in all that?"

"Not really," I whisper, but it's a lie. I haven't peeled off my yoga pants and hoodie yet. Definitely not protocol for the floor, but acceptable for warm ups. Truthfully, the late August heat is brutal, and the air conditioning in the studio seems to be on the fritz. But when I put on my tights and leotard this morning, I felt exposed and bare and vulnerable. I haven't felt that way in a leotard since I was twelve and my breasts first popped out. I remember feeling so conspicuous. Thankfully, they never grew bigger than an A cup, and I realized all the other girls were popping out too.

"There will be no talking at the *barre*," Ms. Kladinski says.

I'm even hotter now.

Her threat saves me any more talk about my outfit, though. I focus on keeping my knees turned out and my bottom tucked. I suck in my stomach. Thankfully it will stay flat. The pregnancy test was negative. Phillip did not leave a permanent mark on me, not like that. But I still feel like he marked an "A" across me with a scarlet Sharpie.

My eyes scan the windows lining the back wall of the studio. All I see is the faculty parking lot for the Fine Arts Building and a small patch of grass, but I can't help feeling like I'm being watched.

"Eyes forward." Ms. Kladinski's voice is sharp.

I tear my eyes from the windows and back to the classroom. The other dancers stand motionless on their left toes with their right feet poised by their left knees in perfect *passés* I'm not in the pose. I zoned a second too long. I practically jump into position. I can't screw up this audition. My heart thunders more loudly than the piano music.

Focus! I yell at myself.

Ms. Kladinski makes her rounds while we strive to maintain our balance. She pulls a black-haired girl's heel forward. I press mine forward.

"Relax." She taps a dark-skinned boy's fingers. He wiggles them lightly, releasing the tension.

I bounce my hands softly, making sure they're light.

By the time Ms. Kladinski gets to me, many dancers wobble. Some have resigned to resting their hands on the *barre* for balance. I focus and tighten my core.

"Nice."

I exhale lightly, keeping my eyes forward. Best compliment ever. I'm determined to give the rest of this lesson to Ms. Kladinski. No more airtime to Phillip or anyone or anything else.

When we push the *barres* back to the wall and take center floor, I'm immersed in ballet and able to strip my armor, revealing my dancer's skin of leotard and tights. I stretch my legs as far as they will extend in *grande battements*. I point my toes sharply toward the floor with each jump from the ground. I melt and reach and turn.

When the music stops after our final combination, blood thunders through my veins. I bend over, letting my head fall against my knees, panting in relief. The other dancers do the same, gulping air to refill our lungs while our bodies feel like they might combust.

"Nice class today." Ms. Kladinski stands calmly in the center. "Lots of focus. Well done."

I lean over my left knee, feeling the stretch.

"Unfortunately, I can only take twenty of you for workshop, whom I will announce in a moment."

We all know this. That is why we are here.

All eyes are on her. We spent the morning stretching and groaning in hopes of twirling in tutus in the troupe's performances. I stand and slide my feet into third position—a ballerina's equivalent of standing at attention. I don't breathe. I'm afraid to, afraid the moment will slip away, and I won't get picked.

Ms. Kladinski continues in thick staccato. "For those of you not selected, there are several dance classes you can take for credit through the University. It's not too late to force add most of them at the registrar's office. I encourage all of you to stay involved with dance. Again, if you're not selected today, we have auditions every semester as well as drop-ins on the first Saturday of every month."

I try to file away my options—classes for credit, Saturdays, next semester. It's a lost cause. Her words are a blur of letters and sounds.

"And now, if I call your name, please step by the piano. Otherwise, you are dismissed."

A murmur fills the room, but I am still frozen.

Clap. Clap.

The sharp sound of Ms. Kladinski's hands clapping quiets the room instantly. Lips are zipped. Everyone stands in position. Poised. Waiting.

Ms. Kladinski calls names; names I don't know, names I've never heard and names that sound familiar, like people from my old school, from my old studio. She calls Ashley and a muscular Asian boy, who held his balance for eternity during the audition. I count dancers, knowing it cannot go past twenty—8, 9, 10. She's halfway done. I inhale and exhale. 11, 12.

"Claire Lassiter," Ms. Kladinski says. I breathe. I want to jump up and down, to hug someone, to scream, but none of that is proper conduct. I reverently take my place by the piano, smiling, feeling heat rush to my cheeks, trying not to shake right out of my pointe shoes. Ms. Kladinski calls seven more names, but all I hear is blood coursing through my ears.

Thank You, God! I scream in my head, over and over again. *Thank You for this.*

"Thank you. Dismissed," Ms. Kladinski says. Those not called shuffle off the floor toward their dance bags, unknotting ribbons on shoes, and wiping sweaty foreheads with towels. I watch them, knowing I could've been one of them, but I'm not. Not today.

29
HANNAH

TODAY IS THE FIRST SATURDAY after our first week of classes. It should be a day of rest, relaxation and roommates, but I'm alone.

Claire has auditions.

Kat's somewhere in Tennessee playing her first game of the season. I couldn't resist singing a few bars of "Rockytop" to her last night as she packed. She couldn't resist throwing a pair of soccer socks at my head.

Palmer went home to see Keegan, which has me extremely worried. I like Keegan and all, but I don't like the idea of him pressuring Palmer. In fact, now that I think of it, he always pressures her to do things his way. The whole thing makes me a little queasy, but that could be the second strawberry waffle I ate at breakfast with Claire.

I take a spin class at the sports center and shower. Our bathroom is a disaster area. So is our room. It's driving me crazy, making me physically angry, like if I don't clear everything out of the way I'll start throwing stuff. Maybe it's a good thing everyone's gone, so I can clear all this crap out of the way.

I start with the bathroom, throwing Palmer's Lancôme in her bin under the sink, shoving a handful of Kat's hair elastics in her bin and putting the rest in Claire's.

I try to tell myself we're still finding places for everything, but it looks more like everything is taking over our place. I gather water bottles and pop cans and take them to the recycler by the main entrance. I spray the mirrors in the bathroom and the full length one on the back of our door. There's something soothing about erasing the streaks, leaving a perfect even shine.

I pull my sheets off the corners of my bed and decide to do Claire's too, because, well, because she's a mess and her bed's a mess. It might be a nice surprise for her when she gets back from auditions. Not to mention, I can barely stand to look at it. I know she's been through a lot, but that is not an excuse to live like an animal. I find her textbooks scattered across her sheets, her cowboy boots lodged in the corner, a granola bar wrapper and a paper coffee cup. *Eww*! What kind of person leaves food in their bed? Under her pillow I find a pen, a spiral notebook and a worn out Bible with a black leather cover.

My inward rant is stopped dead in its tracks. She has a Bible. She's a Christian. Just like me. We're not so different after all. That's what I get for judging her. Why do I have to be such a pain? I just want everything to be perfect. I'm trying so hard to make everything perfect. It's as if God wanted me to see Claire's heart for what it is, not exactly like mine, but with a loving space for Him. It's as if He prompted me to strip Claire's sheets, so I would find her

Bible. Claire is messy. She doesn't approach things like I would, but she's a Christian.

The tension in my shoulders and my forehead loosens. I was the one who invited Claire to be our roommate. I remember the first day I met her. She seemed like a beautiful fairy. She still does.

I whistle a Rihanna song I heard at spinning while I haul the laundry down to the machines in the basement. Back in our room, I exhale. It looks so much better in here. I hold out my arms and twirl, reveling in the space to spin safely. I crack the window, letting in some fresh air and spy Sammie and Owen grinning at me from the picture on my desk. I thought I would appreciate the separation, but I miss O's squirmy body climbing on my lap and Sammie's constant stories. I promised I would Skype over the weekend, so I fire up my laptop.

Before clicking into Skype, I scroll down my messages.

"*Ha!*" Zach sent me a friend request on Facebook.

Instinctively, I click "yes" and browse his profile. He has lots of pictures with friends and with girls. He always seems to be alone when I see him. I didn't give him any credit for having his own group of besties. I shoot him a message:

HI ZACH. FUN TO SEE YOU ON FB. WHAT DO YOU THINK ABOUT THE UPCOMING BOTANY EXAM? PRETTY FAST, HUH? AND OVER HOW MANY CHAPTERS? HAVE A SUPER DAY ☺.

I try to Skype home, but no one answers. A strange hollow thump throbs in my heart. It feels a bit too empty in here. A bit too quiet. I was looking forward to the funny faces Owen and Sammy were sure to make and the sound of their cute voices. I blow some stray frizzes out of my face. As I click off Skype, I see Zach has already responded. At least somebody out there is talking to me.

YEAH, BOTANY EQUALS B-O-R-I-N-G. I HAVE A PAPER DUE FRIDAY TOO. I'M LYING LOW ALL WEEKEND. WANT TO GRAB PIZZA TONIGHT?

I drum the keys on my keyboard lightly, so they won't actually type yet. It would be fun to have a boy fawn over me a bit. Zach seems innocent enough, and it's not like I have big plans. It's not like I have any plans. I mean, Claire and I are supposed to do dinner, but she'd probably come along. That is something great about Claire. She's not picky or demanding. In fact, she's very easy going. How could I have gotten so frustrated about something like her sheets?

I wonder what A.J.'s doing tonight. Probably a romantic dinner for two with Mean Maggie. That settles it.

PIZZA SOUNDS FUN. I'LL BRING MY ROOMMATE, CLAIRE. THE OTHER HALF OF US ARE OOT. BRING YOUR ROOMIES. WHICH PIZZA PLACE AND WHAT TIME?

RAGAZZA IN THE STUDENT CENTER IS SUPPOSED TO ROCK. SEE YOU GUYS AT 7. THAT WORK?

SEE YOU THEN.

And it's done. I've agreed to meet Zach for pizza. Oh well. It'll be fun. Claire and I were just chatting about Ragazza anyway. I can't help grinning a little. Seriously, Zach's a boost for a girl's ego, if nothing else.

I bound down the steps. Folding sheets and T-shirts, I

214

contemplate what Zach sees in me and why A.J. doesn't see the same thing. What would it take to make them switch viewpoints? And why can't I like Zach in the same way I like A.J.? A.J. is off the market, and Zach is into me. It would be so much easier the other way around. But Zach is a little annoying and not as cute as A.J. What a mess.

With laundry folded and sheets back on our beds, I've run out of things to entertain myself. I text Palmer, Kat and Claire, even though I know they're all busy. I wish Claire's audition would be over or Sammie and Owen would Skype. I flip open my *Theories of Learning* book, but all of the theories turn themselves inside out and upside down. I am so not in the mood to study—especially this. A couple of weeks ago I would have killed for an entire Saturday to myself, no Owen or Sammie to follow me around or use my phone or change the channel. But I've had enough alone time for the day. I wish I could take Ziggy for a walk. He'd cheer me up in a hurry. I open our mini-fridge, stare at its contents and shut it again. Turns out all I really need is *half* a Saturday to myself.

I roam down to the mailboxes, but the mail's not here yet. Figures.

I pause at the lounge. I've passed it a hundred times, but I've never entered the formally decorated parlor. Does anybody ever go in here? If I went to school here in the fifties, this is the place A.J. and I would study for Botany, probably chaperoned.

Why do I keep thinking about A.J.? I haven't talked to him since I met Maggie. I've thought about him, though. Lots. I've run over the day we ate bagels. He never suggested it was a date; just that he was hungry too. It's just a fluke we have Botany together. And people do study together who aren't dating. But I took it all to mean fate, destiny, true love, or at least freshman boyfriend.

My hand runs over a velvety, pale blue couch. It's pretty in here and quiet, but not the empty, lonely quiet of my room—more peaceful quiet. In the corner is a baby grand piano. I heard someone plucking away at the keys yesterday.

Instinctively, I sit at the smooth bench. It's been a while since I've played. My fingers fly through Beethoven's "Fur Elise." It's the first piece I ever had to memorize, and I could play it half asleep with my eyes shut. The melody carries me away.

Next I play a "Tarantella." The music illustrates someone trying to shake off the deadly poison of a tarantula bite. I'm trying to shake off the poison of jealousy, of coveting something I can't have, of wishing I could hang with A.J. on this Saturday afternoon.

I am lost in plucking out staccato notes and using the pedal to blend the slower parts of the piece. When the song is over, I roll my neck, cracking it, releasing the stress I've piled there.

Now something sweeter, nicer.

My fingers flow easily through the first verse of "Amazing Grace." I play Chris Tomlin's modern version with an updated refrain. The words fill my head as my fingers dance across the keys.

God's amazing grace is always there for me.

So why do I get so anxious?

I have darling roommates, a picturesque college, and a fab dorm room. My family loves me. I'm healthy. I don't need a boyfriend. I just want one. I really, really, really want a boyfriend. I know God loves me, and I know that should be enough. I'm not convinced, but I am comforted. I'm lost in the music, and I play every repeat and refrain. When I play the last note, I hold it and absorb the warmth of God's love.

Somebody claps.

I turn slowly, puzzled by the echoing hands.

A.J. stands four feet away, propped against the couch, clapping.

30
KAT

AS MY CLEATS CLICK ACROSS the parking lot from our bus, the heat of the Tennessee air stirs something inside me. Like a reptile under a heat lamp, I soak up the sun. Every bit of the drawl I'd tried to harness into a staccato Midwest accent unleashed itself when we crossed the state line on the team bus. It's ironic that our first game of the season is against the Vanderbilt Commodores. If my family hadn't moved in the middle of last school year, I might be playing for them instead of Clarkston. In some ways I wish I could escape back down here. Between the crazy incident with Tony and the goofy way Nicholas has been acting, I'd like to ditch 'em both and start freshman year over again, at least socially. I'd let my mouth relax and draw out my words and breathe in the scent of magnolias and drink sweet tea every day. But I couldn't leave my roommates. They'd have to come with me.

Vanderbilt is good. Really good. But I'm so pumped; I don't care about their record. As we gather on the sidelines, I almost bust out of my skin. I stretch and jump and retighten my ponytail. I check the shoestrings on my neon yellow cleats, making sure they're double knotted. As a freshman, I know I won't start, but I think I'll explode if I have to sit.

The first half of the game flies by. I'm immersed in the action as if I'm on the field. I'm sweating and breathless from the intensity. Although we're tied 1-1, Vandy's dominating us. They've had way more shots on goal. We just can't seem to clear the ball.

After only two minutes into the second half, Coach calls me over.

"Kat, I am going to put you in. Are you ready?"

I look him straight in the eyes and jerk my head up and down, too overwhelmed to speak. He places his hand on my back, ready to send me onto the pitch.

Over the loudspeaker the announcer's voice echoes, "A substitution for Clarkston. Courtney Stewart will be replaced by freshman, number 20, Kat Wiley."

I shoot onto the field like a ball on a throw-in. Almost instantly the ball comes my way. I catch it with my chest, drop it to my feet, and dribble around an incoming Vandy girl. I pass to Molly, but it gets stolen by another Vanderbilt player. Minute after sweaty, intense minute continues like this. Close chances, nice tries, no success.

A loose ball gets down inside our eighteen, and a Commodore heads the ball toward our goal. The tips of our goalie's gloves brush the ball as it lands in the net. 2-1.

"It's all right!" I shout, clapping my sweaty palms together. "We're still in this game. Show 'em what we've got!"

A Vandy player tries to pass to her teammate, but I steal the ball. It's mine now, free and clear. I dribble and shoot— strong, hard, and sure.

Nine out of ten times, I can nail this shot in the top of the net, but not today. Instead the ball hits the crossbar and bounces back into play—a mistake I cannot allow to happen. Molly gets a foot on it, but the Vandy girl is too fast and steals it from her feet. I close in to regain what is mine.

Tweet tweet tweet!

Game over.

A throb begins at the crown of my head then plummets through me. As it passes behind my face, my forehead wrinkles and my eyes well. I scowl, angry at the tears, not allowing them to surface. The thing, the blob, the angry, defeated glob slides down my throat leaving a lump. It hammers my chest and thuds in my stomach like a deflated game ball. This game could have been ours. The other team is awesome, but so are we. We could've tied and gone into overtime, if I hadn't hit that blasted crossbar. I will not let that happen again. I cannot ever let it happen again.

I shake hands with the other team and tell them, "Good game," although I can barely strangle out the words. I replay my shot over and over in my head repositioning my foot, changing my angle, my force.

The six-hour drive back to campus is brutal. The chipper chatter that filled the bus on the way here has been replaced by quiet whispers. My teammates are plugged into their iPods, buried in schoolbooks, and snoozing. I gaze out the window, watching the South dissolve and with it the sunlight, as I'm transported back to Ohio. Rolling into campus, I text Hannah and Claire, hoping to get my mind off the game.

WHAT'S UP?

CHOWING PIZZA – COME JOIN US! WE WANT DEETS OF YOUR GAME

LOST 2-1 TOTAL DRAG NOT HUNGRY ATE ON BUS.

SORRY, SWEETIE. COME ANYWAY. WE MISS YOU ☺

MISS YOU TOO. FEEL LIKE CRASHING. SEE YOU WHEN YOU GET BACK.

I'm so not up for joining them. I thought I would be. I hoped I would be. I hoped their companionship would erase the bitter taste in my mouth. But what I really need is some time to myself. The halls of the dorm are deserted. The echo of my shoes thud along the narrow corridor leading to our room. I've come home from losses before. Of course I have, but those were different. I was leaving a loss and coming home to something. But what am I returning to now? No Mama's fried chicken sizzling on the stove, no Alex making light of my team's loss, no glow from Daddy's office off the kitchen, or the whir of the dishwasher. Just emptiness and silence.

I unlock our door and switch on the light. Hannah's message board has "Welcome home," scrawled in purple marker with a drawing of a cat. I snort. She is a goof. Palmer's stylish throw pillows and curtains make our old room and old futon look like a showroom. The smell of Claire's sweet perfume trails through the air. My soccer stickers and pictures of players are plastered all over my desk. In a way it's like home, like a new home.

I throw my bag under my bunk. Then I change into my comfiest shorts and Alex's T-shirt—the one with the Kool-Aid guy on the front that I "borrowed," because it's huge and soft and orange. I switch on the TV to see what we've DVR'd, but the screen is blurred as tears slice across my eyes.

"Don't be a homesick sissy," I say to myself, angry at the tears, at myself, at my weakness.

HOW'D YOUR GAME GO? Nicholas texts.
CRUMMY!
WANT TO GET A CHAI AND TELL ME ABOUT IT?

"No!" I shout. I don't. I want to have a pity party with a bad TV show. But it's not working out so well. I'm just sitting here wallowing, which makes me angry, which makes things worse. And a chai sounds nice, homey almost, and to be honest, so does Nicholas. Like a piece of pecan pie with whipped cream melting down the sides.

SURE. GIVE ME A FEW.
DEAL.

Out in the quad, the air is cool and crisp in my lungs, so crazy different from the Tennessee heat of this afternoon. The sidewalk leading out of the quad is canopied with giant trees, bowing their branches from both sides. During the day it's swarmed with groups of girls gossiping, guys giving high fives, runners with their earbuds moving to their own beat. But now, there's no one but me plodding along under the green, leafy roof.

I eye the long, straight open stretch, taunting me to take off. I started doing sprints the first time we moved. The kids at my new school teased me about my corduroys, which had been fashionable at my previous school. I came home flustered, about to cry like a baby, but not wanting Alex to make fun of me or my parents to worry. So instead of letting them see my tears, I went outside and ran sprints up and down my street. It's been my coping mechanism ever since. Whenever I take off racing down the sidewalks, everyone in my family knows I have something to vent—a bad test grade, a catty classmate, Alex getting on my nerves, PMS, a loss on the field. Missing a goal tops the list.

I slide my iPod from my string bag and set my earbuds in place. Inhaling deeply, I mentally set my finish line as the brick archway ahead and speed to it, lifting my thighs so high, I'm almost marching in midair. I stop, bend over at the waist and catch my breath. After a few seconds, I turn around and sprint back, feeling my heart banging in my chest, feeling like I've gotta stop or I won't have enough air to continue, but nothing will make me stop before I get to my mark. A stray student passes, but I run with invisible blinders on, picturing the cross bar and mentally sending the ball into the goal.

The Bundys' twangy Nashville harmonies trickle into my ears and slice through my stress like my feet slice through the air. As I sprint, I envision myself flying past the uniforms of the Vandy players. I pant for breath, exhilarated, alive. If I'm going to be on top of my game, I need to be faster and in better condition than anyone else. I gulp a mouthful of evening air and take off one more time.

When I reach my goal, the *thump thump* in my chest is the reward for my labors. I walk with determination toward Corner Cup.

Nicholas waves from a booth on the side of the shop. Of course he got here first. Of course he ordered my drink for me. That's why he's way ahead of me on the friend-o-meter. He's always been the kind of friend I wish I were.

"Hey." I sit across from him, and he slides me a steaming cup. "Yum. Thanks." I blow on it and take a sweet, spicy sip. "Ya know I was all set to say no to your invite, but you completely got me with the chai. You sure do know my weakness."

"Sorry you only came for the tea." He's all collegiate in crinkled khaki shorts, and something about his hair looks different. Did he get a makeover? If I didn't know him, I'd take Nicholas for a sophomore or junior. Of course I'm still wearing Alex's Kool-Aid shirt and my hair in a knot, not to mention I'm sweaty from the sprints and my pulse bumps around in my head.

"I didn't mean it like that." I pause. "I wanted to see you. We haven't had much chance to chat since we got here, ya know?"

"So I'm guessing you guys didn't win?"

"Nope." I avoid eye contact and stare in my cup.

"Want to talk about it?"

"Nope."

"I'm a good listener." Nicholas's green eyes are wide and look genuinely concerned. I slump back into the soft booth, like a ball with a slow leak and let it all out. I give him a play-by-play of the game. He nods at all the right times and sees the injustice in it all. It actually feels good to get it off my chest.

"So, you as a freshman got to play half the game?" Nicholas turns the attention away from my misfire and our loss.

"Well, all but two minutes of half the game." I shrug.

"Isn't that the best thing that could have happened?" He stirs the ice in his coffee with his straw. The cubes clatter dully against his plastic cup.

"The best thing that could have happened is that I played the entire game, made my shot and we won." I draw out my words and smile for the first time since I left the field.

"Well, sure. That's not asking for much, is it?" Nicholas laughs. His laugh is warm and comfortable, like my cup of chai.

"Right. I'm not askin' for much at all." I laugh, feeling a little lighter.

YOU OK? WHERE ARE YOU? HANNAH TEXTS.
GRABBIN A CHAI. BE BACK SOON.
K

I look at Nicholas. "My roommates are wonderin' where I am."

"They seemed really nice the other night when we were all hanging out here."

"They're the best." I catch myself smiling. "How 'bout you? I haven't met your mystery roommate yet."

"Do you need to get back?" Nicholas asks, shaking the ice in his cup.

"Probably." I look at the time on my phone. It's 11:30 p.m. "Wow. You kept me out later than I thought." I drink the dregs out of the bottom of my cup. I can't believe how easy it's been just hanging here with Nicholas. But I guess it's always been easy around him.

"Let's hit it. I'll walk you back to your dorm."

We slide out of the booth, and he opens the door for me. Stars dot the sky, and we fall into an easy cadence. "Weren't you gonna tell me about your roommate?"

"He's a nice enough guy. Let's just say he's looking for

something different than I am."

"What's he lookin' for?"

"Jason is at The Brewery right now and probably will be until it closes." Nicholas points down an alley to one of the supposed "hot" bars.

"Oh. That kind of somethin' else." I nod. "So, he goes out a lot?"

"If you count every night since move-in day a lot, then yeah." Nicholas raises his eyebrows.

"That stinks. It puts you in such a bad spot, Nick. I'm really sorry."

"*Ehhh*, it's fine really." He pauses and looks at me. "Like I said. He's nice enough. During the day it's cool. And he asks me to join him at night. I just don't want to. He hasn't puked or anything, but he comes home smelling like, well, like a brewery." Nicholas laughs it off.

He laughs so much, and for as serious as he is about his studies, he never seems to get upset, ever, about anything.

"Well, here you are." He bows in front of my dorm.

"Thanks."

"For what?" Nicholas rubs his hand through his red curls.

"For everything, really." I glance around at the giant oak trees lining the front of the brick building. "For escorting me home and for the chai and for listenin' to me rant on and on about soccer." I nod, feeling a little too emotional. "Just for, ya know, understanding me."

"I told you before, Kat. Any and every time." Nicholas leans forward, and before I understand what's happening, his warm lips brush mine. It's just a quick peck, sweet and friendly and then he's standing tall again. I should say something, something like "you shouldn't have done that," because he shouldn't have. Should he? Or "that was nice," because it was. Wasn't it? Or "I didn't see that coming," because I didn't. But no words come. Not one.

"Night, Kat," Nicholas says.

"G'night,Nick."

31
PALMER

MY TIRES BOUNCE AND THUMP over the grooves in the torn-up road. As I swerve an inch, the muscles in my neck tighten, so does my grip on the wheel. I swear I'm going to scrape the concrete wall dividing the narrow lanes. I turn the steering wheel tightly and slow to a crawl, holding my breath as I take the sharp curve of the exit ramp. My entire body is rigid.

I am a horrible driver. I don't mean to be. I just am. I hate having to focus on ten locations at once—in front, behind, beside me, at signs and lights and pedestrians and merge lanes. I would much rather be in the passenger seat, daydreaming and noticing the details of a split-rail fence, or the way cows cluster in a field.

The familiar intersections and signs are a relief. I square my shoulders. Almost home, I know when I have to change lanes, where lanes merge and when my turns are coming up without exerting the same concentration required for

Statistics. Now I can turn up my music without being distracted. My hand brushes the cover of my journal as I reach into my purse for a handful of M&M's.

My journal. Hannah suggested I journal, but I didn't. Not yet.

My brain is dull. Like in the morning before my first cup of coffee, I feel I can't get Keegan's caffeine surging through my veins soon enough. He is so much a part of who I am, and I'm trying to see his side of all this, but he seems so angry. I want to pretend our fight didn't happen—to write it off as a bad night or a lovers' quarrel—and move on with things. I need to see his eyes. I need to feel his warm hand in mine to wake up from this bad dream.

I didn't call my parents to give them an update of my arrival time, because I didn't want to risk getting into an accident in the whole challenging act of finding my phone and trying to dial it while driving, so they're not expecting me yet. I'll go to Keegan's first and home second.

I pull into the left side of Keegan's driveway, checking my headband in the mirror. The backs of my legs ache as I get out of the car—partly from the drive, partly from cramps. I hate my period. How can that make the backs of my thighs and calves hurt anyway?

I stand tall, smooth out my cotton dress, adjust one of my wedges and walk toward the door. My bravado dissolves as I ring the doorbell. My stomach feels like the goopy oatmeal the dining hall was trying to pawn off as breakfast this morning—lumpy, mushy, and all stirred up. It sat in my stomach all through my nine o'clock class and the entire way here. The lump from my stomach pushes through to my backbone, shooting a shiver up my spinal cord, making all the little dark hairs on my arms stand on end. Sweat trickles from my forehead as I hear the doorknob jiggle.

In one motion the door swings open, and Keegan's standing there. One look into his silver eyes and I'm immediately lost in his strong arms and warm body. I feel like a scared baby bird, wrapped safe and warm under the comfort of its mother's soft, feathery wing. It's like I never left the nest. "Palmer." His deep voice rattles softly as he strokes my hair.

Why did I doubt him? This is how it's supposed to be, how it's always supposed to be. My dorm room at Clarkston seems a million miles away. All that matters is this porch. This boy. This moment. I don't ever want him to let go.

And he doesn't until I've almost gotten my fill, until the goose bumps are gone, the perspiration has evaporated and the pit in my stomach has dissolved.

"I missed you," I say softly, not wanting to break the silence, but wanting him to know.

"You don't know the half of it, Palm. Nothing's the same around here without you." Keegan shakes his head, and even though we've released our embrace, he maintains constant contact with me, sliding his hand from my back down my arm to my hand, which he holds firmly but softly.

We sit on the step of his front porch for maybe an hour or more talking, catching up on all the little things that seemed too silly or too hard to explain over the phone. Keegan tells me all about Colt from Denver, his soon-to-be roommate and fellow teammate, who skis and snowboards during the off-season and has a crazy impressive antique baseball card collection. I tell him about Freshman Comp and my teacher, who told us unless we write like Jane Austen, there is no way we will earn an *A* in her class.

We talk like we've never left each other's sides. As I

listen to his voice, a magnetic force pulls me closer and closer to him. I wonder how I had any doubts, why things seemed so weird when I was just a couple of hours away.

We detour to my house, where Mom tells me (1) I look like I've lost weight, even though I'm completely bloated; (2) she's not sure Claire or her mom are stable (duh!); and (3) she's glad I brought my laundry home, because the machines in my dorm could destroy my clothes.

After my daughterly catch up session, Keegan and I escape to the nearby shopping district. We spend a few minutes in the athletic store and more than a few minutes in the locally owned boutique, where I buy a darling, tweedy skirt. We share a savory pizza topped with olives and feta cheese at Reno's, talking nonstop about everything and nothing. Afterward we grab ice cream cones and sit on a black iron bench in the middle of the square.

I take a lick of dark chocolate trickling down the side of my cone and shiver.

"You getting chilly?" Keegan asks, rubbing my arm with his hand.

"A little."

"It's summer." He laughs, turning the corners of his eyes upward, which sends another shiver over me, but not because of the chill.

"Summer for you, but I'm well into the fall semester." I wink at him and bat my eyelashes, loving his attention, basking in this time with him without distractions or distance getting in our way. "I think it's the ice cream." I take another lick as if trying to prove my theory. "And it was warmer before."

"Let's warm you up." Keegan kisses me.

This isn't the first time today his lips have touched

mine. Once I stood on my tiptoes, just to kiss the back of his neck and inhale his fresh scent of Irish Spring mixed with the ever-lingering saltiness of sunflower seeds. But this kiss is different. It's full of how much we've missed each other, how much we can't let go of one another. I forget we're surrounded by shoppers, and melt into Keegan—our lips moving, his tongue warm and soft. I press myself against him, trying to fit tighter into his embrace, eliminating any of the spaces separating us.

A flame pulls from somewhere deep inside of me, warming my core, flowing from my toes to my brain and everywhere in between.

"Warmer?" Keegan whispers, his lips sliding from my lips to tickle my ear.

"Uh huh." I nod, searching for his lips again, not wanting this to end, not wanting him to stop kissing me like this.

"We should go." He stands and pulls me up, holding my hand.

I obediently follow, like a puppy on a leash. He's right. We shouldn't make out in front of half of Hoover Heights. Back in his car, my mind is still in mid-kiss. I feel dizzy and flustered and disoriented. It's a feeling I like—all warm and swirly and consuming.

We end up back at Keegan's house, kissing on his couch in the family room. But it's dark and no one's around.

"My parents are out for the night," Keegan whispers, sliding the spaghetti strap of my dress down over my shoulder and kissing my collarbone.

I exhale at the lovely, intense feeling his lips give me. They move back up my neck, and his hands move around my waist and ribs. I'm like Play-Doh and can be whatever shape he wants me to be, fitting perfectly into his hands. But when his hand slides up my skirt and toward my panties, I stiffen. I push his hand back down. Every gross thought about my period and him getting anywhere near all that snaps me out of this spell.

"What's wrong?" He kisses my collarbone again. But this time the shivers don't take me away, because his hand is creeping right back up my leg toward my ugly underwear, the ones I reserve for this time of the month.

"Stop." I push him away again.

"What's wrong with you, Palmer?" He pulls away from me. "I thought we already went through all this. I thought you changed your mind."

"What?" I try to shake the steamy trance.

"Why did you come home this weekend?"

"I wanted to see you."

"Why? So you could tease me again? Who do you think I am? A toy to play with on the weekends?"

"What?" I shake my head. My temples pulse with a headache seeping its way into my skull.

"You said you loved me. You said you wanted us to be together!" Keegan's shouting now, like I've lied to him.

"I didn't lie. I do. I do mean that!" I shout, then lower my voice, mainly because the shouting hurts my head. "FYI, I have my period, Keeg. You don't want to go there."

"Oh." Keegan zooms to the other side of the couch. "Oh. Oh. I didn't know." His hands are up in the air as if he's asking for mercy. "Why didn't you say so?"

"What?" I ask, for the zillionth time.

"You could have told me. Now I'm all turned on. I'm a wreck." Keegan stands and paces around the room.

"How is this my fault? You hate talking about my

period! You cringe at the word *tampon*." I shake my head, scattering tears.

He winces.

"See!" I point at him. "Caught in the act."

"Okay. Okay." He's still pacing. "True. Not my favorite topic. But why did you let things go so far? Why did you come home this weekend if you didn't . . .?" Keegan rubs his stubbly hair cut.

"If I didn't what?" I straighten my dress.

"Never mind. This is crazy." Keegan storms out of the room.

"If I didn't what, Keeg?"

32
CLAIRE

SETTING MY BAG DOWN ON the concrete porch, I dig
around for my key. Three weeks into the semester, you think
I'd find a good place to keep it. I tap the pockets of my
jeans. Nope. I slide my sunglasses from my nose to the top
of my head, hoping for better vision. I pull out lip gloss, a
textbook, three binders, my newly acquired library book,
pens, pencils, markers, two scarves, and my phone, but no
key card.

"Oh, come on."

Kyra, a towering, blonde field hockey player who lives
in our corridor, clomps up the stairs next to me.

"Hi ya, Claire."

"Hey."

"Locked out?"

"Uh huh." I smile meekly, relieved to walk in with her.

"Thanks, Kyra. See ya," I say, as she heads up the
stairwell.

"Sure thing, Claire. Later."

I've got to find that card, but the thought is lost when I hear Hannah's aggravated voice. The door is open and I see Hannah and Palmer deep in conversation.

"I mean, I feel badly for Claire."

I freeze. My stomach flops like the contents banging around in the bottom of my bag. I try to melt into the doorframe.

"I can't imagine some guy doing that to me. But it happened. It was crummy, and it's over, right? It's not like someone died or something. She's so consumed by what happened with that Phillip guy, she's forgotten to be our roommate. And she leaves her stuff everywhere."

I watch Hannah pick up my hoodie from the floor—*so that's where it is!*—and toss it atop a pile of notebooks on my desk.

I never promised to be neat. I didn't know it bothered anyone.

"She completely blew off our roomie dinner."

My forehead burns. I lean back onto my heels, unable to enter the room or turn around and flee. I feel like I'm stuck in the middle of a tightrope, about to lose my balance.

"You don't know why she skipped dinner." Palmer slaps her magazine on the floor. "You've gotten a little anal about those Han."

Hannah blows her hair from her face. "I'm just trying to keep us all together." Hannah's voice shakes. "And I have an idea where she was. She's hiding—from everything. Some gorgeous, smart, older guy has sex with her. She totally admitted she was crushing on him, and she got tipsy and kissed him and went back to his hotel room. Duh? I'm sure he thought she *wanted* to sleep with him."

The hungry pit in my stomach from skipping dinner morphs to nausea. Heat crawls across my cheekbones. How can Hannah say all of that? Even though some of it's spot on. I have been hiding. I did skip the roomie dinner on purpose. It's all too much. I'm used to being a loner. And it's near impossible to sort through what happened with Phillip when we're all in the room together. I feel weird opening my Bible in front of everyone, or like a slacker for taking a nap or sleeping in when they're home, or rude if I close the door to the bedroom so I can have some alone time. I've been taking long walks and sitting on benches, trying to think through everything, trying to pray.

Did Phillip think I wanted sex? I keep asking myself that too. Is Hannah right? I second guess myself for the millionth time.

No. I struggle to twist myself out of the knot tightening around me. God told me this wasn't my fault. I said no. Even the counselor I finally got the courage to meet with last week, told me over and over, "It wasn't your fault, Claire."

It wasn't my fault. I might need to see her again. Soon.

I want to yell something at Hannah, but my lips are stuck to my teeth. I trusted her. She was the one who invited me to join this roommate party. She's supposed to take my side. I feel as if someone is plucking out my hairs one by one. Maybe I should stop trusting everyone. I can't live with her, can I? I can't even face her. Can't even speak. But it's not like I can bail from college or like there are extra dorm rooms sitting around.

I'm stuck, again. I'm going to have to pretend it never happened—like I never heard–just like all those times I had to pretend I didn't hear Mom crying or like I didn't notice her locking herself in her room for days on end. I've learned how to do things by myself. I thought college was going to be different, but maybe it's going to be exactly the same.

Strategies spin through my head. I can sleep until they've all gone to class, disappear for the day, and come in late. As Hannah pointed out, I'm not on her schedule anyway.

"You need to ease up, Han." Palmer raises her eyebrows. "Keegan's pushing me to have sex, too, and it's not as easy as just saying no. You have no idea what it's like. Things are so different in the heat of the moment. It's surreal."

"I have no idea?" Hannah points at Palmer. "First of all, I'm sick of you standing up for Claire. You're supposed to be *my* best friend. And second," she flicks out her second finger, "I'm sick of you thinking Keegan's so great. Keegan's a jerk. I know you've been together forever, but think about how he's treating you. That's not the way you treat someone you love! And you shouldn't treat us like we don't matter, just because you're having relationship issues." Hannah sounds like she's about to break down crying. I thought she was angry, but she actually sounds hurt.

"Foul!" Palmer shouts at Hannah. "You are my best friend, but you're not acting like it. Don't' get jealous of Claire. I thought we were all in this together. And it's more than just issues. I really think Keeg and I are through this time." Palmer wipes a tear from her cheek.

Hannah's rant about me has turned into a riff between the besties. Now they'll blame me for their fight. I squeak—too loudly. Hannah jerks her head toward the door.

"Hey, Claire." She glues a fake smile on her face.

But I can't fake anything anymore.

"From now on, I'll just stay out of everyone's way." I

run down the hall, my bag hitting my thigh every other step.

"Claire, wait!" Palmer calls.

But I don't. I can't.

I bolt down the stairs and back out the entrance. I plop down on an iron bench, cold and unforgiving, like Hannah's words. A bike rack flanks the other side of the entrance. I wish one of the bikes was mine and I could pedal away.

But where would I go? I've been running away from my life for so long, and all along I was running to this place. College was supposed to be the answer to my prayers. I worked my tail off in high school to get the scholarship, so I could afford college. I need this degree to make something of myself, to get a job that gets me out of an old apartment in downtown Cleveland. Clarkston was five hours from home, plenty of space to forget the loneliness that's haunted Mom and me ever since Dad left. My roommates were fairytale princesses compared to the girls I rode the bus with in high school. All my roommates have two parents and lovely clothes and bright smiles. They're the girls who never talked to me in school. I thought my roommates were different, that they didn't care that I didn't have designer jeans and a big house. I guess not, at least not Hannah. Palmer stood up for me a little, but she has her own problems.

It helped a little when I told these girls about the rape, these girls I was starting to trust, these girls I was considering must be what sisters were like. Sharing with them was like extracting a bit of the nightmare out of my brain, like Dumbledore pulls his memories and stores them in the Pensieve. Talking to the counselor, Amy, helped a little more. But we didn't get to any of the healing part, just the telling part, this time. The memories aren't gone. The monsters still lurk around every corner and in every quiet moment I feel the pressure of Phillip's body, and I hear the scream I couldn't make escape my mouth. The thud of someone knocking echoes in my ripped up heart.

I slide out my phone.

Mom answers on the first ring. "Claire, how are you?" Her voice sounds like her happiness hinges on my answer. I've been playing along for too long. For years I've said it was no big deal when she missed my dance recitals. I didn't complain my sunglasses were Forever 21 knockoffs of the latest Ray Bans instead of the latest Ray Bans. I nodded and ate the tuna fish and club crackers for days on end, because Mom was too depressed to go to the grocery. When our phones got cut off because Mom forgot to pay the bill, I shrugged. But I've bottled it up for too long.

"Awful!" I scream.

"Mine too!" Mom shouts back.

"No fair. This is my time to vent. My roommates are talking about me behind my back."

"Arnot is seeing another woman behind my back."

All my anger is sucked out of me, like getting the wind knocked out of me. This is how it's always been. Mom needs more help than me. No huge surprise about Arnot, but nasty just the same. I curl up into a corner of the bench, defeated. Stomped on by my roomies and the one place I sought sympathy isn't sympathetic, only pathetic.

Other students walk by, oblivious to the drama on my bench. I pull my sunglasses from my bag and cover my eyes.

"His wife," Mom whimpers.
"He's married?" Gross.

"Yeah. Guess so." Mom sniffs. "Oh Claire, I didn't want to tell you, because I know you like Phillip so much, and I didn't want you to worry about me.

"That's a whole other story. How'd you find out?" I say like a robot, used to listening to Mom's getting dumped stories.

"I hadn't heard from Arnot in two days." I hear Mom blowing her nose.

"Right." Cradling my phone on my ear, I start braiding a thin strand from my part down one side of my head. How fitting for Mom to have a major drama, just when I really needed her.

Mom inhales. "So I texted him."

"And?" I start on a second braid next to the first, weaving my hair in and out and over and under.

"And I get a text back immediately. His name pops up on my phone, but it's not from him." Mom sniffles and snuffles. "It read, 'Who are you? And why are you texting my husband? Never use this number again!'"

"Oh, Mom." Okay, so I feel a bit selfish and jerky. She has a right to be needy. This guy is the worst.

"He seemed too good to be true, and he was," she squawks between sobs.

"He and his nephew both." Oops! I meant to just say that in my head, but I'm pissed at Arnot, sick of taking the back seat to Mom's traumas, and wounded by Hannah's words. I'm out of armor and filters, just down to my raw skin.

"What do you mean?" Mom asks.

I've practiced how I'd tell her a thousand times—on our plane ride home, in my bed, walking to class—but rehearsals are over. It's show time. "I didn't want to tell you, because of Arnot." I swallow, trying to detain the tears enough to spit out my story. "Phillip raped me." I look around, hoping no one heard.

LAURA L. SMITH

"What?" Mom gasps.

I shiver, feeling nauseated as I think about retelling what happened. But I've started. I can't stop mid pirouette. And at this point, what do I have to lose? Things can't get any worse. I stand and stroll down the sidewalk leading through the quad.

"That night, after the Eiffel Tower, he took me back to our hotel. He asked me to go to his room." I wipe the sticky tears slipping from under my shades with the back of my hand. "I don't know what I was thinking. I was so stupid, Mom. I just thought…" I sniff and rummage in my bag for a Kleenex. "I never thought about a boy and a hotel room. It was Phillip, and he was charming, and I trusted him. He told me to trust him, and I did."

Mom's voice contorts like a rubber band snapping. "In his room, you two had sex?"

I nod and then shake my head, not that she can see. "*We* didn't. *He* did. It was like I wasn't there, but my body was. I don't know, Mom. One minute we were talking and the next he pushed me down and forced himself on me. When he reached for the phone, I ran."

"Why didn't you tell me?" Mom asks, crying too.

"Because you were crazy about Arnot. Because I drank wine and wore a short dress. Because I let him kiss me. Because I'm so scared, Mom."

"You should have told me."

Really? I doubt it would have helped if I'd told her. She's too messed up in her own problems to help. Strangely, though, I feel like one of the bars from my cage has been removed. Not having to hide this from Mom anymore is liberating. I run my fingers down my skinny braids and pick up my pace.

"I couldn't tell you."

"Did he hurt you?"

"A little," I confess. "There was a lot of blood, but I'm all right."

"Blood? Where was I?"

"Out with Arnot. I cleaned it up. I went to bed. I didn't want you to worry."

"Did you kick him? Did you scream for help?"

Why does everyone ask that? Why didn't I think to hurt him or yell? I answer, "No and no. I couldn't move. I couldn't think. It was like I was paralyzed. Like it was a bad movie I was watching, but I couldn't do anything."

"You need to get to a doctor," Mom mumbles.

"*Mmm hmm.*" I say, remembering Hannah's identical words. Maybe she cares a little, maybe Hannah does, too, and maybe I will go see a doctor, but that's not what matters most. What matters most is that even though I still have to carry the burden of being raped. But I'm not going to carry the burden of hiding it anymore.

It's all out there. My roommates know. Mom knows. Even a plump, forty-something woman with mousy brown hair knows. There's no turning back now, whatever that means. Whatever they want to think. However they want to judge. Although my body feels raw, the pressure of Phillip's body smothering me is lighter. Just the relief of letting Mom know, even if she's incapable of helping, lightens me.

"Hey, Mom," I say.

"Yeah?"

"Arnot's a jerk!"

"Indeed." She sighs. "I'd like to wring his nephew's neck."

"At least we got to see the Eiffel Tower," I offer, my

voice still shaky.

Mom sniffles. "That's true. The Eiffel Tower and everything else too. Maybe there is a little good in all this." She sighs loudly. "My heart still hurts. I thought Arnot was the one."

I never thought he was, but my heart hurts too. *Mom, remember we were talking about me?* I shout it in my head, but instead I ask, "Did you text his wife back?"

"Not yet. I was too in shock. But, I'm going to. If I were Arnot's wife, I'd want to know the truth. What she and Arnot do with the truth is their business."

It sounds like Mom has a next step, a place to go, a plan of action. Truth is good.

"Claire, baby, I'm so sorry," she murmurs.

"Me, too," I say, tucking my hair behind my ears.

"You okay? I wish I could come down."

I could try to guilt her into coming, but it's pointless. She can't miss a day of teaching to drive down here and hold my hand. Plus, I'd probably end up holding hers. What good would it do? I need to do this on my own.

Not completely on your own. I'm here, Claire, and you need Me.

That is so true. I do need God. Now more than ever. Comforted by His presence, despite the scene in my room and the drama on the other end of the phone, I breathe in the scent of leaves on the verge of changing colors—a new season, a new chance.

Thanks, God. I know. I just don't always remember.

"I'm fine, Mom, really." I roll my eyes, telling them not to tear any more. "I just had to tell you."

"You can tell me anything, sweetie. But maybe you should see a counselor, too. They have those on campus, right? We'll work through this. We always do."

"Yeah. There's hope for us." I won't tell Mom about my counselor, yet. Maybe I'll let Mom think it was her idea. Seeing Amy again would be good. I have a lot more to tell her.

"Tomorrow, I'll start sending bombs to Arnot's office. It seems like a good place to start." I pick up my pace, noticing dark rain clouds rolling in over the quad.

"Okay, so we both have our to-do lists." Mom cracks up. "I love you."

"I love you, too, Mom. And I'm sorry about Arnot."

"Me, too. Really, really sorry," she whimpers.

33
HANNAH

"I AM SUCH A WITCH!" I yell. Wishing away the awful, stinging words I said. "I didn't mean any of it. I can't believe Claire heard me. Oh, Palm, I'm so sorry! What am I going to do?"

"You have to do something." Palmer glares at me.

"What can I do? Palm, I'm sorry. You're right." I sit down next to her, closing the space between us. "I don't know what it's like to be pressured into sex, because I'm not even being pressured into kissing! Nobody likes me. A.J. has a girlfriend." I sob. My stomach churns; like that time I ate raw oysters on a dare and spent the entire night vomiting in the bathroom. I plead with my eyes for Palmer to forgive me, for her to let me fix at least that piece.

"It's all right." Palmer wipes a tear from her cheek.

I lean over and hug her. "I'm really, really sorry. You're my best friend in the world. You always have been. I just

251

hate seeing Keegan treat you like this. You deserve so much better."

"I know."

"I completely slammed Claire, and she is driving me crazy, for the record, but not as bad as I made it out to be. I just feel like I keep picking up the room, and she keeps dumping all her crap all over the place. I didn't mean for her to hear, and I didn't mean what I said about the rape." I grab a Kleenex, hand one to Palmer and blow my nose loudly. "I wanted us all to meet for dinner and get caught up, and I had it in my planner. I wrote a note on the dry erase board." I bounce my leg up and down, and feel my face flush. I can't sit. I stand up and toss my tissue in the trash.

"Then Kat texted she had late practice." It doesn't take me long to pace to the end of our tiny room. I stop at the wall and turn around. "And Claire didn't even send a message. It's like she's in some kind of dream world half the time. Then we saw Zach at the dining hall, and he sat with us instead." I stomp my foot. I look to Palmer for confirmation of how awful this all is, but she just looks at me, letting me get it all out. I only rant like this once or twice a year. I hate it when I do. I hate myself like this. But when I get this way, I can't stop. I feel the anger and the anxiety gushing out of me, nonstop.

"And it wasn't supposed to be dinner with Zach. He talks and talks and talks, and no matter how nice he is, he bugs the daylights out of me. And if he is going to sit and yap at me all through dinner, I'd at least like A.J. to see and be jealous."

"It's all my fault!" Tears flood my face. "I'm not even mad at Claire, am I?"

"Of course not, sweetie. You love Claire. We all do."

Palmer sniffs.

"I'm mad at me. Mad I don't have a boyfriend. Mad things aren't falling into place like they're supposed to. Mad I'm not good at anything. Claire has her ballet, and Kat's got soccer. You have every boy on campus drooling after you, and you'll find out in a couple of days if you made the magazine staff, which you will. I know you have this stuff with Keegan. I'm sorry. I've been a crummy friend, too. I haven't been a good listener. I was completely insensitive. I'm trying so hard to make it all work." I gasp for air and sit back down.

"I don't know what I'm going to do," Palmer says. "He's so angry. We've broken up twice since I left for school three weeks ago. And in between we fell in love again. I'm all jumbled and tangled." Palmer waves her hands around frantically, grabs another Kleenex, hands one to me, and dabs her eyes. "And you are good at things, tons of things. You were Class President and in the National Honor Society, for crying out loud. You can sing and play the piano. You're so organized and pulled together. Maybe you're trying too hard to make everything perfect, Han."

I scowl. "I want to try hard. That's the one thing I do well, right? A-for-effort, Hannah, that's me. I want our room to be cute, and for us to all be best friends, and to get all A's, and to find a boyfriend." I blow my nose again, standing up. "And I don't think that's too much to ask, Palm. I mean I did it all in high school, right? And our room is cute, and we can all be besties. Can't we? Or did I ruin that?" I pace back and forth. "Did I screw up our chances to be best friends? I'll never forgive myself if I did."

"We're already best friends. I mean *all* of us, Kat and Claire, too. We depend on each other and balance each other.

But that's not something you do. That's something we are."

I let that thought land on my brain. I try to tackle everything through a to-do list. What if friendship does itself? What can I control? What have I accomplished? The room.

"And the room rocks," I say. "Did you see the room next door? Hideous! They need to apply to Extreme Makeover Dorm Edition." My pulse slowly returns to normal, as I realize not everything is chaos.

"Hilarious! They should," Palmer says. "But you can't make *everything* pretty and polka dotty, Han."

I collapse back on the futon next to her, feeling like a popped balloon. "I want to," I squeak.

"I want to, too." Palmer's eyes cloud over. "I want everything with Keegan to read like a romance novel, but it's more like a chorus from a Taylor Swift song. I want things how they were, but instead they're how they are." She bites her lip.

It's hard for me to believe things aren't perfect for Palmer— that she feels out of control too. She's always been the gorgeous one with the boyfriend, the tennis star, the homecoming queen, the editor of the school newspaper, and I've always been her friend.

"Claire's got so much baggage, Han. Maybe she *is* in a dream, or more like a nightmare." Palmer tugs on the green bracelet strung around her wrist. "Keegan was my boyfriend. I love him. I mean, I did love him." Her mouth twists. "And I'm a wreck about him trying to have sex with me. Someone Claire barely knows did this to her, but he didn't just try. He did it." She unties her bracelet and sets it on the desk behind her.

"And I'm whining because chatterbox Zach talks to me.

Too much, I'd like to add." I blow my nose. "I sound like an elephant." I breathe all jaggedly, like I can't even get a handle on my oxygen intake. Nothing flusters me more than when I mess up.

"A cute elephant." Palmer hands me another Kleenex.

"How am I going to fix things with Claire? I've ruined everything!" Hot, sloppy tears flood my face. "All I wanted was for us to be there for each other, and I totally ditched her."

34
KAT

"WHO'S GOING IN FOR SECONDS?" Molly shouts. She stands and rubs her hand through her spiky, black hair. "I'm absolutely famished. I think it's the extra laps Coach had us run after practice."

"Me." I grab my tray and return to the burrito bar, where I make myself a giant wrap loaded with guacamole, black beans, lettuce, cheddar cheese and pico de gallo.

"It's better with sour cream." Tony plops a spoonful of sour cream on the side of my plate.

"Thanks." I laugh. "How was y'all's practice?"

"Crazy. Coach thinks we're robots, not people. I swear he expects us to make every shot."

"Sounds like our coaches have been conspiring."

Tony follows me back to my table. His tray is piled with three burritos and a salad.

"I haven't seen you in a while," he mumbles, through a forkful of Tex-Mex. "Except, you know, across the fields."

I stab a bite of burrito and swirl it in the sour cream. "Yeah. I knew it would be demanding playin' a sport and takin' classes, but I had no idea how crazy it would be. I'm wakin' up early for practice, stayin' up late trying to get all of my course work done, and wavin' to my roommates on the way in and out of our room. I was supposed to meet them for dinner, but when it started to rain at the end of practice, I didn't have the energy to trudge across campus in the downpour. I'm wiped."

I pop a bite in my mouth. "How do you manage it all? Any advice for a freshman athlete?"

"I don't know. You get the hang of it." He downs half a glass of milk. "Listen, Kat." Tony leans across the table. "About that day, what was it, a week and a half ago, outside Corner Cup."

I take another bite, waiting to hear what he'll say.

"I could tell you were a little freaked. The K2 is just my unwind mechanism. You know, keeps the stress level down, so I don't explode."

I nod, my hand shaking a little as I keep eating.

"I'm here on scholarship. There's no way I could afford to go here otherwise. Not to mention the scouts are already hovering like buzzards, and it's only my junior year. I want to play pro. There's so much on the line." He stabs some lettuce with his fork.

"I've felt pretty high strung myself lately."

"See. You know what it's like." He nods and jams the salad in his mouth. "So the K2, it's legal. It's relaxing. It just takes off some of the edge. That's all. Like a glass of wine."

"Just helps you chill." I nod, my mind racing with the paper I have to finish writing tonight. "Doesn't the smoking mess up your breathin' on the field?"

Tony crunches on a chip. "Dunno. Haven't noticed. I mean, I'm always winded after a game or practice, but so is every other guy on the team." He shrugs. "I figure a lot of the guys are drinking or getting high to unwind or doing steroids to perform. What I'm doing is nothing in comparison."

Molly's and Courtney's chairs squeak as they push them back from the table, stand and grab their trays. I hope they didn't hear. Any talk about chemicals could bring any player, or the whole team, down. Way down. "Exam tomorrow." Courtney waves.

"And I have a paper." Molly frowns. "See ya, Kat. See ya, Tony."

"G'night, y'all."

When they've cleared from the table, I lean forward and whisper, "I'd heard people drank and stuff, but if anyone finds out, underage players could get kicked off the team, right? I can't believe anyone would be so stupid!"

"Right. Making drinking and drugs *so* not an option." Tony dips a chip in sour cream. "Not for serious athletes like you and me. Ya know, a lot of these guys," he tilts his head to indicate our teammates, "don't care what happens after college. You and I have our eyes set on higher sights. We train harder than them. We eat better than them." He points his fork to our salads and milk. Not that I eat healthy all the time, but a lot of the players are chugging sodas and making meals out of French fries. "We all find coping mechanisms. Mine are caffeine and K2—both legal. Both within our athletic guidelines."

"Smart." I steal one of his chips and dip it in the swirl of salsa and sour cream on the side of my plate. My brain feels like the mixture of sauces. What are my coping mechanisms? How am I going to find chill in the midst of all these pressures?

I gulp the rest of my milk and wipe my mouth. "All this talk about findin' ways to get everything done reminds me I still have to study for a quiz and write a paper tonight. I've gotta hit it."

"It's pouring out there. Want a ride?" Tony asks.

I glance out the windows at the deluge of rain. It sounds like it's pelting the glass so hard, it just might get in.

"Yes, please."

We dash from the dining hall to Tony's beat up car.

I feel déjà vu of when Nicholas drove me home from soccer in the rain. Was that really just a few weeks ago? My whole life seems completely different now.

At my dorm, ready to hop out, Tony grabs my arm.

"What?" I ask, looking around to see if I've forgotten something.

"You really tear it up out there, Kat."

I retract my other hand from the door handle and sink back into my seat, a shiver shooting down my spine. "Thanks. Ya know, I've been tryin', but everyone on the team here is so strong. I hardly stand out anymore. I even whiffed a shot in our game against Vandy." I wasn't expecting to tell Tony any of this. The last thing I want him to think is I can't handle myself on the field, but after our chat at dinner, I know he feels the pressure too.

"Wasn't that two weeks ago? Let it go. Everyone misses sometimes." He leans a little closer.

"Not you, I'm guessin'."

Tony laughs, his dreads shaking against his shoulders. "Not in awhile, but I have plenty of screw ups on the field."

"Right." I shake my head. His hand is still on my arm,

connecting our soccer woes and us.

"Really," he whispers and kisses me. His kiss is warm and strong and urgent. It seems to say, "I understand what it's like out there. I get it. I need you to get me, too. We need this connection."

Time is irrelevant as I let my stress dissolve in the warmth and strength and vulnerability of Tony's lips. Before my brain focuses on what's going on, he pulls back, gives my mouth one last little kiss, and says, "We're good for each other, Kat. Good luck with that paper."

"Thanks." I give him the rock, our knuckles connecting for a brief second, scoop up my ball, and exit into the rain.

35
PALMER

I CHECKED THE DANCE STUDIO already.

Hannah took the dining hall and uptown.

It's getting dark outside as I make my way into the library. Claire could be crouching in any of the clusters of tables, sofas, or the hundreds of cubbies here. The squishing sound of my Hunter rain boots on the carpet seems amplified as I walk through the silent aisles.

Whenever I feel like I'm losing my composure, I run to the bathroom. Maybe Claire does too. I duck into the restroom, wishing the door didn't squeak so loudly. I look under all of the stalls. No Claire.

Leaving, I catch a glimpse of my sloppy self in the mirror. Despite my umbrella, the rain smeared my mascara. I dampen a rough, brown paper towel and dab under my eyes, erasing the black smudges. I center my silver cross on its chain, so it falls in the center of my clavicle.

My damp hair looks like a fashion "don't". I fluff my

tresses with my fingers, tucking strategic pieces behind my ears. "There." Now I look intentionally mussed, instead of a victim of the weather. A coat of Lip Glass looks more like rain than make-up, and is the perfect touch.

I pull out my phone to text Hannah with an update, but see a message from Keegan. Why is he texting me if he hates me? He attached the song "Free Falling" by John Mayer. Keegan and I watched that acoustic John Mayer concert on TV one rainy Saturday. I've sung along to the song, but never thought about the lyrics.

"I'm a bad boy 'cause I don't even miss her."

Did he text me to tell me he doesn't miss me? Perfect. Just what I needed to hear. The whole song is full of contradictions, just like Keegan and me. John Mayer, whose version is way better than Tom Petty's, sings praises to the girl and is totally thinking about her, but at the same time knows he's hurt her and doesn't care! Dang it, Keegan! I want to shout, but the library's silence is stifling.

I slide my phone back into my purse and bump my textured journal cover.

When I write a paper for English or that article I submitted to *Quad Angles*, the student magazine, my fingers fly across the keyboard of my MacBook. But when I need to sort out my feelings or reflect on my day, I prefer my journal. Why haven't I opened it in so long?

I make my way out of the ladies room to the sofas with a good view of the door. At least I'll see Claire if she comes in or out while sitting here. I shift into the squishy seat and slide my cloth-covered book out of my black leather bag. After digging for a minute, I find one of my favorite pens. It makes my words bold and easy to read, solid like my thoughts.

I open to a blank page and jot down the lyrics from "Free Falling," which are stuck in my head. I write Keegan's name in bold letters down the margin of the page, contemplating how they fit together. And then, as if by themselves, the words flow.

I love Keegan. I have always loved Keegan, for as long as I can remember loving anything or anyone. Well, that's not actually true. Before Keegan, there was my family: Mom, Dad, Tia, and don't forget Thunder. I smile thinking of my sweet, gray kitty and doodle a kitten next to her name. *And God, I have always loved God. Always. So I have always felt love, but it has not always involved Keegan.*

Hmm. I shift my weight.

So even though I feel like I need him, like he defines me, he doesn't actually define me. Keegan is part of me. He has been an important part of me for a long time. Does he always need to be part of me?

I nibble on the end of my pen. Does he?

Before coming to Clarkston, I spent every day with Keegan and did almost everything with him. But here, my roommates fit into a lot of the slots Keegan used to. I study with them and eat with them and laugh with them and watch movies with them. I share with them about my day and my classes, and although they don't always get it, they understand me better than Keegan about some things.

Really? I think back to Keegan making fun of my writing. My roommates urged me to apply for *Quad Angles*, listened to my story ideas, gave me suggestions. Keegan told me I didn't need to major in journalism, because I would be a perfect wife without the degree. At the time, I'd been a flutter with him mentioning me being his wife, not realizing he wasn't supporting my passion.

Maybe Keegan just wants me to be passionate about him.

PASSION – I write in swirly letters. *Things I'm passionate about: God, my family, writing, my roommates, fashion, Keegan. Keegan—kissing Keegan makes me feel alive, on fire, wanted, needed, nervous.*

Why did I write Keegan makes me nervous? Because I'm afraid of what he'll do next. Afraid he'll want me to do something I'm not ready to do. The last time I saw him, having my period was a blessing—a way out, but only a temporary one. What happens next time? How will I tell him no again? Could I tell him no again? Would he explode if I did?

EXPLOSION! I write.

Light bulb! Keegan can't stand it when I decide—when I do something for me. He's only happy when he's in control. Most of the time I like him to be in control. But not always. I close my book and kiss the cover.

Thank you, God. I know You've given me this pen and page to find myself, the real me, the person You created. Thanks for the clarity.

Rubbing the soft cloth of the cover like a lucky rabbit's foot, I tuck it back in my purse. I've been so crazy busy with classes and going home the other weekend. It's a gift to sit with my thoughts. I reach for Keegan's bracelet, to twirl it around my wrist, but remember I left it in the dorm. I picture Hannah's tantrum, and Kat bursting into tears last night, because she's overworked and exhausted, and poor Claire traipsing off to who knows where.

Maybe we've all been too busy to sit with our thoughts. Maybe we all need a weekend on the couch, relaxing and regrouping. I stand, looking forward to the wet walk home to process.

36
HANNAH

I SLUSH ALONG THE SIDEWALKS toward our dining hall, a damp chill dripping down my neck. All of campus seems to be hiding under a giant umbrella. I feel hollow, like those plastic eggs used for Easter egg hunts—cute and perky on the outside, but someone has taken out the candy inside. The prize, the sweetness, the value is gone.

No one stands at the entrance checking ID's. Workers clear tables and empty trashcans. Only a few students are scattered throughout the hall finishing dinner. It doesn't take long to figure out Claire is not one of them.

I check the student center. I feel like a ghost floating through the food court. The irresistible smells of mozzarella melting on pizza and French fries sizzling in oil fill the air, but I'm not the least bit hungry. The only thing I'm craving is a chance to patch things up with Claire—to fix what I've broken. I walk aimlessly past the food lines and the tables littered with trays and text books, scanning the faces of countless students, not caring if they notice me staring at them.

Feeling helpless, I head to the exit. I pull out my phone. No messages.

It's raining harder now. Squinting at the rain spraying my face, I pop open my umbrella. Between my umbrella shield and the torrents of rain, would I even see Claire if I walked right past her? Would she want me to?

The streets of downtown seem like they've been evacuated. I duck into the bagel shop.

"What you in the mood for?" asks a guy with bleached blonde hair and spacers in his ears.

"Just looking for someone," I mumble, glancing at the picnic tables, not seeing a trace of anyone even slightly Claireesque.

The pizza place next door is empty. The workers don't even notice me slide in and out as they toss dough in the air and fold white cardboard boxes for deliveries.

The rain blows past my umbrella and in my face. Stray stringy hairs frizz from every possible follicle on my head. There are more restaurants, but I can't make my feet take the necessary steps to get there. I'm drenched all the way through my shoes to my skin. Even my bones feel soggy.

Feeling utterly defeated, I take the shortest route I know back toward the dorm. I clutch my purse to my side, somehow feeling if I can protect Claire's hoodie I packed in case I found her, I can protect some fragment of warmth and safety for her, even though I'm to blame for fracturing her fragile shell. The grayness of the rain melts into the darkness of evening. It feels like it takes an endless, empty hour to get back.

I slide my key and stomp my feet once inside the dorm. I prop my open umbrella on a doormat along with a collection of others to dry. I pull off my damp jacket and shake it out.

Okay.

Home.

Safe.

But what about Claire?

I'm drawn back to the lounge with the piano like a magnet to metal. The room is dark, but the piano light has been turned on, illuminating the keys.

I think back to the day A.J. found me here. I'd love to have him find me again. I'd love to have him find me and wrap his strong arms around me or offer me the thick Clarkston sweatshirt he usually wears. But he isn't here. No one is. I am completely and totally alone.

And truth is, that day A.J. liked my music, he ended up talking on and on about Maggie and their squabbles, and I am so not up for that right now.

I finger the keys, playing "A Little Fall of Rain" from *Les Mis*. It feels good not to think, or organize, or plan or strategize, but to let my fingers flow back and forth and up and down the keyboard. The absolute emptiness I felt searching for Claire seems a bit less painful.

My piano prescription heals me as much as it can. The rest of my healing needs to come from finding Claire, apologizing to her for being such a witch, learning how to manage my life, finding a way to accept my imperfections.

I think you mean it needs to come from Me. Time to let go, Hannah.

I stand, waving away the notion of letting things go, just when I need to hold on so tightly. How else could I fix things? I walk up the stairs, water squishing in my shoes with each step. Our hall, although lit, seems dark and dreary.

In front of our doorway, Claire sits huddled in a wet lump.

"Claire!" I run to her, fishing her hoodie from my bag. "I am so sorry!" I burst into tears.

She looks up at me, blankly, as if she doesn't even recognize me. I drape the sweatshirt over her shoulders.

"Can't find my key card." She shrugs.

"I didn't mean any of it."

Claire doesn't snap at me. Instead, she stands up, slides her arms into her sweatshirt and tilts her head. "Thanks."

"I love you, sweetie! I really, really do. I am so glad you are my roommate, and I didn't mean anything I said." I sniff. "I'm so mad at *myself*." I unlock the door and step into our dark room.

"You are?" Claire's eyes twitch as she follows me.

"I thought college was my end all, my ultimate calling, you know. I'm a planner, an organizer. This was going to be my world. But I'm failing."

"Hardly." Claire curls up in the corner of the futon, shivering.

"I can't dance, and I don't have a sense of style like you. I can kick a ball, but I'm meant for intramurals not varsity like Kat. Even Palmer's tragedy seems like a thrill for me, as pathetic as that is. I wish I could get one boy, just one to like me, but she has a boyfriend who's obsessed with her. And I got a 'C' on my exam today." I toss my purse on my desk. Crap! I hadn't meant to let that slip out. I was going to go in during office hours and beg for extra credit to raise my grade, and no one was ever going to know.

"You didn't tell me you got a 'C.'" Palmer's voice penetrates the room. Even though she's soaked, Palmer looks like she stepped out of a magazine—damp tendrils perfectly placed across her olive skin, her dark eyelashes thicker and heavier than normal with moisture. "That explains everything, Han." She winks and walks over to the coffee maker. "Claire, sweetie, where were you? We must have looked at least half of the hiding places on campus!"

"You were looking for me?" Claire asks, eyes wide.

"Hannah organized a search party. I'm surprised you didn't see the flares," Palmer says, and walks into the bathroom, where I hear her filling the pot with water.

Claire smiles a little and shivers.

I walk back into the bedroom and peel off my soaked jeans and shirt, replacing them with soft pajamas. "Need some dry clothes?" I ask.

"Not yet. Thanks. I, um, I just need a minute."

"Really?" Palmer asks, walking past me with the coffee pot full of water back to our family room. "You got a 'C'!"

"Uh, yeah," I grumble, setting my shoes over a vent to dry, avoiding eye contact.

"I'll be lucky if I pull 'C's' in everything." Claire sighs.

"Enough about my bad grade!" I groan. "Claire, please, please, please forgive me?"

"I do." She looks down. "We're roommates." Claire's words are slow and quiet, as if she's thinking about each one before she says it out loud, which is the opposite of what I did, letting every evil thought I'd ever had just blast out of my trap earlier. "You were right about some of the stuff you said. I have been completely lost in what happened with Phillip, and it's affecting everything I do, including my grades." Her voice sounds as shaky as she looks.

I sit next to her on the futon.

"Aren't you on scholarship?" I try to blow my damp bangs out of my eyes, but they're plastered against my forehead. I brush them away with my fingers.

"Only if I keep a B-average." Claire hugs her knees to her chest, making her even smaller. "See, I want to let go of what happened, I really do, because it hurts so much, and I'm so scared." Claire sniffs and points to the picture of the Eiffel Tower on our wall. "But I love Paris. I've always loved Paris. It was #1 on my bucket list. Now every day when I go to French class, I smile for a second, and then totally freeze at the thought of what happened in that hotel room."

A sweet, spicy scent wafts through the air as Palmer hands us steaming mugs of tea. The cup feels good on my shivering hands. I hold it and hover over its warmth.

Claire takes a long drink. "Thanks. I don't deserve this. I've been a crummy roommate. But I'm going to try to do better." She pulls her hood over her head, so her face peeks out like a little child. "I am a slob, and I've been sticking to myself, because it's safer."

I rub Claire's leg. "You're not a crummy roommate. I don't think you have to let go of Paris, just of the pain?" I question my words, hoping they're what Claire needs to hear.

"Palm, you're the best." I gulp the warm cinnamon tea. It slides down my throat, soothing my shivery angst.

Palmer sits on the other side of Claire. "I was thinking about this tea the whole wet walk home. I thought it would be rude not to share." She blows at the surface of her mug.

"You know, I thought I could run away from everything here at college and completely reinvent myself." Claire's words drop one by one like raindrops. "I wanted to get away from Mom's depressing, nervous energy. I thought here I could escape the memories of Dad and what he did and then what Phillip did, but it feels like everything followed me." She exhales. "And the craziest part is, part of me wanted it to follow me, so I wouldn't forget the fear or the pain, so I don't dissolve like Mom did when Dad left." Claire pauses. "Mom just stopped being normal, because she pretended nothing happened, like nothing was wrong, when everything was."

"Seems to be going around," Kat chirps from the door.

"Let me get you a cup." Palmer hops from the couch. "You look like you could use it."

"I sure could use something," Kat sighs.

"What happened?" I ask.

"Same old thing. I should not be allowed to talk to boys, period." Kat pulls her sweatshirt over her head. "I need to change. You've got the right idea, Han. Jams are the uniform of choice."

37
PALMER

I REFILL EVERYONE'S TEA CUPS, inhaling the cinnamon and hoping it will flow all the way down from my nose to my heart, which feels a little more settled, but still achy.

We're all in our pj's now, cozier, more relaxed, but there's also something in the air, something fragile—so close to shattering or shining, depending on which way we lean. Like our flannel pants and tea cups and polka dotted accessories are the only things holding us together.

"I sure hope this is caffeinated." Kat raises her eyebrows as I hand her a mug. "I feel an all-nighter comin' on."

"Not for me. I can barely talk about this for another minute, let alone an hour," Claire pleads. "I called my mom before someone let me in the dorm." She takes her cup from me with shaky fingers and smiles. "I'm glad I told her everything, but I'm completely drained and completely

277

starving."

Kat laughs. "Sorry. Not laughing at you, Claire Bear. I should probably talk about the mess I'm in for awhile, but don't know if I have the energy for it either. I meant an all-nighter 'cause I have piles of homework I need to get finished before sunrise. Caffeine?" She looks at me.

"Sorry, sweets. It's herbal."

"Dang it!" Kat laughs.

"Claire did you not eat?" Hannah asks.

Claire shakes her head.

"Oh my goodness, sweetie," Hannah and I say in unison.

Hannah digs in a bin and pulls out a banana and one of the granola bars Claire always seems to be eating and brings them over to her.

"Here," Hannah offers. "Sorry about dinner." I see how sorry Hannah is. I know it's killing her that she blew up. The "C" was the trigger. I should have known.

"It's over." Claire shrugs. "Fall's starting. A new season. Okay?"

"Okay." Hannah smiles and wipes a single tear.

"Okay, girls," I say, sitting. "You guys might not want to talk anymore, but I need to talk to you. I need some girly advice." I savor a warm sip of the tea as it slides across my tongue. "When I was at the library looking for Claire, I had a sudden realization."

"You were looking for me at the library?" Claire looks at me sweetly.

"We had to find you, sweetie."

She smiles and burrows deeper into her sweatshirt.

"So when I couldn't find Claire, I started journaling about all the crap that's going on with me and Keegan, and I figured some stuff out. I'm just not sure what to do with it. I need your help."

"What'd you figure out?" Hannah asks, cozying up next to me.

"I figured out Keegan is a great boyfriend when he calls the shots." I exhale and sit up straighter, gathering my words. "Everything was so easy in high school. We did the same things. We had the same friends. We wanted the same things. When he wanted something, we did it, and it worked, almost all the time."

"He *has* always called the shots." Hannah looks at me.

"Really?"

"I hinted about it before. And Ally came right out and said it one time, but you were livid. See the thing was, you were happy." Hannah blows her bangs. "But if he wanted to see you, you dropped us for him."

My eyes sting. Hannah's right. "Sorry," I whisper.

Hannah rubs my knee. "He didn't ask you to do anything terrible, and you never missed anything really important. He's totally into you, Palm. He was just controlling, that's all. And now, he's out of control." She nods, like that sums it up.

"Okay." I tuck my legs under me. "So now Keegan's asking me to do something I don't want to do. Actually two things."

"I know he wants to sleep with you," Claire says. "What's the other?"

"He wants me to transfer to Polaris State."

"You can tell him to go jump in a creek." Kat sneers. "No way is he gettin' you away from us."

"Amen, sister." Hannah squeezes me.

"Thanks, guys. I'm not going to transfer, and I'm not

ready for sex."

"So now what?" Hannah asks.

My lip quivers, and tears well in the corners of my eyes. "Crap. I was doing so well. That's the part where I have no clue. I know I should dump him for good, but…" My lips pucker then pout, unable to form more words without crying.

"And I thought the fact I just made out with Tony in his car was messed up." Kat taps her rings on her mug.

"Get out!" Hannah shouts.

"True." Kat shakes her head. "It was nice, too. I just have no business kissin' boys."

"Didn't you just kiss Nicholas like last week?" Hannah's eyes bug out of her face.

"Bingo."

"I'm dying to kiss a boy!" Hannah screams. "How unfair is it that all of you have boys chasing you down, doing more than you want, and I'm chasing boys around wishing for a little hand holding or a peck on the cheek."

"Zach is ready and waiting." I raise my eyebrows at Hannah.

"That so does not count!" Hannah stomps her foot.

Claire laughs, just a little squeak at first, but then an all out giggle.

I join in. Hannah's outburst was priceless. And I have to laugh at the irony of our situations, so I don't keep crying.

"Glad I could provide the comic relief." Hannah laughs too, and Kat snorts.

"I hope you figure out things with Keegan." Claire smiles. "I really do. And, Hannah, I hope you find a boyfriend, a sweet one. You deserve one." Claire's eyes dart back and forth before lowering. She starts braiding a thin strand of hair on the right of her face. "And, Kat, I hope you figure out what you want. But somehow it makes me feel less alone, knowing you're all right here with me."

"It's like we're all playing four square," I blurt.

"How do you mean?" Hannah asks.

"Remember playing four square on the playground as a kid?"

"Sure." Claire stops braiding to look at me. "I hate that game."

"Really?" Kat asks. "What's to hate?"

"The cool girls always ganged up on me and tried to get me out." Claire rolls her eyes.

"But you are the cool girl," Hannah says.

Claire opens her mouth wide and closes it again. "Not according to my school. I'm the pipsqueak ballerina girl."

"No. You're not that at all," Hannah says. "You are petite and beautiful and creative and unique. You know that day I met you at orientation? I was smitten with your braids and your skirt and your smile and the way you weren't clinging to anyone, but strong enough to sit by yourself."

"The strong part is an act, but thanks." Claire looks at Hannah. I think they might have officially made up.

"I promise to never gang up on you, Claire Bear." Kat grins. "But I want to hear more about the four square thing, Palm. I love that game."

"Well, it's like four square, but we're not trying to get each other out." I pat Claire's arm. "We're trying to keep each other in. We're all in this game together, but we're each in our own squares—A, B, C, and D."

"Which square am I?" Kat asks, leaning forward.

"A, of course. I have a feeling you were in A every day at recess."

"I hung out in A every once in awhile." Kat tugs my

hair.

"So we all have different problems with guys. That's our game. And we're all playing it together." I roll my shoulders back, more and more confident as I explain.

"But we're facing completely different situations, coming at it from different angles. Right?" Hannah asks.

"Four Square." Claire nods. "I like it. As long as you guys are helping me stay in. I could really use the help."

"You've got it." Kat smiles.

"Problem is…" Hannah taps a pen on a pad of paper she's holding. "We need a ref, because we sure are having a hard time figuring out the rules by ourselves."

"You can say that again." I put down my teacup.

"We need a ref," Hannah starts, "because we sure are…"

Kat slaps her. "Funny girl."

"Seriously," Hannah continues. "We do need someone wiser to help us out."

"The only clarity I've had since we've been here is when I manage to spend some time with my Bible," Claire admits.

"I've been runnin' around so crazy from soccer to class, I've barely even thought about God." Kat looks down at her socks. "Dang it. I do so much better when I talk to Him."

"God was there when I was journaling tonight. He really showed me what I needed to know about Keegan," I say, feeling warm all over, and not just from the tea.

"I feel Him here right now," Hannah whispers, eyes glistening. "Here in our midst."

Our room is silent.

Goose bumps prickle my thighs.

"If two or more are gathered in my name, there I am,"

Claire whispers. "Jesus says so in Matthew."

Kat taps her rings. "So where do we start?"

"Right here. Right now." I reach on my bookshelf for my Bible.

"Okay." Hannah picks up a pad of paper. I read something the other day on my Bible App. I think I'm supposed to share it with you guys." She taps her pen on the page. "In Matthew 28, Jesus ascends to heaven and tells the disciples they need to stick together, and that even though they might forget, He would always be with them."

I feel a quiver in my stomach and exhale. "I haven't been very good at remembering He's with me lately." The tears come again, warm and wet.

"And we all need to stick together," Kat says. "Palmer, you and I talked about that the day we went shopping. God brought us all together."

I nod, remembering. "Little did I know how much I'd need you guys." I roll my eyes upward, but when I blink, more tears fall.

"How amazing that He knew we'd need each other," Claire whispers, her voice almost inaudible.

He knew all along.

What happens next? Keep reading about the roommates in *It's Over*, Book Two in the Status Updates Series

1
KAT

AS WE TURN ONTO MY street, my eyes are transfixed by the alternating blue and red lights coming from my driveway. My roommate Palmer places her hand over mine, but I can't register why. Why would there be a police car at my house?

"That's weird," I mumble.

"It's all right. It's probably nothing." Palmer's voice shakes a little. Why does she sound nervous?

"Wonder if the neighbors are all right?"

"The cops are at *your* house," Palmer whispers.

We park, get out of the car, and walk in slow motion up the driveway, past the flashing lights, past the static of police radios. Palmer carries my laundry bag as I lug a duffel bag and my backpack to the front door.

"Sorry, miss, you can't go in there." A burly policeman with a brown bushy moustache blocks my way.

"I live here," I manage to mutter through the lump in my throat.

"Wait here." Moustache Man stares straight ahead.

"What am I waitin' for? It doesn't look like he's doin' anything," I squeak to Palmer.

Daddy's Rav4 races up the driveway. His tires squeal like a NASCAR speedster, and he springs out of the driver's seat—so not normal for Daddy. He's usually really calm, in control.

I look to Palmer for some explanation of the *Twilight Zone* scene. Palmer's chocolate eyes shine. She shakes her head.

"Where's my boy? Where's my wife?" Daddy's voice bellows as he sprints toward us, almost knocking Palmer and me over with his tall frame. "Kat?" he whispers, straightening me like a book he's knocked off a shelf, placing his strong hands on my shoulders, but just for a second.

"Are you Mr. Wiley?" the policeman-turned-bouncer demands.

"Who do I look like? Of course I'm Mr. Wiley!"

Everything's turned inside out. Something is so terribly wrong. Goose bumps climb up my calves. Tears scald my eyes.

From somewhere inside the house comes a shrill cry. What is that? Is that Mama? Daddy charges past Moustache Man to the sound of her wails. I try to follow, but the policeman grabs my arm a little too hard.

"My mama needs my help!" I fight to get free. His grip remains firm and burns my bicep.

"Hey!" I try to swat him away.

"We're helping her, miss. You'll have to wait. Your dad's with her. After my partner talks to them you can go in." The policeman's voice sounds like it's coming from a swamp—dark, muddy, and gurgly. Nothing he says makes sense. None of what's going on makes sense. I bang my head against his navy blue chest like a football player charging the other team, but he won't budge. I bang and I bang and I bang and I bang, until I can't lift my head another time. I collapse against his stone-hard chest, not caring about his sharp badge poking my forehead or the stale smell of cigarettes lingering on his shirt.

"C'mon, Kat." Palmer's voice punctures the dark cloud encasing my body. "Let's wait over here."

Palmer must have the remote control for my body, because I can't make myself move, yet I end up on our porch swing, swaying back and forth, holding her hand, staring at the flashing lights.

I never thought I'd be friends with someone like her. Rich. Gorgeous. You know the type. I met Palmer—Hannah too—when I first moved to Ohio last year. They were inseparable BFFs at the high school I transferred to. When we found out we'd all be attending Clarkston College in the fall, we decided to be roommates. Add Claire, the ballerina from Cleveland whom Hannah met at orientation, and we're oddly a perfect fit.

I notice how cold Palmer's manicured hand feels against my hot, sweaty one. The continued glare from the top of the police car gives me something to focus on. I don't know if I sit here for a minute or an hour or a week, but eventually Daddy's in front of me, blocking my view of the blue and red streaks.

"Kat." He puts his strong hand on my shoulder.

I look up, trying to focus but can't shake the blurs of light from my brain. I find Daddy's straw-colored hair and bright green eyes among the streaks of light, and then the rest of his face comes into focus. Mama swears my brother, Alex, looks exactly like Daddy did when she met him. But right now Daddy's face is twisted, like it's made out of Silly Putty.

"Alex was in a car accident." The words drop like bowling balls on a wooden lane, crashing and echoing, then rolling forward faster and faster as they barrage the row of neatly placed pins, sending them flying in different directions before they crash to their sides.

"What happened?"

"I don't know." Daddy covers his face with his enormous hands. He stays covered up for what seems like hours. The police walk out of the house, right past us with just a nod, and head back to their car.

The slam of their doors snaps Daddy's attention back to me. "He was on his way home from the pool and another car came around the corner." Daddy shakes his head in disbelief. "They say the other driver must have never seen him." He clears his throat and continues, "The police came here to tell Mama. All they had listed was our phone number from Nashville, but they got our address from Alex's license plate. Mama called me."

The cops pull out of our driveway, almost silently. My eyes follow them disappearing into the dusk.

"Where is he?" I ask, searching Daddy's face for answers to the questions too painful for me to form, too impossible to ask.

"He's at Mercy Hospital in ICU." Daddy's gaze is somewhere above me, and his voice is whispery, like a cloud I can stick my hand through. "There's internal bleeding. They're doing surgery."

"We have to go." I grab Daddy's arm. "Get Mama."

"What?" Daddy clears his throat. "Right, let's go."

"Oh, Kat. I'm so sorry." Palmer hugs me, her Burberry perfume surrounding me. "I'll be praying for Alex and for you. I'll text Hannah and Claire. Let me know if there's anything I can do, okay?"

I hug her back, afraid to let go, afraid of what will happen if I emerge from the perfume cloud and let the next play of this awful game begin. If only she *could* do something!

"Make this all a dream," I say. "Or . . . or," I choke,

"make Alex's surgery go all right. I need the best surgeon in the world. Pray for the best surgeon in the entire world," I blurt, releasing her and turning to look for Daddy. He's gathered Mama into his car and is getting in. Did they forget about me?

"I'll take you," Palmer offers and grabs my hand.

ACKNOWLEDGEMENTS

Thank you, God, Author of the Universe, for giving me stories and words and the tools to write them—may this story glorify You.

Thank you, Brett, the love of my life. Nothing about our marriage is complicated, just pure and true and right and perfect.

Thank you Maddie, Max, Mallory and Maguire for believing in and supporting your mom. Your hugs and visits into my writing nook are priceless.

Maddie – you get a special thank you for all of the soccer insight you gave me while writing Kat. You made her time on the pitch come truly alive.

Thank you, Amy Parker for supporting and encouraging me every step of this writing journey. Your grace is overwhelming.

Thank you my precious writing twin, Tammy Bundy. Your eyes, edits, comments, suggestions and encouragement help shape everything I write.

Thank you Birch House Press for providing a beautiful home for my stories.

Thank you strong, bright, talented fellow authors; Laura Anderson Kurk, Jennifer Murgia, Stephanie Morrill and Rajdeep Paulus. You are air in my writing lungs.

ABOUT THE AUTHOR

Laura L. Smith believes in God and true love. She
believes if she bangs hard enough on the back of
her wardrobe, she'll get to Narnia someday.
She believes eating chocolate is good for you.
She believes part of her soul lives in France, part at the
beach and the other part in Oxford, Ohio, because when
she goes to those places she feels at home. Laura, her
husband, and their four children live in Oxford, Ohio,
home of Miami University. Her other novels include;
Skinny, Hot, Angry, It's Over and *It's Addicting*.

www.laurasmithauthor.com

www.ingramcontent.com/pod-product-compliance
Lightning Source LLC
Chambersburg PA
CBHW051411170626
46809CB00006B/2121